Mermaids on the Moon

Also by Elizabeth Stuckey-French

The First Paper Girl in Red Oak, Iowa: Stories

Mermaids
on
the
Moon

A Novel

Elizabeth Stuckey-French

DOUBLEDAY

New York   London   Toronto   Sydney   Auckland

PUBLISHED BY DOUBLEDAY
a division of Random House, Inc.
1540 Broadway, New York, New York 10036

DOUBLEDAY and the portrayal of an anchor with a dolphin are trademarks of
Doubleday, a division of Random House, Inc.

The publisher gratefully acknowledges Weeki Wachee Springs LLC for the
use of lyrics from "The Mermaid Theme Song."

Book design by Caroline Cunningham

Library of Congress Cataloging-in-Publication Data

Stuckey-French, Elizabeth.
  Mermaids on the moon: a novel / by Elizabeth Stuckey-French.—1st ed.
    p.   cm.
    1. Synchronized swimmers—Fiction.   2. Mothers and daughters—
Fiction.   3. Missing persons—Fiction.   4. Women swimmers—
Fiction.   5. Florida—Fiction.   I. Title.
PS3569.T832 M47 2002
813'.6—dc21   2001058405
ISBN 0-385-49894-2

June 2002
First Edition
10   9   8   7   6   5   4   3   2   1

For Ned, Phoebe,

and especially Flannery

Acknowledgments

Many, many thanks to Deb Futter, Anne Merrow, Gail Hochman, and Estelle Laurence. Thanks also to Florida State University, the Florida Humanities Council, and Robert Fichter, Nancy Smith Fichter, and Laurie Peeler of the Lillian Smith Center for the Arts. Quincy Hamby of Artzania gave me the inside scoop. Janet Burroway, Claudia Johnson, Pam Ball, Lu Vickers, and Beauvais McCaddon offered invaluable suggestions and support. Hats off to Bev Wells, Pam Mitchell, Katie Clark, Tony and Betsey Brown, and everyone at Cornerstone Learning Community for all you do for children. Bill and June Stuckey and Chuck and Jeanne French listened and said the right things. And without my husband, Ned, all this would be only a dream.

"Salvation is a last minute business."

—Robert Mitchum in *The Night of the Hunter*

Mermaids
on
the
Moon

One

The Fantasy Doll Theater had no telephone, so France drove out to tell Bruno about her mother's disappearance. The theater, where Bruno staged his Fantasy Doll shows, was thirty miles north of Indianapolis, on a county road a few miles from the town of Cedar Valley, up on a rise where the wind always blew. There was a magnificent view, but France was sure Bruno never noticed the rise and fall of the corn, rolling out for miles, the endless green grid broken up occasionally by a farmhouse glowing white under oak and maple trees. This morning, as usual, rain clouds filled the sky. France pulled up next to Bruno's van with the bashed-in side, a van he'd bought from a family who didn't have the insurance to fix it. She hated the sight of it.

When she got out of her Toyota she felt assaulted by sounds. A row of rocking chairs, with Bruno's wooden dolls propped up in them, rocked and squeaked in the wind. Other dolls spun around

in a tin merry-go-round, ringing bells as they went. His theater
and workshop were in what used to be an old general store. Big tin
tubes—wind catchers—stuck up through the roof. FANTASY
DOLL SHOW—2 DOLLAR ADMISSION read the hand-painted sign
over the door.

Bruno began carving dolls soon after he and France started
seeing each other again. A farmer mowing ditches near Bruno's
house knocked down one of the cedar posts lining the county
road, and Bruno'd helped himself to the post and crafted his first
doll. He carved and painted a face, attached movable arms and
legs made of pine, and after he finished, he announced that he'd
found his calling. He figured out how to use wind power to make
his dolls move and dance, sure they would draw a crowd.

Inside the dim, barnlike room, which smelled of mouse turds,
was a little stage crowded with brightly dressed wooden dolls, and
facing the stage were rows of chairs set up for the audience that
never came. Bruno crouched on the stage among his dolls, wearing cutoffs and a tank shirt, oblivious, as usual, to the chill in the
air. He'd played football at Indiana and had kept that build, even
though he never exercised anymore. His golden brown hair was
still thick and wavy. The lightly etched lines around his eyes
looked as though he could wipe them away if he wanted to.

At the moment he was tying an ivory-colored bonnet under
the chin of a doll wearing a ruffly, Little-House-on-the-Prairie
dress. He dressed all the dolls in clothes he found at the thrift
store, and he painted their lips and eyes and fingernails. They all
had nameplates hanging like reading glasses from their necks.
Wilma. Peanut. He didn't seem surprised to see France, even
though he hadn't been expecting her until evening. It was her

weekend to stay with him. "Francie Pants, meet Francie Pants," he said. Francie Pants was the first doll Bruno'd based on her, and she felt surprised and slightly offended by the doll's attire. "I can't decide," Bruno said, adjusting the doll's bonnet. "She sings, but should she play an instrument too? Maybe a fiddle."

"How about a washtub?" France suggested. She sat down on the edge of the stage, tucking her skirt around her legs. She'd never worn prairie clothes in her entire life. Right now she was dressed for work in a bright knit shirt and long black skirt, and when she left here they'd be covered in dust. "You forgot the corncob pipe," she told Bruno, trying to keep her tone light.

"Don't get prickly," said Bruno, grinning at her. "This here's the inner France. The one you try to hide. Your inner Pioneer."

"Whatever," France said. She'd rather he'd dressed it like a werewolf. "You've got three more dolls to make," she reminded him.

"One doll at a time. That's my motto."

Bruno was downwardly mobile. He lived in his parents' old frame house in Cedar Valley, which was stuffed with junk he'd collected and junk his parents had left behind when they retired to California, and he refused to either clean it up or move. He'd gone from managing three of his father's Mr. Donut restaurants to construction work to carving birdhouses and now dolls. If it weren't for France he wouldn't have even considered selling the dolls—he peddled firewood in the winter and produce in the summer for pocket money. But France knew she shouldn't nag him about making more dolls, or he'd dig his heels in. Besides, that wasn't why she'd come.

"Mom's gone," France said. "Nobody knows where she is."

Bruno was still fiddling with the new doll's bonnet. "Maybe she swam off with the real mermaids," he said. Unlike her father,

Bruno didn't overtly make fun of her mother for donning a tail again at age sixty—could someone who dressed up dolls and put on Fantasy Doll shows cast any stones?—but he often referred to Grendy and her swimming partners as fake mermaids, contrasting them with the real ones who were out there somewhere.

Where had Grendy gone? Bruno's guess was as good as any. The only place she'd ever talked about going was back to Florida, and she got her wish three years ago, in 1997, when Mermaid Springs hosted a Mermaids of Yesteryear Reunion. All former mermaids were invited back to put on a special retrospective show. France and her father encouraged Grendy, who'd been a mermaid at Mermaid Springs from 1958–61, to attend the reunion. France's younger sister Beauvais had been dead for two years, and Grendy needed something to help her through the shock, so she grew her hair out, lost ten pounds, and went. The reunion was such a success that Mermaid Springs scheduled the older mermaids for regular performances. Earlier this year, in the spring of 2000, after North retired from the ministry of Cedar Valley Methodist Church, he and Grendy bought a second home in Mermaid City so she could participate in the Mermaids of Yesteryear shows. North acted like he thought the whole thing was ludicrous. "Why would people pay to watch fat old ladies swim?" he'd asked France, and, although she'd frowned at him, she'd wondered the same thing. Grendy refused to be offended. "Merhags, that's what we are," she said.

Over a hundred mermaids had come to the 1997 reunion, and quite a few wanted to swim in the first monthly shows, but after a while only a few diehards were left. The older mermaids weren't paid, just given free passes, and gradually most of them decided that it wasn't worth the trouble. Now there were only four left, and one of them was Grendy.

"Everything gets clear underwater," Grendy'd said, speaking to France from her home in Mermaid City. "I'm happier underwater than I've ever been on land. It's my salvation."

At first North had grumbled about hating Florida, but then he took a part-time job as an assistant pastor at Mermaid Springs Methodist and began playing golf again, and France, relieved, thought they were mellowing into their new life.

Then, this morning, she got her father's phone call from Florida. France lived in the Broad Ripple section of Indianapolis, in a large sunny studio apartment with unadorned white walls, furnished with a leather couch and armchair, a trunk doubling as a coffee table, a white iron bed, and a few other things she'd taken from the house she'd shared with her ex-husband, Ray. She had just finished the *Star* and was washing the coffeepot. She felt dread before she'd even said hello.

"I've got something to tell you," her father said, sounding almost gleeful. "Your mother's run off."

"You're lying." Her parents had been married for thirty-nine years.

"Hold on," he said. "Hold on. She left me a note that says she has to go find herself and she'll be in touch. She took the old Volvo."

"Find herself?" Her mother would never say that. "When's she coming back?"

"No idea. But there's no reason to be alarmed. She's a grown woman. She just got a bee in her bonnet."

"Why wouldn't I be alarmed?" France sat down at her kitchen table. "How could she leave without saying where she was going? And what about Theo?"

"It was a bit self-centered," he said piously, in his minister's voice. "She left Theo behind." Theo was Beauvais's six-year-old son. He had been strapped in his car seat, in the car with his mother, when a teenager in a Jeep veered over the center line and hit them head-on, killing Beauvais but leaving Theo unharmed. Beauvais had never revealed who Theo's father was, so North and Grendy took custody of him. France couldn't believe her mother had gone off and left him.

"Maybe something happened to her," France said. "Maybe she's been abducted."

"You've been watching too much TV," her father said. "Remember, she's done this before."

When France was eight and Beauvais six, Grendy disappeared for over a week. What France mostly remembered about that time was staying at the neighbors' house while her father went to Tucson to bring her mother back. The neighbors' house was dark and scary, with unfamiliar sour smells, small portions of food and strange rules—only one glass of milk per meal and lights out at seven-thirty. France and Beauvais slept in their sleeping bags in the living room, and as they lay wide awake in the twilight, Beauvais would tell her that their parents were never coming back, that they were now the Hunts' children and she'd better get used to it. After their mother returned there was never any discussion about her leaving, no explanation given. They all pretended it hadn't happened. But it had happened, and it was happening again. France, to her horror, was overwhelmed with the same fear and anxiety she'd felt back then.

Pressing the receiver too hard against her ear, she realized she was now outside, on the balcony of her apartment, watching a man try to start his Corvette in the parking lot. The engine stuttered and stuttered but wouldn't catch. She shivered. It was too cool for August. She could hear water still running in the kitchen. "Are you there?" she said into the phone.

Her father sighed. "I'm sorry."

"For what?"

"That this is so upsetting to you. How do you think it makes me feel? I'm the one who got left."

"I thought she was happy," France said. "I thought you were both happy."

"Join the club," said her father.

"Are you going to stay down in Mermaid City?"

"Oh no," he said. "Theo and I are coming back to Indiana ASAP. But the thing is, I can't take care of him by myself."

France felt the last piece of solid ground dissolving underneath her. "What are you saying?"

"I'm wondering if he could come stay in Indianapolis with you. Your mother's the one who took care of him. I'm too old to take care of a six-year-old."

"You're only sixty-six."

Her father lowered his voice. "He makes me nervous. There's something wrong with him."

"What? What's wrong with him?"

North laughed, a strangled little sound. "He's obsessive. He acts like a cat. He memorizes scientific facts and recites them at strange moments, but when you ask him a simple yes or no question, he can't answer. He avoids kids his own age. Can't get him to throw anything away. He has these terrible outbursts. I'm afraid he's mentally ill."

"Have you talked to a doctor?"

"Your mother won't admit there's a problem. But he's getting worse. I just can't handle him."

"What makes you think I can handle him?" France said, hating the whiny tone of her voice. She felt as if she were being sucked backward into a vortex. "Poor Theo," she said, to steady herself. She loved Theo, she did. He *had* seemed a bit strange when she saw him last Christmas at her parents' house in Cedar Valley. He paced back and forth, twiddling his fingers as he sang Christmas carols in his flat, toneless voice. She'd tried to talk to him, but his mind was somewhere else. "Don't you think he's gone through enough changes?" France asked her father. "He's probably freaked out about this."

"It would just be till your mother comes back."

"If she does," France said, and told her father she had to go.

Bruno hung a nameplate around his new doll's neck. Francie Pants had tons of freckles and irritatingly wholesome blue eyes. That thing is not me, France thought.

"Theo will love her," Bruno said.

She told Bruno about her father asking her to take Theo.

"Theo's a real treat," Bruno said. "Nothing wrong with Theo." Last Christmas, France had taken Theo to visit Bruno's studio, and he'd fit right in. He'd walked over to Wilma, the cowgirl doll, who was perched on a wooden rocking horse, and snatched the blond wig off her head, plopping it down on his own. He was exactly the same size as the dolls.

"Put that filthy wig back," France had said, but Bruno was

laughing, so Theo'd ignored her. Later, Bruno and Theo went into town to get hamburgers, and, at Theo's suggestion, they put Wilma in the front passenger seat to ride along with them. Bruno never put the wig back on her, deciding he preferred her bald.

Bruno would be a terrible father, France had thought. He'd let a kid get away with anything. He wanted to marry France and have children, but marriage, France told him, was hard enough with no kids. Her first marriage had spooked her. She met Ray during her junior year at Purdue, when she was living in a sorority house and slowly losing her mind because of it. Ray, whose parents paid the rent for his off-campus apartment and the insurance premiums on his BMW, was halfheartedly working toward a degree in business administration. He spent all his money on clothes and all his spare time playing pool. He voted for Reagan. He and France had nothing in common, but they did not perceive this to be a problem. After they married they began to have violent arguments where they hurled things at each other. Sex got to be horribly self-conscious and somehow beside the point. They supplemented their own college furniture in the townhouse with office furniture Ray stole from whatever job he happened to have. France was relieved to be able, after five years, to leave it all behind, which she did when she got her first decent paying social work job and could afford to live on her own.

But the social work job also took a toll. It required her to investigate child abuse cases and to be a surrogate parent to abused and neglected foster kids for whom she could do next to nothing. She'd decided by then that she did not want children. Her own, or anybody else's. She wanted peace and quiet and order. But she also

wanted Bruno, who was as resistant to changing his life as she was
to changing hers.

Bruno poked his new doll in the stomach. "How's my serious
gal?" he asked the doll. Francie Pants was the only doll he'd made
who wasn't smiling. What was the significance of that? France
didn't really want to know.

She sat down in one of the plush chairs meant for his audience, and Bruno came over and sat down beside her, hulking in
the little chair. He smelled slightly funky, but at least he'd cut off
the ponytail. She took his hand, which was thick and square and
rough and covered with nicks. His hands were one of the sexiest
things about him.

He turned her hand over and studied it like a piece of wood he
was about to carve. "You going down to Florida to find your mom?"

This idea had not occurred to her. "Maybe." She rested her
head on his bare shoulder and had the sudden desire to crawl on
top of him, funky smell and all.

"Go talk to her mermaid pals," he said, wrapping his arm
around her. "They'll know where she went."

"But what about your show?" She wriggled away from him.
"How'll we get your dolls to the gallery?"

"You'll be back by then. If not, we'll think of something." He
tried to hug her again, but she couldn't sit still. The idea of him
winging the doll show made her nervous.

"The jig'll be up," she said, "if Naomi finds out."

"I could always show somewhere else," he said.

France buried her face in his chest and groaned loudly. They'd
had this discussion many times. It was very important to France
that Bruno show at Naomi's gallery, and he knew it.

The problem was that Bruno was a man, and the gallery, where France now worked, one of the best in Indianapolis, was called WomenSpace. Naomi was adamant that they only display the work of women. "They've been underrepresented for too long," Naomi said, and France agreed. France had led Naomi to believe that Bruno's dolls were made by a woman, and Bruno had gone along with the deception, neither of them ever imagining that the dolls would be so popular. They were selling for one thousand dollars apiece, and now the anonymous dollmaker was scheduled for a solo show. Naomi had indicated, in an offhand way, that perhaps, after the doll show, she and France could talk about the possibility of France buying into the business—after all, France had discovered the dollmaker, along with many other artists, and made the gallery lots of money. France had been saving her money for just this purpose, but she'd simply nodded, also in an offhand way, not wanting to reveal how excited she was about the prospect of owning a share in WomenSpace.

Bruno leaned over and kissed France good-bye. "Stay and hear Francie Pants sing," he said. "She really adds a certain something." He stood up and padded into his control room. Tinkling piano music, coming from the speakers, filled the theater. "Paper Roses." The dolls began to spin and move—he'd turned on the wind power. Francie Pants, the serious gal, scooted forward and began to sing in Bruno's falsetto voice—she had a tape player in her back. *"Oh how real those roses were to me . . ."* A nightclub performer called Baby Tangerine, who wore a black sheath and black nail polish, played a keyboard. Heidi, in a polka-dot dress, squeezed an accordion. Minnie, decked out in cat's-eye glasses and a cloche hat, sewed wildly on a sewing machine. Wilma the bald cowgirl rocked on her wooden horse. *"Like your imitation love for me,"* sang Francie Pants. Peanut waved and waved from her bar stool. In spite of herself, France waved back. If she went to Florida, she might jeopardize Bruno's show at WomenSpace. And her own future there.

She got up in the middle of the Fantasy Doll Show and walked outside into the gloomy morning light, where she stood on the hillside, gazing at the roofs of Cedar Valley. She'd always been the one to deliver the dolls to WomenSpace. How would they get there if she left town? She didn't want Bruno to do it because she was afraid he'd blurt out the truth. Surely she'd be back in time, but if not, she and Bruno could work something out. Right now she needed to find her mother. Theo needed his grandmother. The wind began to blow rain, a misty drizzle that coated her face, retreated, and coated her face again. It felt as though it would never quit raining. For the entire summer it had been raining all over Indiana, all over the Midwest. The creeks and rivers were rising and the corn leaves drooped like pennants from their stalks. In Indianapolis the air smelled like wet garbage. Here, it smelled like hogs. France stood there on the hillside, raindrops clotting her eyelashes, and decided to go to Florida and find her mother.

WomenSpace occupied a prominent position on Broad Ripple Avenue, surrounded by bars and restaurants and flanked by cross streets lined with boutiques in tiny bungalows. When France walked into the gallery around noon, the place was full of the usual Saturday browsers, mostly wives of professionals wanting to inject a little whimsy into their lives. She waved to regulars who'd become friends—Cadence Kidwell and Caroline Pearson—and greeted the part-time employee, Amy Peters, who was behind the jewelry counter surrounded by customers.

Naomi and France had painted the walls of the front room a delicious apple green, and the ceiling and hardwood floor orange. This month, along with the ubiquitous landscapes and streetscapes, they were featuring the art of a police dispatcher who carved and painted wooden monsters. France had discovered the monsters and their maker at an art fair in Fort Wayne. They were also showing a group of bottle cap figurines, oil paintings of circus scenes, and dioramas of fruit people, including a fruit wedding. WomenSpace was France's playhouse. She never bought any art for her apartment, because she wanted to keep the two places separate. The gallery was filled with all the objects and color and activity she wanted, and, most important, it was all under her control—she could step in and out of it as she wished.

When France started working weekends at WomenSpace she'd been newly divorced from Ray and still working at Child Protective Services. The gallery, quiet and stimulating at the same time, felt like a treasure island, and she'd taken to it right away. She'd first met Naomi at a Rally for Choice at the state capitol, but she'd seen her around at various gatherings and meetings in support of women's rights. Naomi had invited France to lunch at Three Sisters Café and from there they'd struck up a friendship. Gradually, as the gallery prospered, France was able to quit her social work job and work full time at the gallery. Her great gift, as Naomi often reminded her, was her unerring taste. France had a knack for choosing the best art to display, and everything she chose turned out to be a hit—old clock parts transformed into mobiles by Dr. C. E. Perry, boxes covered with plastic teething beads, thermometers, and baby teeth by Jacinta, a mother of seven. And Bruno's dolls.

Today Naomi was in the backroom behind her desk, doing paperwork. Naomi was a short, busty woman whose energetic personality made her much more attractive than she appeared at first glance. At the moment, though, doing her most hated task, she looked frazzled, her red bob sticking out every which way from running her hands through it. She wore her trademark white blouse, adorned today with a celluloid likeness of the Jetsons pinned to the collar.

France plopped down across from her and told her that Grendy had fled. "I'm really worried about my father," she told Naomi. "You should've heard him on the phone. This forced cockiness. It was scary." She told Naomi what her father had said about Theo's behavior.

"Theo's probably got one of those syndromes," Naomi said. "I'll ask Roger about it." Roger, Naomi's husband, was a psychologist.

"Maybe it's ADD," France said.

"What does Mr. Donut think?" Mr. Donut was Naomi's nickname for Bruno, whom she'd never met. Because France never told Naomi about Bruno's true vocation, she'd taken the liberty of putting him back into the most promising position he'd ever had.

"He thinks Theo's just dandy," France said. "He thinks I should go to Florida to find Mom."

"But you really can't do anything in Florida, can you? You can't find someone who doesn't want to be found."

"Maybe she does want to be found," France said, and told her about the first time Grendy left, how her father had tracked Grendy down and gone to get her. "I'll be back before the doll show opens,"

France promised. She picked up a snow globe from Naomi's desk and shook it, watching the blizzard swirl around Santa Claus. Naomi had fifty snow globes on her desk—all Christmas scenes.

"It'd be so amazing if the dollmaker came to her opening," Naomi said. "See if you can talk her into it. Otherwise, the *Star* won't have anyone to interview!"

France was running out of excuses for the nonexistent female artist. "She never goes out in public," France said. "I didn't want to tell you, but she's misshapen. She has a hump."

Naomi was staring at France, who blushed. In the other room a woman said, "Put this on my Christmas list!" Laughter. The door chime sounded.

"A hump?" Naomi squinted and leaned toward France. "Is it you? Are you the dollmaker?"

To her dismay, France's blush deepened. "Of course not," she said, aware that she was acting guilty. Part of France, a part she was ashamed of, liked being suspected of being the artist. She had an excellent eye for other people's art, but she wasn't an artist. She envied their audacity. I think I'll just glue my children's teeth on this box! Wow! Am I glad I broke this old clock! Even though some things about Bruno drove her insane, she admired him. She wanted to make things instead of just selling them. But she hadn't carved the dolls, and she wasn't going to compound the lie. She wished she'd never lied to begin with, but it was too late now.

It all began one winter day when France had stopped by the gallery to pick up her paycheck. She'd left her car in the alley behind the gallery, and when Naomi slipped outside for a smoke she saw Wilma, the bald cowgirl, who'd recently been riding shotgun with Bruno and Theo, in the backseat.

"Oh my God!" Naomi shrieked. "Where did you find that?"

"A friend made it," France said, wishing to God she'd covered Wilma up with something.

"Who? Who?" Naomi said. "Would she let us display it?"

"Uh, I don't know."

"Take it out! Let me see it."

So France took Wilma out and Naomi carried her inside and showed her to Amy and a customer, Alison Jester, who were hanging about drinking coffee. Alison wanted to buy it on the spot.

Naomi kept pressuring France, asking who'd made it, wanting to know if the gallery could show it, wanting to know if the artist had more dolls.

"I don't think this person would want to show them," France said.

"She's a recluse? An outsider artist?"

France wanted to say, she's a he, but instead she said, "Bingo."

Naomi clutched her arm in the intimate way she had. "We don't have to reveal the name of the artist. We could show her anonymously." And France, stupidly, promised to talk to the artist about it. Bruno, thinking it was just a lark, said, "Why not?"

Now Naomi was behind the desk, smiling knowingly at France, as if she'd figured everything out.

"I really didn't make them," France said. "Really."

Amy stuck her well-coifed head into the room. "That weird woman's here. The one who paints tea parties in hell."

"I'll get rid of her," France said, getting quickly to her feet, happy to have an excuse.

T w o

At the Tampa airport, France rented a Ford Taurus and started up the Gulf toward Mermaid City. At first the traffic on Highway 19 was horrendous. The small towns of Tarpon Springs, Holiday, and New Port Richey had morphed into one long, continuous strip mall since France had last seen them, in 1975. When France and Beauvais were children, North and Grendy decided that they must visit every state in the United States, so each summer they set out for new destinations. This project was the one thing North and Grendy planned and executed together, the one thing they were both enthusiastic about, the one thing they actually completed, and Florida was their grand finale.

Back then, when they drove up Highway 19, France, who was thirteen, sulked in the backseat while their father drove, his shoulders hunched with exhaustion, and their mother sang the mermaid anthem—"*We've got the world by the tail! We've got the world by the tail!*" Grendy loved singing in the car, and she usually sang old-timey hymns from her childhood, "Leaning on the Everlasting Arms" and "Is Your All on the Altar?" but this was even worse. Beauvais found the whole idea of mermaids enthralling. "We're going to see the mermaids! We're going to see the mermaids!" For France it was too embarrassing for words, the idea of anyone, especially her mother, wriggling around half-naked in a garish tail. Even today she found the idea appalling.

As she approached Mermaid City, there were no other cars in sight. The four-lane highway went straight for as far as she could see, low clouds hanging above it like a long string of laundry. Raggedy palm trees grew sporadically in the median and dense pine forests lined the road. Mermaid City itself could hardly even be called a town, let alone a city. It was a haphazard community consisting of Mermaid Springs, a few strip malls, side roads where mobile homes, bungalows, fishing camps, alligators, and pit bulls were hidden back in the pines along with new subdivisions full of retirees.

Her parents' home was in a subdivision off Highway 19 called Star of the Sea. Consulting her scribbled directions, France turned right, right again, left, left again: Oyster Road, Stonefish Lane, Pelican Place. The houses, gussied up double-wides, seemed to be locked tight, curtains drawn against the sun. The neat little lawns were green, full of flowering vines and shrubs, but empty of people. Finally she was on Conch Court. Her parents' house, white with light blue trim, sat on a corner lot with the woods behind it. It had a screened porch, a carport, and a mailbox in the shape of a manatee. A large live oak tree grew beside the house, festooned with vines and Spanish moss, branches dipping near the ground. When she got out of her car she felt as if she'd stepped into a stifling Laundromat. There was an earthy, piney smell. Red hibiscus bloomed on bushes near the house, and crushed flowers littered the front steps.

The door was unlocked. Every light in the house was on. She found North and Theo in a bedroom. North was taking Grendy's dresses off the hangers and stuffing them into cardboard boxes. He glanced up, startled, when he saw her standing in the doorway.

Theo was lying on the bed. "Hi, Aunt Frances," he said.

"Why are you doing that?" France asked her father. She was shaking. Maybe he'd found out something terrible.

He stood there, staring at her, tan and fit in one of his striped polo shirts, his wispy white hair standing on end. Over his arm hung a navy blue dress Grendy had had for years, one she often wore to church functions. It was hideous. France was glad she'd left it behind. "She may call and ask me to send this stuff. So, I'm just getting the jump." He put his fist up to his eye. "It's hard, seeing her stuff every time I open the closet."

He was more upset than he'd sounded on the phone. France went to him and gave him a hug. Then she hugged Theo, who did not hug her back. He seemed both smaller and older than he had last Christmas, like a shrunken man, a shrunken tourist man, with his blond crew cut and pale skin, wearing too-big Hawaiian print shorts and a white T-shirt with a big blue stain on it. "I know a real mermaid," he told France. "She's my friend."

"That's nice." France sat down gingerly on the bed beside him, her fingers stroking the chenille bedspread. Her parents had had the same bedspread for as long as she could remember. It was there when she used to take afternoon naps in their bed, her mother reading *Ladies' Home Journal* beside her. The small room was full of mermaid things France had never seen before—a lamp with a mermaid base, a mirror with mermaids painted on the frame. The curtains had a mermaid print. On the wall hung a quilt with mermaids stitched on it.

Theo tugged on France's skirt. "This is Grandma's mermaid shrine." He pointed up at the sparkly ceiling. "She put glitter in the paint," he said, "so she could pretend she was sleeping underwater."

North was shaking his head to show his disapproval.

"Tell me more about what happened," France asked her father.

North grunted. He didn't sit down, but leaned against the dresser, folding his arms on his chest, and began talking about Grendy's departure as if he and France were continuing an ongoing conversation. "That night I went out for dinner," he said. "Went to eat oysters with Ernie Elder and some men from church. When I got home all the lights were on. There was a pan of string beans on the table. Like she'd just been snapping them and got up and left. And she took *my* raincoat. Theo was in his room reading. She didn't tell him anything about where she was going or why. I found the note in the middle of our bed." He pointed at the bed where Theo was now pretending to be asleep.

"Did you two have a fight?" France asked him. Her parents, as far as she could remember, had never had a real argument. She'd never even heard them raise their voices, let alone brawl the way she and Ray used to, breaking every dish in the house. Her father sniped at her mother, and her mother pretended to ignore him, a martyr's smile fixed to her face.

France expected her father to take offense at this question, but instead he smirked. "Not that I know of." He went on to tell her that her mother and Theo had been at Publix supermarket between five and six, buying groceries, and that when he called her from the church to tell her he wouldn't be home for supper because he was going out with the men's group, she'd only complained about the weekend tourist traffic, which was their little joke, and said she'd see him when he got home. The last person to speak to her, besides Theo, was her friend and fellow mermaid Rose d'Angelo, who'd called her on the phone around seven-thirty to tell her about an extra mermaid practice. Grendy said she'd see her there.

Later that night, after he discovered her note, he'd called her local friends and acquaintances. Even though they'd only lived in Mermaid City for a few months, she had many of these. Grendy was a club person. Along with being a mermaid, she volunteered at the Humane Society and was active in the Sunshine Bible Class of their church and served on a multitude of committees there. But nobody'd heard from her or seen her, not even their sick neighbor, whom Grendy had been checking up on twice a day. The next morning North called France and then Grendy's out-of-town friends and relatives. Nothing. "Seems she got a bee in her bonnet," he said.

His story sounded rehearsed, but so what? He'd probably told it many times already. Besides, most everything he said sounded rehearsed. Perhaps that came with being a minister. France studied his face, but couldn't get any hints. What was she hoping to see? A gesture, an expression, something to indicate whether or not he was telling the truth. "Let me see the note," she said.

He turned and began fumbling around on his dresser. Was he going to claim he couldn't find it? That he'd already thrown it away? No, there it was, he was holding it up.

It was Grendy's handwriting. "North," it said. "This is it. I've got to be by myself and think things over. Don't worry. I'll be in touch. Grendy."

"What does 'this is it' mean?" France asked him.

"Got me." His childishness, which she usually found amusing, was beginning to get on her nerves.

"It's not a joke," she said.

He gave her a professional, concerned frown. "I'm not laughing."

She slipped the note into the pocket of her tissue-soft skirt. "Aren't you worried about her at all?" she asked him.

"She said not to worry, so I'm trying not to. She's obviously not concerned about me. Or Theo." He sounded bitter, but there was something else there too, a new coldness that gave her the willies. "Why'd she have to run off to think things over?" He scowled at France as if she would have an answer.

The day France left Ray, she'd hired a moving company to remove the few pieces of furniture she wanted and was gone by the time he arrived home from his new job at U-Haul. She hadn't considered the fact that he'd simply call her parents, who immediately gave him her new phone number. Instead of yelling at her, he'd begged and pleaded with her to come home, more passionate than he'd ever been before, even though he was just as miserable as she was. She knew how it felt to be cast as the hard-hearted deserter.

Her father was still scowling at her. "You really don't need to be here. How long are you staying?"

"Till I know what happened to her."

"Nothing *happened* to her," he said, mimicking France. "She just left. She's done it before, and she'll probably do it again." He shook his finger at France. "It was probably the Prozac."

"She's been on Prozac for months," France said. She herself had been on an antidepressant for years—she'd started taking it soon after her divorce, and never wanted to go off it. She kicked off her black sandals and stretched out on the bed beside Theo, who lay stiffly beside her, his eyes closed. On the far wall of the bedroom hung a group of framed black-and-white photographs of Grendy in her young mermaid years, photos France hadn't seen since she was a child.

"Did she leave a note when she left the first time?" France asked her father. She knew virtually nothing about the first time her mother fled.

He shook his head. "That time she just ran off, and I called around till I found her, staying with an old college friend out West. This time, nothing."

France had to gather her courage to ask. "Why'd she leave that time?"

"She said she felt trapped. She thought I'd try and stop her so she just ran off." He pinched the bridge of his nose. "She couldn't, or wouldn't, tell me why she felt trapped."

"Have you called her college friend in Arizona? Who is it?"

"Called her first thing," North said. "Somebody who was on the synchronized swim team with her. Sarah somebody.

Sarah Chambers. Said she hasn't heard from your mother in years."

Theo gave a loud pretend snore, and France stroked his arm. He flinched and turned over on his side. Why did she feel so frightened? She wasn't a child anymore, helpless and totally in the dark as she'd been the first time. As Theo was now. "It's not right that you're packing up her clothes," France said. "It's like you're giving up on her already."

Her father stood there, gazing blankly at her. "Okay," he finally said. He dug into the box, grabbed an armful of clothes and threw them on the floor, then he upended the box and emptied it. France saw Grendy's favorite sundress slip out. Theo opened one eye and then closed it again.

"There," North said. "Feel better?"

"No," said France.

"Me neither." He gave her a sheepish smile.

France managed to smile back. Her father was anxious and scared, as she was, but was trying to put on a tough face. She knew him well enough to know this. She gathered up Grendy's sundress and folded it into a neat square. "It'll be okay," she told her father.

"You go right ahead and try to find her. I'm done trying."

"Theo needs her," France said. "I've got to find her, for his sake."

"You guys can stay here awhile," North said, "but if she doesn't come back eventually, I'm going to rent out this tin can. I resigned from Mermaid Springs Methodist. I'm going back to Indiana tomorrow. I'll be glad to be shut of this place."

After North left the room, France got up to check out the mermaid photos. There was young dark-haired Grendy, wearing a one-piece bathing suit and high heels, sitting on the sandy bottom of the spring with her legs tucked underneath her, drinking a bottle of Coke, a fish kissing her ear. There was another one of her, also underwater, but now in her mermaid tail, with her mermaid friend and rival, Lydia Baumgartner, the two of them holding up a sign that said Elvis Fan Club, and Elvis Presley himself ogling them through the glass wall of the theater.

Something butted into her side. Theo was rubbing his head against her. "Meow," he said. "I'm a cat."

France scratched his head. "Good kitty," she said.

"Pretend like my name is Winky," he said.

"Good Winky."

"Pretend like you're my owner."

"What's my name?"

He turned away, seemingly not interested in giving her a name. He pointed up at another mermaid photograph, one that Grendy wasn't in. "That's Martin Milner and George Maharis from 'Route 66,' " he said. " 'Route 66' filmed a show at Mermaid Springs. It had a real mermaid in it. Pretend like I'm a talking cat."

"Okay." Theo was a bit odd, no doubt about it. France turned back to the photos. In every one Grendy looked plump and pleased with herself. "Why didn't she have these framed before?" France asked herself aloud.

"She wanted to be a proper minister's wife."

Startled, France glanced down to see Theo beaming at her. He had a heart-shaped face and widely spaced blue eyes. He'd be a heartbreaker when he grew up, if he wasn't crazy. It dawned on her that Theo, even though he'd already been questioned by North, might know more about Grendy's leaving than he'd so far been willing to tell. She would have to question him gently. "You sure you don't know where she is?"

"No no no," he said, his face turning red as if he was going to cry. "I thought she loved me."

"She does," France said, kneeling to hug him. Again he was unyielding and waited for the hug to be over, but his face relaxed.

France sat back down on the bed, rubbing her temples. She was developing a killer headache, and she was dying to get out of her bra.

"This is the year of the Rooster," Theo announced. He'd sprawled out on the mint-colored wall-to-wall carpet.

"Where'd you hear that?"

"Fortune cookie. In the year of the Rooster, law and order are important. All the bad people will get put into jail." According to North, one of Theo's current obsessions, along with animals and science, was lawbreaking.

"Grandma will be back soon," France said. "She just wanted to be by herself for a while. Sometimes people need a vacation." She closed her eyes and saw her mother walking on some city street, wearing dark glasses and carrying a museum bag, or lounging with a drink on the deck of a cruise ship. Had she gone back out West somewhere? She had no idea what sort of life her mother longed to lead, other than the life of a mermaid.

"I know she's coming back," said Theo, his eyes fixed on the sparkly ceiling. "She wouldn't leave all her mermaid stuff."

"She wouldn't leave *you*," France said. But perhaps she'd left because of Theo. That idea was too awful to contemplate.

Three

Late the next morning, after North had packed up their newer Volvo and headed back to Indiana, France decided to take Theo and check out Mermaid Springs. They drove south down the monotonous, trance-inducing highway, and France remembered a movie she'd seen in driver's ed that had scared the bejesus out of her. *Highway Hypnosis!* Maybe that's what had happened to Grendy. She was hypnotized, still driving.

"How fast are you going?" Theo said from the backseat.

She eased her foot off the gas pedal.

"Roll up your window," Theo said.

She rolled it up till it was open only a crack.

"All the way."

"Why?"

"I'm afraid."

"Of what?"

"Somebody might get blown out the window."

She told him that this couldn't happen.

"Roll it up," he whined. "Please. I said please."

She rolled it up and flipped the air conditioning on high.

After a few seconds Theo said, "Maybe Grandma's hiding in those woods over there." He tapped on the window. "I bet the Hardy Boys could find her. Or bloodhounds. Bloodhounds can sniff people out for miles."

Maybe she's *buried* in those woods over there, France thought, then gave herself a mental slap. She wasn't going there. Not yet.

"A Russian submarine is missing," Theo said. "It's called the *Kursk*. They might have more about it on the radio. Turn on the radio, please. I said please." North had warned France not to let Theo listen to the news, because he'd gotten hysterical when he first heard about the *Kursk*.

"I don't want the radio on," France said. "I don't want any extra noise." She cringed, remembering her mother saying the exact same thing.

They passed a sign advertising the Reptile Show at Mermaid Springs—a grinning cartoon man with a fat snake wrapped around his neck.

Theo said, "That's Jake on that sign. He's a Seminole Indian. He wrestles alligators."

"Who'd want to watch that?"

"I would."

"Except us," France said.

"And Grandma. She took me to the Reptile Show. I miss Grandma."

"Me too," said France. "Me too."

France hadn't been to Mermaid Springs in twenty-five years. Now the sign at the entrance was faded and peeling. The huge parking lot wasn't even half full. In front of the ticket booth stood a tall white plinth topped by a statue of two naked females—with legs, not tails—performing a balletic movement with one girl on the bottom, hand-spotting the back of the top one, who arched above her, one knee bent. Moss grew on the breasts of the top girl. Why were they nude? Why didn't somebody clean off the moss? More bare-breasted statues, statues of mermaids, lined the entryway. Naomi would be horrified, France decided. Both by the tackiness and the sexism. Or maybe not. Maybe she'd consider it a celebration of the female form. France hadn't even told Naomi about her mother and the mermaids because she didn't want to listen to a speech about objectifying women. Bruno, on the other hand, would love it.

France told the warty-faced man selling tickets that she was Grendy's daughter and he didn't charge her the twelve-dollar admission fee.

"Let's go, let's go," Theo said, tugging her through the front gate. He was wearing his Hawaiian shorts again. Bruno often wore the same thing day after day, not knowing, or not caring, if it was dirty. With Theo, she would have the opportunity to nip this habit in the bud. "We gotta be on time for Brett's show," Theo said. "She's the real mermaid. She's my baby-sitter."

According to the program they'd been handed, *The Little Mermaid Show*, performed by the young mermaids, started in five minutes. Theo led the way over a wide wooden bridge, lined with ropes and lanterns, which crossed a stream, and they wound their way down a concrete path toward the sunken Mermaid Theater. A family in bathing suits rushed past them to get good seats. The paths were landscaped with manicured hedges, pink impatiens and ferns, and palm and magnolia trees. In the distance was the spring, where clear greenish-blue water boiled up from an underwater canyon, the origin of the Crystal River. It was there, in the opening of the underwater canyon, that the mermaids staged their extravaganzas. On the other side of the spring the public swimming beach beckoned, its shockingly white sand busy with red-striped umbrellas, its huge water slide gushing. Shouts of happy bathers echoed through the park.

"God it's hot," France said as she plodded along. The air was so thick and oppressive it was hard to breathe. Her tank top stuck to her back. Her hair, she knew, had frizzed out into a bush. "How does anyone stand it here?"

Theo's cheeks were bright red and he vibrated with excitement. "I'm used to it," he said.

"I hope we find Grandma quick," said France. "I can't wait to get back home." She thought longingly of the cool, cloudy climate she'd left behind. If she were home she'd be at the gallery, drinking a café mocha, gazing out the front window at the familiar parade of people—the owner of Artzy Phartzy in her red molded plastic wig, the leather-clad teenage rebels biking toward their hangout under the bridge, the elderly department store heiress with her marmalade cat draped around her shoulders.

"Aunt Frances. Look." Theo pointed to a "posing place," a large plaster replica of a mermaid and King Neptune sprawled on a rock, faces cut out. "Grandpa took a picture of me and Brett there."

"Uh huh." As she watched Theo, she thought again how he

didn't look a thing like Beauvais, who'd had dark hair and an olive complexion like Grendy. Theo resembled France and her father. And, presumably his own father, whom he would never know. Why hadn't Beauvais told them who his father was? France tried again to hug Theo, but he ducked away.

He must have sensed that she was hurt, because he took her hand. His hand felt weak and limp, like a little flipper. "Meow Meow," he said. "Winky is excited to see the show. Pretend like I'm on a leash."

They wandered down into the Mermaid Theater, past the glamour photos of the young mermaids, and over to the food stand. France introduced herself to the bleached blond woman selling popcorn and the young woman in a mini skirt acting as usher. Both of them had just started working there and hadn't known Grendy.

The audience sat in an ampitheater with aqua-colored walls. At the bottom was the glass wall between them and the water. A curtain hung over the glass, blocking their view of the springs. France and Theo navigated their way down to a bench near the front, finding a seat among groups of children and families.

France surveyed the theater, deciding that there hadn't been many changes since 1975. The industrial-strength carpet looked worn; the white plastic curtain over the wall was riddled with tiny holes. The place was definitely down at the heels. While Theo munched his popcorn, France listened to the couple behind her, an older couple obviously out on a first date. They'd come to see the mermaids on a first date? "I've been in the tile business for forty years," the man was saying.

Suddenly, beside her, Theo erupted. He stood up and wailed, his face a red grimace.

"What's the matter?" France asked him, feeling equal parts concern and embarrassment. "What is it?" He kept crying, an angry bellow, louder and louder. She tried to pull him back down, but he resisted, his body rigid. A little girl in front of them, with pierced ears and a purple cast on her leg, turned and gaped. "Theo, sit down and tell me what is the matter," France said. He didn't respond. It was like trying to reason with an angry beast. Or a cave man. His bellowing felt like a club, whomping on her. France had the urge to run out of the theater. Finally she noticed that he was pointing down at the floor. His popcorn had spilled. Was that the cause of this fit? France reached down, picked up the box, and showed it to him. She tried to remember her social work days, when she'd actually given workshops to foster parents on how to deal with kids' behavior problems. All she could remember telling them was to speak calmly. "There's plenty of popcorn left," she told Theo calmly. "If you want more, we'll get more."

Theo promptly sat down, took the carton, and began to eat again. "Meow," he said. "Winky loves popcorn. Pretend like popcorn is good for cats." There was no residue from the tantrum, no sniffing or pouting, no reluctance to let it go. He showed no desire to cuddle. It was simply gone, like bad weather. France's pounding heart slowed. This was one of the outbursts her father was talking about. How often did he throw these fits? This was only her first day with him, and she was already exhausted.

Thankfully, at that moment, music came over the speakers, tranquil music with birds chirping in the background. The lights dimmed and the curtain went up on the great glass wall between them and the spring. It was like looking into a natural aquarium. Directly behind the glass was a fiberglass platform, an underwater stage, which, in 1975, Grendy'd told France and Beauvais, was actually the roof of an air lock where the mermaids stayed until it was time to swim up and put on a show. Beyond the platform was the wide drop-off, the Underwater Grand Canyon—deeper than a ten-story building!—where the water welled out of the ground, water that stayed seventy-two degrees year round. Sunlight shimmered on the slopes of white sand and eelgrass. Fish and turtles drifted by, unaware that they were part of the show. A twin-towered castle, like a playhouse, perched on the far side of the canyon wall. A small copy of Michelangelo's David and a chest overflowing with treasure rested on a hummock near the glass.

"See?" said Theo. "Isn't it awesome?"

"Awesome," France said, and it was.

"Welcome to the Spring of Live Mermaids!" a female announcer said. "Clap loudly! The mermaids can hear your applause!"

An air curtain of frothy bubbles covered the window, then fizzled out, and up from the depths swam a mermaid, a young woman with long dark hair, wearing a spangly pink bikini top and a tail. Naomi would have a field day with this, France thought. The mermaid swam around leisurely, taking hits from her air hose, which looked like a microphone attached to a garden hose. She fed little fish from a chunk of bread in her hand. The announcer's voice came over the speakers, and Theo spoke along with her: "Here dwell a strange and wondrous breed of people, half human, half fish. Legend tells us that these undersea creatures are known as mermaids."

"Brett comes next," Theo announced.

Two new mermaids ascended in a cascade of bubbles.

"It's Brett! There she is! The pretty one! She's my baby-sitter!"

The little girl with the purple leg cast turned again to stare at Theo. "Shhh," France told him.

The new mermaids also had long hair that floated above them, looking magically dry and silky. They were dressed in the same iridescent pink bikini tops and tails as their fish-feeding sister. France remembered Grendy telling her and Beauvais that the mermaid dressing room had a chute, a long dark L-shaped chute, through which the mermaids had to swim down to the air lock, holding their breaths. There were air hoses along the way, but it was hard to find them in the dark.

Loud pop music filled the theater, and the three young women, hovering twenty feet below the surface and directly in front of the glass window, began to lip-sync along with the mermaid anthem, taking occasional breaths through their air hoses, which they waved like bubbling wands.

> "We're not like other women, living lives that are a bore.
> Don't have to clean an oven, and we never will grow old.
> We've got the world by the tail!
> We've got the world by the tail!"

They twirled and flipped in dreamy slow-motion unison, with an eerie freedom from gravity, and then, all in a row, curled their hoses into "chairs" and perched on them, rocking, while they mouthed the words. The mermaid on the end reminded her a little of Grendy, something about the shape of their heads, and the fact that they were both chunky. France wished she could've seen her mother as a young mermaid, swimming in a show like this one.

In 1975, the mermaids had been dressed like hula dancers. Performing underwater, one of them "played" the ukulele while the others stood in a giant clamshell, swaying and dancing. They peeled and ate bananas, dropping the peels for the fish and turtles, and glugged entire bottles of Coke. France was impressed but pretended not to be, because her mother, sitting beside her, had so wanted her to be impressed. Her father sat on her other side, staring fixedly at the mermaids. Something about the way he was watching caused France to feel uncomfortable, so she shifted closer to her mother.

Mermaids train for three months, Grendy'd told her and Beauvais, learning to use the air hoses, taking in just the right amount of air, learning to smile big and keep their eyes open underwater, acting like they can see, even though everything's a blur. Most of the girls who start training quit halfway through, Grendy had said. "I could do it," Beauvais said, bouncing in her seat. Back then she wore her hair in two long braids. For once she was behaving herself. "I'm going to be a mermaid when I grow up," she said. "As soon as I turn sixteen." But by that time, of course, being a mermaid was the last thing on her mind.

Who would want to endure the torture? France had thought. Unlike Beauvais, she'd always been timid in the water, even though she'd had swimming lessons since she was an infant. Once, in frustration, Grendy took five-year-old France to the Y and tossed her into the pool. France felt like a failure when Grendy had to rescue her.

A fourth mermaid, a blonde dressed in a white bikini top and a tail, emerged from the deep, perched sidesaddle on a sea horse. "The Little Mermaid thinks she's hot shit," Theo said. "But she's not as good as Brett."

"Don't say that!" France wanted to clap her hand over his mouth.

The Little Mermaid swam over to join her sisters and they all "sang" a Calypso-sounding song about her birthday celebration. *"We're gonna dance. We're gonna sing. We're gonna make the waters ring."* When they held each other's gauzy tails and spun in a big Ferris wheel, looking erotic and athletic at the same time, the audience applauded wildly, and France clapped along with them. Grendy'd told France and Beauvais that on her first visit to Mermaid Springs, in 1958, when she was eighteen, she'd seen the mermaids drop their air hoses and make a wheel, and she'd decided then and there that she'd rather be a mermaid than a teacher. She'd decided not to return to college, and the next day she began mermaid training with Rose, a former underwater wrestler from Kalamazoo.

Grendy had always loved the water. As a child, living in St. Augustine, she'd spent entire days floating on her back just outside the breakers, her helpless mother watching her from the shore. She convinced her parents to put a swimming pool in their backyard, which caused her father, who worked at a gravel company, to go over his head in debt, but anything, Grendy liked to say, for his darling Grendy. She sang, splashed, swam, and played in that pool year round, even the year when it got below freezing. She could hold her breath underwater longer than any of her four older brothers—all of whom grew up to be petty criminals and ne'erdo-wells—and longer than any boy in the neighborhood; two minutes and seven seconds.

By the time Grendy went away on scholarship to Florida State she was a powerful swimmer, but she was also plump. "I had a large caboose," she told France and Beauvais. Even so, she earned a spot on the college synchronized swimming team, called the Tarpons. The Tarpons were featured in a short movie and Grendy was the lead swimmer, her face the center of a big flower, her teammates' legs the swaying petals.

The Little Mermaid was swimming toward the surface to seek her fortune, when, with a loud, taped splash, an anchor fell into the water, and she heard singing. "A sailor's life's the life for me." The sound of a storm filled the theater. "Man overboard!" A sailor sank down from above—a skinny, pock-faced young man dressed in a sleeveless white shirt, black knickers, and white socks with dirty bottoms. He was soon revived by the Little Mermaid and they danced the dance of love—advance, retreat, twirling in mesmerizing flips.

Grendy'd met North, who, with some of his friends from divinity school, was on a spring vacation, when they came to watch one of her shows. This was in 1961, when she was twenty-one and he was twenty-six. At the end of the show, when she swam up to blow kisses at the audience, she saw North's face pressed up against the glass like the face of a big fish. A big, handsome fish. Four months later, during one of her shows, he held a cardboard sign up at the glass wall. "Marry Me!" the sign said, but since she was underwater, the words were so blurry she thought they said, "Many Mes." She should've taken that literally, she told France and

Beauvais. Grendy and North eloped in September of '61 and nine months later had France.

The rest of *The Little Mermaid Show* followed, roughly, the Hans Christian Andersen tale. Theo cheered and gasped throughout the show as if this were the first time he'd seen it. "Brett is a real mermaid," he told her. "The rest of them aren't. But she is."

"Doesn't she have legs?" France asked him.

"She can change back and forth like the mermaid on 'Route 66,' " Theo said. "She told me. She's special."

France tried to concentrate on the show but she kept thinking she saw Grendy, or flashes of Grendy, swimming in the distance behind the young mermaids, diving down into the canyon, hiding up in the doorway of the castle.

After the show, France and Theo sat in the theater as it emptied, staring at the turtles and fish still swimming by the glass. The older man behind them was still trying to impress his date as they got up to leave, telling her all about his quadruple bypass. The mermaids' absence was palpable. France realized that she felt her mother's presence at Mermaid Springs more strongly than she'd felt it anywhere else, even though her mother was no longer there. Her mother loved this place. France couldn't think of anyone else who would appreciate it, except Bruno. He would want to get right in there and swim with the mermaids. "Are you going to be a merman when you grow up?" France asked Theo.

Theo sneered. "I'm going to be a detective, like Frank and Joe Hardy. And a marine biologist and a veterinarian. And a cave diver. There are three hundred twenty natural springs in Florida. Lots of the springs have underwater caves. There's a whole highway system of underground rivers."

"Hello, Theo." A woman stood at the end of the aisle next to them. "Giving another science lecture?"

"Hello," Theo said, not turning his head. He didn't seem happy to see her.

"Frances? Is that you?"

It was Lydia, one of the Mermaids of Yesteryear, the one her mother loved to hate. Grendy had introduced France and Beauvais to Lydia and her husband in 1975. Back then Lydia was hip in her vest and bell-bottoms and platform sandals, her hair tied back in a big bow. Now she was trying too hard. She was in her late fifties and too thin, her dark hair chopped up in a shag, and she wore black Lycra biking shorts and a flowered belly bra. "You look great," France said. France herself still had shoulder-length blond hair, now lightly streaked to cover the gray, which she pulled back in a ponytail, and when she wasn't at the gallery, she wore mostly T-shirts and cutoffs or jeans, imagining she hadn't changed much since high school. But of course she had. Where was the line between youthful and pathetic? How did you know when you'd crossed it? She stood up and gave Lydia a hug.

"I haven't seen you for years and years!" Lydia said. "It's awful about your sister. Such a pretty girl. Such a sad life."

"Good to see you too," France said, sitting back down. She glanced at Theo.

"Meow," he said. "I'm a cat."

"Still doing the cat thing, huh, Theo?" said Lydia.

Was this Lydia's way of being friendly to him? "Good Winky," France said, scratching Theo's head.

France braced herself for more of Lydia's sympathy, but Lydia took a different tack. "Your mother left us in the lurch," she said.

"We got a show coming up Labor Day weekend, and we don't have anyone to replace her. We don't have alternates, like *they* do." She gestured at the empty spring, but France knew whom she was talking about. The young mermaids. Glamorous, sexy, and lucky, with their whole lives ahead of them.

"What's your show this time?" France said, to distract her.

"Mermaids on the Moon!" Theo shouted.

Lydia's sour expression vanished. "Coralee and Rose and I are the alien mermaids. We wear all green, even green makeup! Your mother was supposed to be the astronaut. She's the only one who can fit into the astronaut suit. She's short. Like you."

"Grandma's astronaut suit is silver." Theo stretched out on his back and began drumming his heels against the bench. "Grandma's the best mermaid," he said.

Lydia, hands on her hips, rolled her eyes. What did she expect? Theo was Grendy's grandson. He was just sticking up for her. France was surprised to find herself feeling so defensive about Theo when just a little while ago she'd wanted to run away from him and his tantrum as fast as she could.

"Very inconsiderate of your mother, taking off like this," Lydia said. "You're skinny, just like your sister was. But she had boobs. Where'd Grendy go, anyway?"

"Lydia's obsessed with boobs, 'cause she hasn't got any," France remembered her mother saying. France surreptitiously checked out Lydia's belly bra. No boobs. France grabbed Theo's drumming feet and held them still. "We thought you might know where Mom went," France said.

"Aunt Frances and I are going to find her," said Theo. "We're detectives. I'm a cat detective and she's my owner. We're searching for clues."

Lydia dropped down onto the bench next to France. Her perfume was too sweet and too strong. "Maybe she told the other girls where she was going," Lydia said. "She sure didn't tell me anything. She wouldn't. She's always been jealous of me. Ever since Elvis."

Theo started drumming his heels again. "Lydia's obsessed with Elvis," said Theo, and France was sure that this tidbit had come from Grendy.

Lydia scowled. "You gotta muzzle this kid," she said. "I am *not* obsessed with Elvis. I never even listened to his records, not after I met him. I wanted to remember him the way he was." She sighed dramatically. "With me."

"Lydia kissed Elvis," Theo said. "It was the highlight of her life."

France forced herself not to laugh.

"There was more to it than kissing," Lydia said. "I had the lead in the show we were doing, when Elvis came. The whole picnic show was my idea. We all rode up on bicycles—underwater! I served the food, while the rest of them sat at the picnic table. Grendy thought she should've had the lead. She wanted to serve the food."

Theo leaped up and trotted off between two rows of benches, twiddling his fingers, trotted back, his eyes averted, then away again. He'd done this last Christmas, when France had seen him in Indiana. For some reason, she didn't want Lydia watching him pace. "How do you have an underwater picnic?" she asked Lydia.

Well." Lydia clasped her hands together. She was gazing out into the spring, as if she could see the scene as she described it.

"We sank a picnic table down to the stage and weighed down the tablecloth with silverware and plates and ketchup and mustard bottles. We had a grill with hot dogs cooking—there were air bubbles, just like smoke. I had a little red-checked apron on and I was holding one of those big soup tureens and we'd put three live mullets in it; then I opened it up and the fish swam out and the audience went nuts. After the show, Grendy and I pulled off the tablecloth, spilling all the plates, and 'Elvis Fan Club' was printed on the other side. He had his picture taken with both of us, but he kissed me on the lips! Grendy was so pissed, pardon my French."

Theo collapsed on the bench beside France, digging his elbow into her thigh. "Grandma's a really really good swimmer," he said.

"Being a mermaid is about more than swimming," Lydia told him. "It's about sex appeal. When the Clairol people came here, they picked me to be in their commercial. I did the Windex commercial, too."

"What's sex appeal?" Theo said.

"Man!" said Lydia. "Glad I didn't have any kids!"

How could someone be so insensitive? "Don't listen to her," France told Theo, kissing his forehead. He smelled like a fresh biscuit. "Kids are great."

"You don't have any," Lydia pointed out.

France decided to ignore this. "Sex appeal," she told Theo, "is when a girl thinks you're cute."

"Like Brett does!" He leaped up and began trotting and twiddling again. At least he was smiling as he ran.

"Elvis sure thought I was cute," Lydia went on. "He invited *me* to have a drink with him. I was so excited! On cloud nine. I didn't tell Grendy beforehand, 'cause I knew she'd try and tag along." She kicked France in the shin, twice, because France didn't look at her the first time. She gave France an exaggerated wink. "I kept the dress I wore. Kind of a Monica Lewinsky–type thing."

"I can't believe it," France said. "Mom never told me a thing about you and Elvis."

"Oh, everybody around here knows all about it," Lydia said.

Theo jumped down the aisle toward the glass wall, wobbling when he landed, his arms waving. He seemed so uncoordinated that France was afraid he'd fall any second.

"Your mom's just jealous," Lydia added.

"How's your husband?" France asked Lydia, so that Lydia would have to mentally juxtapose her husband, whom France remembered as short and unimpressive, with Elvis.

"Del died two years ago," Lydia said. "Cancer. At the end, I just gave him permission to go. I said, 'You can go now, honey,' and he died that night in his sleep." She lifted her chin bravely.

France pictured her father saying that to her mother. "You can go now, honey," and her mother wandering off down the road, a knapsack on her back.

"After Del died I bought my condo here in Mermaid Springs," Lydia said. "Now I have a cleaning woman and a yardman and a microwave and three remote controls. All I need to be happy is my lounge chair and a glass of iced tea. And to be a mermaid, of course."

Theo stood as close as he could to the glass wall, peering into the spring.

"Don't smear the glass!" Lydia yelled.

He ignored her.

Lydia went on. "I'll have to get one of the young mermaids to clean the window, and they hate cleaning the window, but they gotta pay their dues, just like we did." She turned to France. The shimmering light from the water gave her face a scary glow. "Being a mermaid is my life," she said. "Your mother had her church work, and her clubs, and her husband. But it's all mermaids for me. All I've ever wanted to do was be a mermaid. Mermaid Springs was losing *beaucoup* money before our Mermaids of Yesteryear shows started. We bring in the most people, so they'd better not boot us out. Where else could I be a mermaid?"

Was she for real? "Nowhere, I guess," France said.

They sat in silence for a while. Theo was still plastered against the glass. France stretched her arms over her head, wanting to get away from Lydia but reluctant to leave the panorama of the spring. Lydia planted her feet, in their expensive running shoes, on the bench in front of her. "How come you're not married?" she asked France.

"I was married. My ex-husband lives in Baltimore. He sells yachts." A few years ago Ray had sent a Christmas card with a picture of him with his saintly-looking wife and three dark-haired daughters on the deck of a sailboat. They all wore white pants and matching blue windbreakers. Presumably Ray wasn't stealing yacht parts. "I'm seeing someone else now," she told Lydia.

"That dollmaker? Your mom told me all about him. He let you come down here by yourself?"

"He practically ordered me onto the plane." France was getting weary of Lydia's nonsequiturs. "I've got to find Mom. Theo needs her."

She must've sounded desperate, because Lydia reached over

and patted her knee. "Your mother's fine, I bet. She was mad 'cause she had to be an astronaut. That's probably why she left. Or else she ran off after that sexy truck driver."

"What truck driver?"

"Oh." Lydia swatted at her. "Just this guy who was hanging around after the show one day. Talking to Grendy, slobbering over her boobs. It's nothing."

"But who was it? What's his name? Where's he from?"

"Search me," Lydia said. "Just said he drove a semi. I only saw him the once. But he was a hunk. Had these killer sideburns."

France pictured her mother in the cab of a semi, riding through the desert, laughing and nuzzling with a shadowy trucker. A trucker? Maybe he'd be a relief after living with France's father.

"Forget about that trucker," Lydia told France. She gave France the once-over. "Where'd you get all those freckles? How tall are you?"

"Five four."

"Perfect."

"For what?"

"The spacesuit. Are you certified to dive?"

"I'm not even a good swimmer."

"The astronaut doesn't have to do that much. Forget the certification. We've only got three weeks." She checked her sports watch and hopped up. "We're meeting down at Applebee's. I'll tell them you want to take your mother's place in the show."

"I didn't say that."

Lydia laughed. "Come watch our next practice." She dashed up the stairs.

"Tell Coralee and Rose I'm here," France yelled after her. "Tell them I want to ask them about Mom. And the trucker."

Lydia gave a gay little wave and kept going. "They're fixing to lock up for the day," she yelled, and the door banged behind her.

France walked down to the window to stand beside Theo.

He pointed out into the spring. "The castle over there is covered with black algae. That algae didn't used to be in here."

"Time to go," France told him.

He pressed his forehead against the glass. "The whole crew of the *Kursk* might drown if they don't find it soon."

"They'll find it," she told Theo. "Lots of other countries are helping."

He smiled brightly at her. "Are you gonna be in *Mermaids on the Moon?*"

France was getting whiplash being around Theo. He was worse than Lydia at changing the subject and his mood. "No way," she told Theo. "Could you see me doing that?" She couldn't do the cheesecake posing and wiggling and smiling, let alone the swimming. Naomi and Bruno would think she'd lost her mind.

"It would be really cool," Theo said. "You could be like Brett. And Grandma."

"But it's not me." Out in the spring, France pictured the underwater picnic. The mermaids sat demurely at the picnic table, all eyes on Lydia, who was dressed in 1950s' housewife attire. Lydia lifted the lid of a pot and released live fish—presto! The enchanted audience, including Elvis, applauded like mad. France thought she understood why her mother had wanted the part so badly.

Four

Back at her parents' house, France called Bruno and told him all about *The Little Mermaid Show* and the underwater picnic and the Mermaids of Yesteryear and their upcoming show, *Mermaids on the Moon*. She described Lydia. He kept pumping her for more details.

Finally she said, "Have you started on the new dolls?"

"You just gave me a great idea," he said. "I'll make three mermaids. I'll base them on Lydia, Rose, and . . ."

"Coralee. But you've never seen them."

"You can describe them to me."

"Right." She was relieved to hear the enthusiasm in his voice. Then she told him about some of Theo's odd behavior, including his temper tantrum in the theater. "Naomi thinks he has a syndrome," she said.

"He's just weirded out," Bruno said. "Give him lots of love."

"But he's not normal," France said.

"What's normal?"

"You wouldn't know."

Bruno snickered. "Is pretending to be a mermaid normal?" Then he added, "I think I know what happened to your mother."

France waited for him to continue. She could tell by his tone that he wasn't serious.

"In the *Weekly World News*," Bruno said, "there's an article about some guy in Hong Kong who found a mini mermaid in his tuna sandwich. Fishermen over there have been catching mermaids and selling them to restaurants. Human rights activists are in an uproar."

"Thanks," France said. "That's very helpful."

She camped out in her parents' bedroom, among all the mermaid paraphernalia. Theo's small room was lined with books about animals and science. He had the first eight books in the Hardy Boys series. He had a tank of tropical fish. "I take care of them all by myself," he said. The floor was littered with scraps of paper and rocks and shells and stuffed animals. There were jars and buckets full of marbles and pennies and soldiers and race cars. A brightly colored pirate ship and a plastic castle sat side by side, both overflowing with plastic animals and people and their weapons and accoutrements. Every flat surface was covered—clay animals, markers, stacks of puzzles, and board games.

France sneezed. Was she supposed to make him clean up this stuff? Or clean it up herself? Why hadn't her father done it? She couldn't imagine living in a room so crammed full of random, dusty crap. But where to start? France picked some paper up, thinking it was trash, and Theo started to howl. There was something so automatic and mechanical about his howling that it was easy to forget that the sound came from a small scared child. She only wanted to turn off the noise. She threw the scraps of paper back down and he immediately stopped howling. No wonder her father hadn't cleaned the room up.

France had already begun to discover what sorts of things triggered Theo's outbursts. He had to be the one to open the front door, close and lock it behind them. She was not allowed to help him with his seat belt. He would only wear shorts with elastic waistbands and his socks could not be the slightest bit twisted. He had to drink from a certain glass with Halloween figures on it.

That night at supper France was so tired she could barely eat. Theo had begged for macaroni and cheese, which France hadn't had since college because back then she'd eaten too much of it, but she obliged him. She had quickly learned that meals with Theo were a mine field. No kind of food must touch another kind. Toast must be cut in quarters, peanut butter sandwiches in half. Honey was okay on peanut butter crackers, but never on peanut butter sandwiches. Spilling milk on his shirt made him caterwaul. Spilling anything made him caterwaul. Surely his behavior was extreme. Was he crazy? Trying to anticipate and prevent his tantrums was driving her crazy, because something unexpected always cropped up to torment him. She wondered again if Grendy had left because of Theo. Maybe Theo had driven her around the bend. Surely Grendy was tougher than that. And Grendy loved him. He was Beauvais's son.

France quickly finished her macaroni and salad, but Theo took forever to finish his. He could not sit still at the table. He kept scooting his chair back and bringing his knees up under his chin, flopping to one side and then the other, eating only sporadically, dropping food on the floor, always talking. He told her that after Grendy left, his grandfather, who used to get up early to read the Bible, began to sleep late, till even "Geo Kids" was over. Then he sat at the kitchen table drinking coffee until lunch, and after lunch—a bowl of cereal—spent the afternoon at the Methodist church. He wouldn't let Brett come baby-sit and instead took Theo with him to church. Theo was very bored. "He was counseling people," Theo told France. "I had to sit in the lounge by myself and color. Grandma's more fun."

Back in Indiana, Grendy had taken Theo on lots of educational outings—to museums, concerts, community theater productions. North was generally too wrapped up with things at church to spend much time with Theo. This was a familiar pattern from France's childhood. Grendy, even though she was usually involved in one of her schemes, schemes that were often calculated to irritate her husband—running for city council, adopting Great Danes, redecorating the house—always exhorted France and Beauvais to better themselves, and was always trying to educate them in her distant, harried way. Beauvais, of course, required monumental effort. North mostly let the girls alone.

As France remembered it, Beauvais had been a troublemaker since she was three years old. She openly defied her parents, crossing her eyes and calling them buttheads. Grendy once asked Beauvais, when she wasn't yet ten, what she wanted to do when she grew up. "Make you miserable," Beauvais had replied. France tried to please her parents by following the rules and Beauvais tried to get their attention by flaunting them. But no matter how her parents wrung their hands about Beauvais's getting kicked out of school for telling a teacher off or for coming home drunk, France could tell they were secretly awed and fascinated as well as disgusted by her behavior. Grendy lectured Beauvais, saying that her biggest mistake ever was dropping out of college, and North tried to defend Beauvais. "She'll come to her senses."

North and Grendy were both more involved with Beauvais than they were with France, because Beauvais demanded it. She dropped out of Cedar Valley High School her senior year and ran off with a rock band called Mumbo Jumbo. A year later she moved back in with her parents, got a job at the Bare and Ball, and practiced her act in a bikini on her parents' front lawn. Neighbors wrote letters to the editor, complaining. She got her butt tattooed with the words "Get offa that thang." She was thrown in jail for drunk driving. All this took up lots of family time—crying, fighting, and many, many frantic conversations about how to deal with Beauvais. France stayed in her bedroom and read *Seventeen* magazine.

Because of this, Beauvais and France mostly hadn't gotten along. France told herself it was because they were so different, but there was more to it than that. France was afraid of her, afraid of really getting to know her, afraid of being in any way like her, and Beauvais, it seemed, was resentful of France's ability to follow rules, or at least pretend to follow them. She saw to it that France paid a price for this ability. She expected France to cover for her, to lie to their parents, and to smooth things over, and France, feeling guilty because she herself was actually a secret slut, mostly did what Beauvais wanted her to do.

She would sometimes tell her parents that Beauvais was sleeping in the room with her and didn't want to be disturbed, when actually she was out doing evil deeds. The first time France told this lie she was sure her parents wouldn't believe it. "Could you give us a little privacy?" she'd said in an outraged voice, peeking out the door of her bedroom. To her surprise, they turned and hurried off to their own bedroom like soldiers given a reprieve from battle.

Of course, France had rebelled against her parents too, just not as flamboyantly. Grendy had definite rules of decorum, and France was constantly breaking them. There were the small blunders, like the time Grendy had found stolen underwear in France's drawer, Kmart underwear, and she'd lectured France about their poor quality before forcing her to return to the store and pay for them. Or the time France, newly married, invited her parents over for dinner and served the entire meal—barbecued chicken and potato salad—on plastic plates, with plastic cutlery. Grendy got up from the table, went home, and came back with real plates and silverware for North and herself. Then there were the bigger failures, like when France had stopped going to church as a teenager. And she'd gotten divorced from Ray, whom her parents loved madly. On the surface, Ray shone. He had impeccable manners and looked like a preppy Huck Finn. They'd never liked shaggy-haired Bruno, even in high school, because he had a motorcycle and had been suspended for streaking during a home basketball game. Grendy thought that WomenSpace didn't require France to live up to her full potential, and North thought that Women-Space was full of radical lesbians who were trying to convert her.

Her parents never found out how she sleazed around before

and after her marriage broke up, or about her high school affair with her driver's ed teacher, Rudy Quackenberry. But all of these things paled when compared to Beauvais's dramatic life and sudden death.

Beauvais was killed in Lymon, Kansas, a place France had never been and never wanted to see. Beauvais shouldn't have died in Lymon, Kansas. It had no significance for her or anyone in their family. It was the wrong place to die. Like all accidental deaths, everything about it felt all wrong. When she died, Beauvais had a good job at the University of Kansas. She loved Theo and she loved being a mother. She was killed by a drunk driver when she herself had been sober for two years. France couldn't think of these facts without an upswelling of grief and anger, which she quickly tamped down. At first France had persistent daydreams about being in the car with Beauvais and Theo and somehow, at the last minute, steering them out of harm's way. This would lead her into berating herself by cataloging all the things she could have done differently in relation to Beauvais, starting from when they were children: allowing Beauvais into her secret clubhouse under the tree roots, willingly offering Beauvais her Midge doll, going to see her strip shows, and on and on. There was something addictive and self-aggrandizing about this kind of thinking, like fantasizing pornography. She finally was able to squelch these fantasies by focusing intently and relentlessly on the here and now, and by regulating the here and now as much as possible.

Beauvais had been dead for five years, and France was finding her loss slightly easier to live with. But she also couldn't help thinking that Beauvais had kept claims on her parents even after her death by leaving behind her son for them to raise. It was petty to think of things this way, but sometimes France couldn't help herself. And now France was expected to help out again by graciously taking over Theo's care. She watched him, planted in front of her parents' TV, hypnotized by a video about cats, picking his nose. None of this was his fault, of course. But it also seemed unfair that he was so stubborn and volatile. He should be cheerful, obedient, grateful. And normal.

On their second day in Mermaid City, France spent hours on the phone, calling her mother's church and neighborhood and Humane Society friends, using phone numbers she'd found written in the back of the phone book. None of these people were any help. Grendy was always happy, people said. A real ray of sunshine. Couldn't imagine where she'd taken herself off to, or what she was thinking, worrying her family this way. One woman asked, in a hyped-up voice, if France had considered *"foul play."* France told her no, but the words kept popping up in her mind, and when they did she would take a deep breath and tell herself that *foul play* would be considered after she'd ruled other things out. Then, and only then.

Later that day, she and Theo went back to Mermaid Springs and wandered around, asking questions of the employees, searching for leads, hints, signs, anything. France spent nearly an hour sitting on a straw bale, sneezing, watching Theo scratch goats in Petti-Goat Junction. He was particularly taken with an African pygmy goat that kept rubbing his forehead against Theo's belly, making greasy spots on his pale orange shirt. Theo didn't seem to mind. "I want a goat," he said. "Can I have a goat? I love goats."

"You've already got fish."

"You can't pet fish."

"I thought you wanted a cat."

"I want a cat and a goat. Can I have a goat? Please?"

France thought about explaining to him what a pain goats were, that they climbed fences and ate everything in sight, but she couldn't do it. Instead she told him that he probably could get one after his grandma came back and after he got his cat. His face was suffused with happiness, the way it had been at *The Little Mermaid Show.* Just as he could turn into an angry monster he also seemed to enjoy things more intensely than other people. He gazed into the goat's yellow eyes, and his own eyes glittered with joy.

Later, they followed the shady path past flowerbeds full of the same blue plumbago that was in her parents' yard, France slopping along in her mother's flip-flops. They were heading for the outdoor amphitheater where Theo had seen the Reptile Show. Theo ran ahead and then turned and ran back, ran ahead and ran back, again and again, twiddling his fingers excitedly, explaining to her that Jake the Indian was really cool and kept his reptiles in suitcases. But when they got there they saw a sign saying that the Reptile Show was closed. France braced herself for Theo's tantrum, but it didn't come. "Oh well," he said. "I can be adjustable." He puffed out his chest. This was obviously something else he'd heard Grendy say.

France and Theo decided to take a boat ride instead. On the Wilderness River Cruise, drifting down the transparent Crystal River, they sat on the boat's wooden benches under a tin canopy and leaned over the hot metal sides, gaping with the rest of the heat-struck passengers. Huge brown fish glided by. They saw water turkeys spreading their black wings out to dry, pelicans lined up on a tree trunk, alligators buried like car tires in the mud. A dank-smelling breeze cooled France's sweaty head. Moss-draped live oaks and cedar trees arched over them. France expected any minute to see Tarzan swinging out on his vine. How did she ever get here? Just a few days ago she'd been strolling up to the Three Sisters Café in Broad Ripple, the smells of fresh coffee and French bread wafting out, chattering people grouped at tables on the porch, Naomi and Alison waving from their favorite spot in the corner. France thought longingly of the walnut, pear, and Gorgonzola salad they always ordered. She needed to call Naomi to see how Bruno's show was shaping up.

Theo began pestering the boat captain, a florid-faced man wearing a sailor hat. "Are there snakes swimming in there?" Only poisonous ones. "Could an alligator eat a whole person?" Sure, if a person were small enough and tasted good enough. A gator could grab a person's leg and jerk him down before he could yell mama. He'd take his dinner to the bottom, to a little nest he's got set up, and stick him in there until he was ready to eat him.

"Few years back I was taking a tour group out on a glass-bottom boat," the captain told Theo. "We all looked down and there went a gator swimming by, and I said, 'Folks, he's got him a deer.' Then we realized it wasn't no deer. Found out later it was some college student."

What a story to tell a kid, France thought. She glowered at the captain, but he ignored her. He stuck his hand into a paper bag and tossed something out into the water, and the pelicans swooped over to snatch it up. Wasn't that cheating? France had always heard you shouldn't feed wildlife. An egret stood in the sandy shallows as if waiting for them. Captain tossed him some food too. "They all got parts in the show," he joked.

Theo persisted. "Could an alligator eat a mermaid?"

"If she got out in his territory. Or sometimes a gator will swim up where they do the mermaid shows. Last winter they took a three-footer out of the castle."

"My grandmother's gone. She's a mermaid. Maybe an alligator ate her."

"That rhymes!" said the boat captain.

"Stop it," France snapped at the captain, who chuckled, obviously thinking she was an overprotective mommy. Grendy eaten by an alligator. Another vision for them to torture themselves with. Theo hung his head out over the side as if watching for his grandmother, or parts of her, in the river.

"A gator wouldn't eat your grandma, son," the boat pilot said. "I know Grendy. She wouldn't taste good."

Theo turned to face the pilot. "Meow meow meow meow," he said. "I'm a cat. My name is Winky."

France, embarrassed, tried to distract the man. "Do you know where she might have gone? Did she ever talk about leaving?"

"I never fraternize with the mermaids," he said. "Don't want trouble with the wife. Even if I did know I wouldn't tell you. We all got a right to our privacy."

France felt the urge to give the man a huge shove. She imagined a satisfying splash, the panicky waving of his arms, his yelps of terror. But no, he would probably just swim calmly and deliberately toward the shore, shoving alligators out of his path.

"A Russian submarine is missing too," Theo told the captain.

"They found the *Kursk*," the captain said. "Smack dab on the bottom of the Barents Sea."

"Good," France said cheerfully. "Now they can rescue the crew!"

"Meow meow!" Theo cried, spinning around in a circle. "They're safe! They're safe!"

France caught hold of him and pinned him down beside her.

"Sure they're safe," said the captain, winking at France. "Right, Mom?"

Every night Theo insisted that she read him a chapter from his latest Hardy Boys book while he flipped around his bed with excitement. In *The Mystery of Cabin Island*, Frank and Joe Hardy and their best friends, Biff and Chet, were vacationing in a rich friend's primitive cabin on a remote island. It was the middle of winter. Fearsome snow squalls were always approaching. Sinister intruders, often disguised in costumes, lurked about, looking for the rich man's hidden treasure, harassing the boys night and day, stealing food, smashing things up, and leaving coded messages. Some vacation, France thought. But, of course, it was all in the service of solving a Big Mystery.

Five

The next morning, Monday morning, France called Naomi at WomenSpace while Theo writhed and twisted at the kitchen table, all the while managing to shovel in his third helping of pancakes. Naomi was breathless about the doll show, chattering on and on about the preparations—she'd sent out invitations, even though she had no guest list from the humpbacked artist! And she'd hired Green Goddess to cater it. Some odd man—a man!—had come in already that morning trying to sell some of his art. It was terrible, Naomi said—toothpicks glued to rotten wood. She gave him her standard kid-glove rejection by suggesting that he set up a booth at the downtown market and try to sell it himself. Naomi seemed annoyed that France hadn't located her mother yet. "What have you been doing down there?" she asked.

France couldn't resist telling her. "We went to see some mermaids perform."

Naomi was speechless. Finally she said, "Women? In bathing suits?"

"And tails," France said.

"Are they, like, in a tank?"

"No, in a natural spring. The audience sits in an underwater theater. Elvis came to see them once."

"You're such a joker," Naomi said. "I miss your sense of humor."

France tried to explain that she wasn't joking.

"What a throwback!" Naomi said. "Can't believe women still subject themselves to that."

"I talked to one of them," France said. "She's in her late fifties, and being a mermaid was the highlight of her life."

"How sad."

"Not to her."

More silence. "Well, hurry back. I can't manage without you."

France was glad to hear this, and promised to be back before Labor Day, in two and a half weeks. Bruno's opening was the Friday night before Labor Day Weekend.

"Hope you finished all the dolls you promised," Naomi said.

"Huh?"

"Why don't you just admit it?" Naomi said. "I'll find out sooner or later. Why don't you want to take credit for your wonderful work?"

"I can't," France said. "Wish I could, but I can't."

"Humph," Naomi said. "Hey. I checked with Roger about Theo. Could be ADD. Or OCD. Or just plain old depression. Or anxiety. Maybe Tourette's. Worse case, schizophrenia."

"He couldn't narrow it down?"

"There has to be a professional evaluation. But whatever it is, they probably have a medication for it."

France arranged to eat lunch with the Mermaids of Yesteryear in the Mermaid Galley, which was a little canteen lined with windows, its plastic orange tables bolted to the floor. The place had a faint vinegary smell. Old mermaid costumes hung on the walls— faded bikini tops and tails that would fit a twelve-year-old.

France and Theo, carrying their food, crowded in with Lydia, Rose, and Coralee at one of the orange tables. Everyone had ordered hamburgers and fries, since there wasn't much else on the menu. It was the sort of place where all the condiments came in little plastic pouches. The only other diner was a gray-haired man sitting across the room, wearing a cowboy hat and eating nacho chips smothered in cheese. All the mermaids waved hello to him, but they didn't ask him to join them.

Coralee daintily unwrapped her burger. "I'm sixty-five," she told France. "The oldest old mermaid." She had a sweet face, framed by long chestnut-colored hair, and a deep tan. She could pass for forty if you didn't study her too closely.

"Coralee loves to tell people how old she is," said Lydia, who then informed France that she herself was fifty-nine, the youngest old mermaid. Unlike Coralee, Lydia looked her age, despite her shag haircut. Her face was creased and lined, as if she'd worn a tense expression most of her life.

Rose, who wore a voluminous yellow shirt, told France she was sixty-three. Rose had once been an underwater wrestler, but she didn't look the part. She was blond and pale and doughy-looking, and her eyes were rimmed with an unfortunate shade of blue eye shadow. Ignoring her lunch, speaking in a placid, deliberate way, Rose explained to France how she and Lydia and Grendy and Coralee shared a cottage for two summers—1960–61—while they were performing at Mermaid Springs. "Your mother and I were the best of friends," Rose said, and Coralee interrupted and said that she and Grendy were also the best of friends.

France bit into her hamburger and wished she'd ordered the nacho chips instead. "How's your burger?" she asked Theo, who was eating with more focus than usual.

"Purr purr," he said. "That means I like it."

"Hello, Winky," Coralee said. "How are you today?" Coralee's eyes, framed by a fringe of bangs, were dark brown. She wore red lipstick and a brown shirt. She reminded France of a gingerbread woman.

"Meow meow!" Theo said. "That means I'm great!" He looked great too. France had convinced him to wear a T-shirt decorated with snap-on ladybugs and spiders, even though he was certain they'd fall off and be lost forever. He handed her a third pouch of ketchup to rip open for him.

"What a nice kitty," Rose said, smiling fondly at Theo. "You miss your grandma, don't you, kitty?" she said.

Theo dropped the cat act. "Aunt Frances and I are detectives. We're going to find Grandma."

Rose finally began unwrapping her burger. "Your mother was obsessed with being a mermaid," she told France. "She'd never have left here of her own free will."

"What do you mean by that?" France said, glancing at Theo. He was already eating and didn't seem to be paying attention.

"Something must've happened to her," Rose said. Her silky shirt was nearly the same color yellow as the mustard she began spreading on her hamburger bun.

"An alligator ate her," said Theo morosely, still chewing his burger. "Maybe she swam into their territory and one grabbed her and took her down to his nest."

Lydia gave a loud, inappropriate laugh. "You've got an overactive imagination, buddy." She bit off the tip of a fry. "What about that note to North?" she said. "That wasn't an accident." The spaghetti straps on Lydia's sundress kept creeping down her thin shoulders.

Rose admired the condiment art on her bun. "Maybe she wrote that letter under coercion. Did you inform France about the stalker?"

"Stalker?" France was chewing her hamburger but not tasting it. Why hadn't Lydia mentioned this before?

"This guy who hung around here for a few days," Coralee said, tucking her damp hair over her shoulders. Her brown knit top had a low V-neck that revealed a significant amount of tanned cleavage. France, in her blue jean overall shorts, felt like a frump. Bruno was going to have a great time making dolls based on her descriptions of the Mermaids of Yesteryear. No more Hoosier Pioneers!

"That stalker came from Los Angeles, California," Theo said.

"Naturally," said Lydia.

"He pulled this suitcase around with him," Coralee said. "Weird dude. Had like a Prince Valiant haircut. Kept making remarks."

"He was harassing Grendy," Rose said. "Always following her around, commenting on her hair and clothes. 'What's that kind of dress called?' 'Where'd you get your hair done?' It was almost like he wanted to be her."

"She never told me about that!" Coralee leaned over the table, displaying more cleavage. France averted her eyes.

"Grendy asked me to help her." Rose turned to France, revealing a small, glittery earring underneath her white-blond hair. "Your mom's always depended on me to get rid of men. She hated to disappoint them. I'd tell them she'd been called home on an emergency, or she was too sick to get out of bed."

Lydia slapped her hand on the table, causing her dress strap to tip off her shoulder. "You're out of your gourd," she told Rose. "She had a ball stringing them along." She glanced over at France. "Not now," she said. "I'm talking about back then, in the sixties."

"Your mom was such a bubbly, happy-go-lucky girl," Coralee told France earnestly. "Everybody was crazy about her. Not just men."

"Huh," France said. This picture of her mother as a man-crazy, ditzy party girl did not fit with the mother she'd known. She'd assumed that her mother had always been self-contained and businesslike and periodically depressed. She decided not to mention the fact that Grendy had run off once before. It would only get them sidetracked.

For a moment everyone stopped talking. Banjos twanged on the radio in the backroom. Rose snapped wolfishly at her food, sopping up the remaining ketchup on her plate with bits of bun, and Coralee nibbled at her hamburger but left the bun. Lydia's food was long gone. France finished every one of her lukewarm fries. She saw Theo wiping his ketchupy fingers on his shorts, but didn't feel like correcting him.

"When your mom came back here for the reunion, she wasn't the same." Rose dropped her crumpled napkin in the center of her plate. "There was more fear and less of the good old Grendy."

Lydia cackled. "Good time Grendy, you mean." Her eyes met France's and she stopped talking.

"What happened with the stalker?" France said.

Rose whisked a crumb from her mustard-colored shirt. "She asked me to talk to him, so I told him to leave her alone, but he didn't. I complained to management, and all they said was, 'You can't kick someone out just for being weird.'"

Lydia shook her finger at Rose. Her skinny arm flapping reminded France of a bird's wing. "She just uses you. Gets you to do her dirty work." Lydia turned to France. "Sorry, but it's true. Grendy plays Rose like a fiddle."

"Balderdash," Rose said. Her nostrils, red around the edges, flared out—with pleasure? Irritation? Her blue eyes and red nose and mustard-yellow shirt gave her a slightly garish appearance.

"You want to know what was in the stalker's suitcase?" Theo asked. He stuffed the last of his hamburger into his mouth. "A tail!"

Coralee said, "That's right. He went over to the swimming beach, took off his clothes, and he was wearing a woman's bathing suit—and then he starts putting on this tail. You should've seen the place clear out." She had a delighted expression on her face.

"He could've done something to Mom," said France, trying to sound as if this were any ordinary subject they were discussing, instead of the incomprehensible loss of her mother. "Maybe he drove her away." She saw Grendy holed up in a seedy motel, eating boiled peanuts, while a man with a Prince Valiant haircut yelled threats and banged his tail against the door—"Give me your blue dress or else!"

"Grendy didn't even enjoy doing the shows anymore because of him." Rose shook her white head sadly. "The day after she leaves, he's gone too. Might just be a coincidence."

"Where'd he get the tail?" said Theo.

"Through the gift shop," said Lydia. "You couldn't afford one. Costs five hundred bucks."

Theo wrinkled his nose. "I don't want a tail."

"Boys can't be mermaids," Coralee said to Theo in a kind voice. Then she frowned at France. "I don't think your mom was that freaked out about the stalker. But she's still freaked out about the accident."

"What accident?" France said.

Lydia jumped in. "It happened a long time ago. Back in '61."

"Tell me about it," France said.

"Later," Coralee mouthed, and cut her eyes at Theo.

France drained her tea in one long swallow. A small chunk of ice got caught in her throat.

"France is going to take her mother's place in our show," Lydia announced.

France cleared her throat. "I can't hold my breath that long."

"Sure you can!" said Coralee. "I'll train you."

"Quiet," Rose hissed. "Ace." She scanned the room, presumably for the man wearing the cowboy hat. "He was here a minute ago." His basket was still on the table, his napkin fluttering underneath the ceiling fan, but Ace was gone.

"What about me?" Theo said. "I'm already a good swimmer."

"Kids can't be in the shows," Lydia said. "We told you that before."

Theo grimaced like he was going to lose it, and France grabbed his weak little hand.

"We'll find something for you to do," Coralee told Theo. "Okay, Kitty?"

Theo quickly recovered. "Meow meow," he said. "That means thank you."

"I used to run cross-country," France said, "but I've never been a swimmer."

"I'll work with you," Coralee said.

"We can't take her into the mermaid area without permission." Rose fiddled with one of her glittery earrings. "Management would have a hissy fit. Insurance says under no circumstances."

"*Management* doesn't have to know," Lydia said. "For the show, we'll pretend she's Grendy. She'll have the spacesuit on. Ace won't rat on us." She leaned toward Rose. "Are those earrings real diamonds?"

Rose covered her ears so Lydia couldn't see them.

"The show's on Labor Day weekend, right?" France said. "I have to be home before then. I have to work that weekend."

"Work?" Lydia said. "On Labor Day?"

"What do you think we're doing?" Rose asked Lydia.

"We're playing, not working. We do it for love."

"Can't you get that weekend off?" Rose asked her.

"I'll have been gone three weeks by then."

"So what's another weekend?" Lydia said.

"But I want to go back. We're having a show at the gallery that I've been working toward for a long time. Sort of like your show." France could tell by their faces that they didn't see the connection. How could anything be like their show?

"Tell your boss that something came up," Lydia said. "You got a lead on finding your mother and you have to follow it."

France realized it was useless to make more excuses. "We'll see," she said.

Coralee reapplied lipstick without looking in a mirror. France had always marveled at women who could do that. "Meet you at the swimming beach in the morning?" Coralee asked with perfect red lips. "Tenish?"

France, against her better judgment, even though she knew she could never be a mermaid, any more than she could be a real astronaut, promised to be there. She had no intention of actually performing in the show, but she'd find out things about her mother from being around the mermaids. She needed to be around them as much as possible.

She asked Rose and Coralee what they knew about the trucker, but they claimed to know nothing.

All three women said they'd let France know if they thought of anything else that might help her find Grendy. Rose wouldn't meet her eyes, and France had the feeling that there was something she wasn't telling her. As they were walking out into the heat, Rose said, "Your mom thought your dad might have someone on the side. She never said who."

"Grendy was jealous of everyone," Lydia said. "She was even jealous of me, and I wouldn't touch your father with a ten-foot pole! No offense."

Coralee kissed France on the cheek. "Your mom never had a bad thought about anybody. She'll come home when she's ready. Your dad could be a real pill, you know. See you in the morning!" And the three of them walked off together toward the theater, tall Rose, short Coralee, and waif-like Lydia.

"Meow," Theo said softly. "Winky's tired."

"Me too," France said. "But we have to get groceries first."

S ix

In the huge, frigid Publix supermarket, which was surprisingly empty, Theo lagged behind France, collecting coupons from the coupon dispensers to add to the drift of paper in his bedroom. A ladybug had come unsnapped from his shirt, and she prayed he wouldn't notice till they got home. She had found out that, along with macaroni and cheese and peanut butter, he only really liked fish sticks and chicken fingers and pizza and hamburgers and especially, like her, chocolate. At least shopping was easy.

They found themselves in the frozen food aisle, where Theo stopped to stare at the cartons of ice cream. France, thinking he wanted ice cream, put a pint of Ben and Jerry's New York Super Fudge Chunk in the cart. He didn't seem to notice. Still not meeting her eyes, he said, "Me and the trucker and Grandma went out for ice cream." He started walking toward the produce.

In the produce section France pawed through stalks of rubbery broccoli and tried to act nonchalant. She would insist that Theo eat some salad at dinner, or he wouldn't get his ice cream. "What did you and the trucker and Grandma talk about?"

Theo flipped through his coupons.

"Theo?"

He kept poring over his coupons as if he hadn't heard her.

"Theo!" She shook his shoulder, and he jumped back, startled. "What did Grandma and the trucker talk about?"

"I can't think," he whined. "I don't know."

"Well think harder," France said, in a nastier voice than she'd intended.

He cowered against the tomatoes, flinching. "I'm sorry," he said. "I'm really sorry."

A portly black man in a suit, carrying a basket of frozen food, strolled by them, rubbernecking.

I'm not a child abuser, France wanted to tell him. I used to take child abusers to court! "It's okay," she told Theo. "I'm not mad." But he knew better.

He slid down and flopped onto the floor. "Ouch," he said, blame in his voice.

France bent over and helped him up. A tall, foxy-faced woman pushing two bickering toddlers in an oversize cart gave her a sympathetic smile. He's not mine, France wanted to say. I am not one of you. Why did she care what strangers thought of her parenting skills? She wasn't even a parent.

"Winky." France tickled Theo under his chin. "It's important for our detective work. What Grandma and the trucker said could help us solve the mystery. So try and remember."

Theo contorted his face as if he were making a great effort. "I think they talked about the good old days," he said. "I think they did."

France spoke as calmly as she could. "What did they say about the good old days?"

"When Wayne came to see her shows. He said, 'Them were the good old days.' "

"Wayne?"

"That's his name. Wayne Purdy." Theo was sliding down the tomato bin again, and France yanked him up. When she let go he staggered backward, loose as a doll, bumping into the shopping cart. Was he really this uncoordinated, or was he putting on a show? Or was he just tired? She would have to tell Naomi about this behavior, so she could ask her husband about it. But how would she describe it?

Theo hung on the cart, tipping it sideways. "Stop it," she told him, and he dropped to the floor, lying flat on his back. She just stood there. They were supposed to be grocery shopping. At this rate they'd never get home. Maybe she should ignore the way he was acting. She put some hard pink tomatoes into their cart. She'd assumed that Florida would have better produce than Indiana, but she was wrong. "Did Grandma act happy to see Wayne?" she asked Theo, who'd scrambled to his feet to watch the sprinklers mist the squash. What a stupid question. She wanted to ask, Did they kiss? Did they go to a hotel? Did they make plans to run away together? She couldn't really imagine her mother doing any of those things, especially with someone who said, "Them were the good old days," but it seemed there was a lot she didn't know about her man-crazy fun-loving mother.

Theo was now leaning against her. "Wayne let me sit in the cab of his rig," he said. "Grandma told me that Mr. Wayne Purdy was a 'gem.' That's all I remember." He glowered at her defiantly, and France realized how seldom he made eye contact with her. "Thanks for telling me, Winky," she said. "Let me know if you remember anything else."

That evening, after fixing dinner—linguini with pesto for her, plain buttered linguini for Theo, a salad, and then ice cream for dessert—France called her father and told him about Wayne Purdy.

"She mentioned him," North said. "Guy who used to work at Mermaid Springs. Handyman. There's nothing to that."

He was too dismissive of Wayne, France felt, but she decided to move on. "There was a stalker after her."

"That fruitcake with the tail in his suitcase? He was harmless. Nuts, but harmless."

"But she was scared of him."

"She laughed about him," North said.

"Doesn't mean she wasn't scared of him."

"Could you imagine your mother getting scared of some pathetic little person? So scared she'd leave without telling anyone where she was going?"

"I guess not," France said. "But Rose seemed to think she was that scared."

"Rose likes to be the knight-in-shining-armor," North said. "Always trying to solve problems that don't even exist. She's a lesbian, by the way. She'd fit right in at WomenSpace."

France decided to dive in. "Somebody said she left because you were a real pill to live with."

Her father just laughed. "No doubt about that," he said. "But she's known that for years."

France felt defeated by his flippancy. "I just can't believe she hasn't called us."

"If you get a bee in your bonnet," said her father, "and you run off, you're only thinking of yourself. Try not to take it personally. She'll call or come back eventually."

He was probably right, but his insistence on minimizing France's feelings was driving her mad. And why did he keep repeating the idiotic phrase "bee in her bonnet"? "They also mentioned some accident she was involved in, back when," France said.

"I don't know what that would be," he said. "Anyway, why would that cause her to take off now? Something that happened years ago?"

"They said she still felt guilty about it," France said. "Coralee's the one who told me."

"Coralee," North said. "Now there's a case of arrested adolescence." He chuckled. "How's Theo? Has he been acting weird?"

France glanced over at Theo, who was licking the bottom of his ice cream dish. Where would she begin? "Not any weirder than anyone else," she finally said.

"He needs some discipline," North said. "We let him get away with too much. Maybe you can get him in shape."

Again France tried to remember all the suggestions she'd given the foster parents she'd worked with, tips for managing problem behavior, things anyone in their right mind would think of themselves. How could she have known that someone saddled with kids wouldn't even have a mind left? "He's getting *me* into shape," she told her father.

After they hung up, she got Theo settled with a video about jungles and took the phone out to the screened porch to call Bruno. The warm air felt comforting after the air conditioning, and the fading golden light on the doublewide across the street transformed it into something regal. She could smell meat cooking on a neighbor's grill.

France almost cried when she heard Bruno's voice, when he said he missed her. He said that the Wabash River was overflowing its banks. She described Theo's recent antics and he said that Theo, like most kids, probably just craved a routine. France couldn't think of a way to make him see that Theo wasn't like most kids, so she just agreed.

He still hadn't started on the mermaid dolls—he was waiting for physical descriptions of the mermaids. She described the three women as best she could. "Perfect, perfect," he kept saying. "Love the eye shadow. And the cleavage."

"Are you going to give them tails? How will they stand up?"

"They have to have tails. Big sturdy tails. They'll be land mermaids."

France didn't want to hear anymore of Bruno's silliness. She told him that Naomi thought she'd carved the dolls.

"You?" Bruno made a spitting sound. "Your hands are smooth as a baby's. Does she really think you could carve wood?"

"Maybe she thinks I wear gloves. I don't know. It's ridiculous. She knows I'm a total klutz."

"What've you found out about your mom?" he asked, and she told him.

"My money's on the affair," he said. "Pappy's on the prowl again. Remember Tammy Vickers."

"How could I forget?" France said. Actually, she did forget about Tammy most of the time, and she regretted ever telling Bruno about her. "That was ages ago," she told Bruno now. "Water under the bridge."

"Milk over the dam," Bruno said.

"What?"

"Get real," he said. "He probably never stopped messing around."

For a few seconds France felt so angry she couldn't speak. Then she found her voice. "How the hell would you know? Do you have proof? He *is* a minister."

"So was Jim Jones."

"Just because someone messes up once."

"Sorry. Forget I said it."

France glanced over and saw Theo standing in the doorway. How long had he been there?

"Winky," she said, holding out the phone. "Come talk to Bruno."

Theo ran for the phone. "How's Wilma? Did you take her for any more car rides? Is your big wind tube still sticking? Meow meow meow. I love you."

Theo had never told her he loved her. How did Bruno do it? She decided not to tell him that she'd been asked to swim in *Mermaids on the Moon*. She didn't want him to think she might not be back in time for his gallery show, because if he thought that he might not carve the new dolls. Also, she was angry at him for making the remark about her father. When she got back on the phone she said good-bye right away.

After she hung up France decided that she and Theo should

take a walk. At home she power-walked around Broad Ripple every evening. She hadn't done it here because of the heat. But to hell with the heat. It could only make her sweat. She went into Theo's room, where he was lying on his stomach moving plastic knights around on the carpet, and told him they were going for a walk. He stood up and his face began to melt into an expression of—terror? rage? sadness?—as if the very worst thing in the world had just happened. His face grew redder and redder and he began screaming and crying, louder and louder, like a fuse had been lit and he was catching fire. "What's the matter?" she kept asking. She tried to touch him but he danced away. She asked him to stop, begged him to stop. "Stop it!" she yelled, as loud as she could, which wound him up even more. She felt the urge to shake him, so she left the room and sat down on the couch.

The living room had been furnished by someone with ADD. The couch was orange velour and the chairs red faux leather and the carpet rust-colored. It probably all came from garage sales. At home, her parents' house was furnished with North's parents' antiques and oriental rugs. How could they stand this room? The only evidence that North lived here was a small bookcase in the corner, filled with history and philosophy books. She couldn't wait till she was back in her own soothing apartment, back at the gallery with all its handpicked charm. Able to take a simple walk around the block without a major battle. No way could she deal with these battles on a regular basis. In the other room, Theo was still railing. France felt so inadequate she wanted to rail herself. She'd never imagined she could lose control so quickly.

After ten minutes or so Theo came out, no longer crying, but acting as if he might go off again. "I don't want to go for a walk," he told her.

"Okay," she said. "Why not?"

"The drainage ditch. It'll suck me down."

How would he react if something truly bad ever happened? How had he reacted when his grandmother left him? France was glad she hadn't been here to contend with that. But he really didn't seem to be faking. For him the drainage ditch must feel over-whelmingly scary. She tried to convince him that he had nothing to fear, but he kept shaking his head and whimpering.

"How about if I go just around the block, and you stay here and read?"

"Then you'll get sucked down," he said. "Just like the *Kursk* submarine got sucked down. Maybe that's what happened to Grandma!"

France told him that the *Kursk* crew members would soon be rescued, even though she had no idea if this were true. In order to protect Theo, she hadn't listened to or watched the news since she'd been here. She also told him that his grandma wasn't in the drain—wouldn't somebody hear her calls and pull her out?—and she promised to walk as far away from the drainage ditch as pos-sible. Finally, after she assured him that she'd be back for his bed-time ritual, he agreed to let her go. He relished his bedtime ritual—Hardy Boys chapter, three songs of her choice, and then a lullaby, her prayer, his prayer, which was always the same, "Thank you for the animals, especially cats. Please let the *Kursk* be saved and let Grandma come home tomorrow," and then a good night kiss. By the time she finished all this she was ready for bed herself.

France stumbled out into the deepening dusk. The air felt

soggy and smelled metallic, like a bog. The cicadas made an elec-
tric, pulsing sound. Forget the power-walking, she decided. Moving at all felt like a big effort. She waved to a woman who was
yanking vines from her hedge. The neighborhood was livelier at
this time of day, although nobody under sixty seemed to be in the
vicinity. A white-haired man, bare-chested, in excellent shape,
jogged by with a beagle on a leash and gave her a smart salute. She
turned the corner, staying a good two feet away from the drainage
ditch.

Because the houses were so much alike she found herself
searching out differences. An old fishing boat and the rusty boat
trailer underneath it were nearly covered with kudzu. Another
house had two gorgeous little palm trees framing the front walk.
If she ever lived here, which she wouldn't, she'd never get used to
seeing palm trees. Right now she felt very fondly toward the palm
trees, and everything else she saw, but maybe she was just relieved
to finally be alone, thinking her own thoughts. It wasn't just Theo
who was getting on her nerves. She was still annoyed at Bruno the
busybody. She needed to forget about both of them and concentrate on finding her mother.

As she walked she went over the possible causes of her
mother's flight. It didn't sound like the stalker was a real factor.
Rose did seem a bit overzealous in her protection of Grendy. Had
that in itself driven Grendy away? Didn't seem likely. Wayne
Purdy from the good old days? She needed to get more information about him. And the accident. She'd pump Coralee about that
in the morning. Why had Coralee volunteered to give her mermaid training? Coralee seemed too generous to be true. And then
there was the hint of an affair. France didn't even want to think

about the possibility of her father having another affair. Did having one affair, years ago, place you under suspicion for the rest of your life? She hoped not. She herself had had an affair with a teacher, Rudy Quackenberry, when she was in high school. And she'd had a fling before her marriage to Ray broke up. But she was only a kid both times—teens and early twenties—and her father, when he had the affair with Tammy, was older, and a minister, and should've had more sense. Even as she thought about it, she knew she was being ridiculous. Good sense had no part in this kind of equation. For instance, there was Clinton and Monica Lewinsky. And North and Tammy Vickers.

Tammy Vickers had been a member of her father's first church, in Illinois, when France was ten and Beauvais was eight. One Sunday morning, before the sermon, North announced to the congregation that he had something to confess, because he couldn't live with himself anymore. "I have met the enemy," he said, "and he is me." He went on to say that he and Tammy, a soloist in the choir, who wasn't there that day—everybody immediately strained to see—a young woman with a perpetually annoyed expression and little wire-framed glasses had been "intimate." North stood there in front of everyone, crying, saying he had to get it off his conscience, he was so sorry and had learned his lesson. France had no idea what being intimate was, and nobody explained it to her, but she knew it must be awful. She remembered two things about this incident, two things that penetrated her haze of humiliation. One: the way her mother, who was sitting beside her, dressed in the red-and-white-striped summer dress North had just given her for her birthday, kept staring at North and muttering disturbing, animal-oriented things:

"Cat's out of the bag now. Horse is out of the barn." Two: she was sure that her mother, who'd already run off once to Arizona, would surely leave again.

After North's confession, Beauvais, white face framed by her braids, got up, clawed her way out of the pew, and lurched out the side door. Grendy sobbed quietly beside France. Many members of the church filed up to the front to hug North, as if he were some kind of hero, and France found herself feeling almost proud of his bravery. At the same time, she was enraged that only a few women came over to comfort her mother. Her mother was allowed to sit and cry until, finally, France led her out the back door and walked her home, resenting the fact that she and her mother had been lumped together. It wasn't that she approved of her father's behavior—she was furious at him—but who wanted to be linked with the victim?

Later, Beauvais and North showed up at home together. What had the two of them talked about on the way home? France wondered. She was lying on the couch pretending to read a Nancy Drew book. North headed straight upstairs to try to salvage his marriage, and Beauvais, standing there in the Hang Ten culottes that North permitted her to wear to church, even though they were the same as shorts, gave France a self-satisfied smile. "It didn't surprise me," she said. "I always knew Dad was a faker."

Did Beauvais's downhill trip begin that day? How tidy it would be to attribute all Beauvais's problems to one incident. There were surely many factors influencing the roles they all adopted. Back then, of course, she wasn't thinking of causes and motivations. She was ten years old.

For weeks after North's confession, France expected to come

home from school to an empty house, a plate of oatmeal cookies set out on the counter like the ones her mother had left the first time. Every afternoon when she opened the kitchen door and did not smell cookies, she let out a gasp of relief. After a while she stopped consciously expecting her mother to leave, but the fear had never really gone away. Whatever had caused her mother to run away to Arizona must have been worse than Tammy Vickers, she'd finally decided. Something really bad.

Like whatever had caused her to run away this time.

A bell tinkled behind France, startling her. A bicycle studded with little American flags wobbled past, a large woman hunched over the handlebars. France realized that she'd come around to her parents' house again. The subdivision was small, and she'd completed the loop too quickly. She was hardly sweaty at all, and would've circled around again if she hadn't seen Theo, standing on the screen porch, waiting for her.

They were up to Chapter VI in *The Mystery of Cabin Island*. At the end of the chapter, the Hardys and their friends were returning to the cabin with provisions, when Chet stopped short.

"*For a moment, Chet could only point. Then he declared in a strange, hollow voice, 'There! In the woods! A ghost!'* "

Seven

The next morning, France and Theo met Coralee on the Mermaid Springs swimming beach. Coralee had positioned herself in a lounge chair facing the sun and pulled down the straps of her navy blue tank suit for maximum exposure. "I've heard all I want to about skin cancer," Coralee said. "This is my only vice."

France and Theo were both pasty white and slathered with sunscreen. France had gathered her hair back in a messy sort of bun, and she wore an old turquoise-and-black-striped swimsuit that was faded and frayed. She spent so much time at the gallery that she never went out in the sun anymore. Why hadn't she bought a new suit in Indiana? She dragged one of the white plastic lounge chairs over beside Coralee and parked herself under a big red umbrella.

"You sure don't have your mother's skin," Coralee remarked. "She has the prettiest skin. Naturally tan." Coralee wore a minty smelling lotion. Her face was meticulously made up—waterproof makeup, undoubtedly—and her long brown hair was still wet from an earlier swim. Her legs and arms were muscular, as if she worked out with weights. France felt like the Little Match Girl sitting beside her.

They sat facing the springs. Although Highway 19 was close behind them, they might've been on a remote tropical island, one with a tacky resort. The roped-off swimming area was already full of splashing, boisterous groups of people. Theo walked across the sugary sand and waded into the water, pale green near the edge and darker green farther in. To their left was the spring where the mermaids performed. To their right loomed a huge water slide, and past that the river turned and disappeared. The same river they'd taken the boat ride on. The Wilderness River Cruise. Theo stood like a stump in water up to his knees. Was he thinking about alligators? Even in the shade the bright sun hurt France's eyes. She began digging around in her totebag for her sunglasses.

The sky above them was deep blue, but dark clouds nested in the West. This time of year it rained nearly every afternoon, Coralee told her. She pointed out some French tourists—she knew they were French by their skimpy bathing suits and superior haircuts. She also pointed out the Albritton clan, a local family who was always there—a bunch of sloppy sisters and their passel of rambunctious kids. Theo sat down in the water.

"Theo loves the water," Coralee said. "Your mom tried to teach him how to swim this summer, but he's having a hard time. Got no muscle tone. So you're going to take him? I think he'd be better off with you."

France brushed a strand of hair out of her eyes. Beads of sweat had formed on her nose. She was still digging around in her bag. "I don't know a thing about taking care of kids," she said.

"It's on-the-job training," Coralee said. "I've got five kids. Sixteen grandkids. And they all live right here! Well, not right here, but in central Florida. Close enough for me to do lots of baby-sitting. My house is always full of people." Coralee smiled to indicate that she liked her house being full of people.

"Sounds awful to me," France said, and then wished she hadn't. "I love living alone," she added, remembering the time Ray smashed an entire tea set against their locked bedroom door.

"Not me. I love having them all close by. My granddaughter is in *The Little Mermaid Show*. She baby-sits for Theo. I take the younger grandkids up to Wild Adventures in Valdosta. In my spare time, ha ha."

"Theo's crazy about Brett," France said. She finally pulled out her new sunglasses and put them on. She liked the authority they gave her. Theo was wading deeper into the water. Was he safe out there?

Coralee lay back in the chair. She had donned big black sunglasses. "We'll start in a minute," she said. "I want to even up my tan first."

France, keeping an eye on Theo, decided to take this opportunity to find out more about her mother and the accident. She asked Coralee to give her the details.

In the summer of '61, Coralee said, Grendy had been helping to train a new girl, and she and the new girl went up into an air lock—a big plastic clamshell, not the castle that's there now—to wait for their turn in the show. But there was bad air in the clamshell. Both girls started to pass out. Only Grendy managed to swim up to the surface.

"Linda was the girl's name," Coralee said. "Linda Huddle. She didn't make it. Nowadays there'd be a lawsuit, but back then they could hush the whole thing up. They paid off her parents. It was so sad. Grendy never got over it."

"She never told me about it," France said, settling back in her own chair. Maybe her mother had been so racked with guilt she had to get away from the scene of the accident. But why all the guilt? It obviously wasn't her fault. And why all the secrecy?

Theo began splashing back toward the beach as if an alligator were chasing him.

Coralee kept talking. "A few nights after it happened I came in from a date with Kenny, my high school honey, and Grendy was sitting there, at the kitchen table, crying. That was the second year we four girls lived together, in one of the cottages they used to have for the mermaids. We actually had a curfew! Anyway, Grendy was out-and-out sobbing. She kept saying, 'I let her die.' "

"How awful," France said. It was painful to imagine her mother so distraught. Why hadn't she told her husband and children about it?

"It was awful," Coralee said with relish. "Just terrible. She said she felt so bad she was going to leave, that she didn't deserve to be a mermaid anymore. The next morning she quit the mermaids and went off to Chicago to marry North, even though she didn't think she really loved him."

"She didn't love him?" France had always assumed that her mother stayed with her father and put up with his philandering because she was so in love with him.

Theo was now floating on his stomach, hanging perfectly still in the water like a drowned person.

Coralee patted her arm. "I'm sure she came to love him, over the years."

"Maybe," France said. Marriage certainly hadn't caused whatever love there'd been between her and Ray to blossom. Then, of course, his stealing and her affair had squashed what was left of it.

"Your parents couldn't have come from more different backgrounds," Coralee observed.

This was true. North had grown up in Oak Park, Illinois, where his father was also a Methodist minister, and his mother a musician—she played harp with the Chicago Symphony. North was their only child. They were always vaguely disapproving of Grendy and her Southern working-class origins. They didn't even appreciate the fact that Grendy named Beauvais after North's mother's family, or the fact that Grendy was always striving to seem cultured and refined. She went through phases of wearing Indian saris and Japanese kimonos. She visited all fifty states so she could say she had. She drove Cadillacs and Volvos, even though they could only afford old ones. Grendy's parents both died of heart attacks before France was six. "No wonder," she'd overheard her father say once. "They both drank booze and smoked and ate potato chips nonstop."

Coralee dabbed at her face with her towel. "When Grendy joined the Mermaids of Yesteryear, Linda wouldn't leave her mind. I think that's why she left."

France couldn't imagine her mother, who always seemed so sure of herself, getting into such a state about something that happened so long ago.

"She's changed so much," Coralee went on. "When she came

back in '97 it was like she'd gone into low gear. She's as friendly as ever, I don't mean that."

"What was she like before the accident?"

"Full of herself. That's a good thing—don't get me wrong. Always laughing and joking and touching people. A real social butterfly."

France pictured Grendy with butterfly wings, flitting from person to person. But something was missing from this description. "I don't really think she liked people all that much," France told Coralee. "When I was a kid she used to hide whenever someone rang the doorbell. She hid from people in the grocery store. Had me answer the phone and lie for her. She wanted to be a good minister's wife, but I don't think she really liked it." She didn't tell Coralee about the times when Grendy lay around in bed for weeks with the lights off, watching the TV with sunglasses on. She would call France or Beauvais in to change the channels for her.

Theo kept rolling over and over in the shallow water. Was he imitating some animal?

Coralee said, "To be honest, Grendy was even fatter back then. Lydia used to call her Sea Cow. But her weight never seemed to bother her, not a bit. She'd go to the drugstore for hot fudge sundaes and I'd just drink iced tea—unsweet—to keep my figure."

As long as France could remember, Grendy was always going on and off diets, but she never lost weight. France often caught her eating ice cream and candy on the sly. North never commented on Grendy's weight or her dieting, but he flirted with other women, young women, in the church. That was enough of an incentive for

Grendy to pretend to diet, evidently expecting miracles because she was willing to make a halfhearted effort.

"Such a perfect life she'd led," Coralee said, "and then wham! She kills someone. Or, rather, thinks she did. It really was an accident. I tried to convince her of that."

France watched Coralee, whose face seemed to grow harder as she talked. It was no wonder Coralee couldn't talk Grendy out of leaving, France thought, seeing as she was practically blaming Grendy right now.

"Not that I've had real *bad* hardships," Coralee said, "but I took care of everyone. Still do. Not that I mind. My dad died of bone cancer when I was sixteen. But we won't go into that. I helped my mom around the house because my sisters were always too busy. Then I had my own kids and now there's the grandkids and they all depend on me." Coralee pointed at Theo, who was jumping up and down like a frog in the shallow water. "Your boy's having fun," she said.

He's not my boy, France wanted to say. She was dying to slip into the water. Even sitting under the umbrella she was drenched with sweat, and she felt slightly dizzy. "Are you sure you want to train me?" she said. "Don't you want a break from training people? You just said . . ."

"Honey, I love people," Coralee said. "Don't pay my bitching any mind. I'm really a very nice person." She stood up and stretched, checking on her tan. Her chest and shoulders were a nice nutty brown. "If I sit here any longer I'll just say something else I don't really mean." She stood up, unwrapped a towel, and produced some swimming goggles and flippers. "Let's go out and I'll give you some pointers. Then you can practice and I'll watch your boy."

"Thanks," France said. She pulled off her sunglasses, feeling vulnerable and exposed. Should she trust Coralee with Theo? She pictured Theo's limp body on the beach and Coralee being led away by the police yelling, "But I'm a nice person!" France had to stop being paranoid. Coralee was just a tad resentful of Grendy, that was all. And of the fact that she had no solitude. But who wasn't resentful about something?

France sat in the shallow water, which felt like an ice bath, and pulled on the flippers and the mask, her lower half going numb. She and Coralee swam out till they could no longer touch bottom. "You've got to practice treading water with your legs straight," Coralee said. "Remember: always come up slowly and always exhale while you're ascending. And you've got to smile at all times. Even if you're the astronaut."

France dove into the water, flogging it with the flippers. Everything came into focus with the mask on—the legs of the swimmers, the darting fish. Someone stepped on her head, pushing her down. She struggled up to the surface, ears popping, and sucked in a breath of air. She yanked up the mask and glanced over at Theo and Coralee, who seemed to be doing fine. Coralee was helping Theo float on his back. For a while she practiced treading water with her legs stiff, but people kept bumping into her.

She needed to get out into deeper water, away from the other swimmers. She slid the mask back down, dove under, and swam out toward the diving platform. She found herself imitating the undulating way the mermaids swam, pretending she was wearing a tail, hoping no one was watching her. Besides not being a strong swimmer, she had terrible stage fright. At her first piano recital she'd frozen in fear in the middle of her performance and had to be led off the stage by her piano teacher. She swore she'd never put herself in that position again. Beauvais, who loved being up in front of people, whizzed through her first piano recital. Beauvais was a cheerleader in junior high. She played Mrs. Hale in *Trifles*. She would've been a perfect mermaid.

France stopped swimming, lunged backward, and tried a flip, flailing about, water going up her nose, bobbing up to the surface like an awkward kangaroo. How did the mermaids manage to stay down and do acrobatics at the same time?

She glanced over and saw how close she was to the Underwater Grand Canyon, the source of the spring, the place where the mermaids swam. The roof of the underwater Mermaid Theater sat on the surface of the water. The mermaid shows didn't start till afternoon, so the place was empty. She wanted a closer look, but the boundary rope for the swimming area was in her way. Would anyone really notice if she swam over there now? The lifeguard, a teenage boy, was talking to an Albritton girl who stood beside his chair. Coralee and Theo were both floating on their backs. She'd just do a quick dive under the rope, swim over there, turn and come back. No problemo.

France dove down again, as deep as she dared, and began swimming toward the canyon. She could see it in the distance, like a huge blue room. There was the storybook castle on the hill, and beyond that, the statue of David, and the treasure chest. And there was the great glass wall of the theater. A large turtle swam in front of her, back end sagging as if it were weighted. She almost expected to see Grendy, in a mermaid tail, sitting beside the treasure chest, waving to her. Here I am! You found me! The whole place was a mirage, and France wasn't going to get there and back after all. She had to take a breath. She heard the lifeguard's whistle just as she broke the surface. All the swimmers, and most of the sunbathers, including Coralee and Theo, were gawking at her.

"Stay in the roped area!" the lifeguard bellowed.

France dog-paddled toward the shore, fighting the impulse to duck underwater and hide. So much for being inconspicuous. Now Coralee wouldn't want to have anything more to do with her, would think she couldn't be trusted. She yanked off her mask and slogged out of the water in her flippers, dripping ice cold water, feeling like the Creature from the Black Lagoon. She lowered herself onto her lounge chair, hiding her face in a towel.

Coralee left Theo digging a moat at the edge of the water and came up to sit beside France again. "What were you trying to do?" she asked France.

"Had so much fun I got carried away," France said, and then, wanting to head off any criticism, quickly added, "Tell me how you learned to be a mermaid."

Coralee began toweling her hair. Her makeup was still flawless. "I grew up right near here, over by Homosassa Springs," she said. "I was the middle of five girls, and we were all mermaids. I'm the only one who stayed here. Even when my mermaid days were over, I kept on working here. I trained the new mermaids, and even did some choreography, whatever they needed me to do, just so I could keep swimming here."

"Why do you like it so much?" France said. She wished she'd asked her mother this question.

"Down there I'm one of the fish. Fish don't talk. They ignore me. Everyone up here always expects me to smile and be a nice person. And I am a nice person. Don't get me wrong."

Why would anyone feel compelled to insist that she or he was a nice person? "I know you're a nice person," France said. "Mom always said so." Actually, France didn't remember her mother saying much about Coralee at all. Or Rose. "So what's the story on Rose?" she asked Coralee.

Coralee set her sunglasses back on her face and jerked at her chair arms till the chair reclined. "Rose's a dear," she said, flexing her red-painted toes. "She's gay. Lives with a partner over by the Gulf, a woman dentist. She used to live in Cassadaga, the little town where everyone's a medium. Everyone can speak with spirits. It's not far from here."

"So she's psychic?" France asked. If Rose was psychic, she should be able to tell them where Grendy'd gone.

"Not any more," Coralee said. "Says she lost her powers, or some such nonsense. I think they're all a bunch of loonies. Anyway, Rose has always had a sort of crush on your mom, no doubt about that."

"Maybe Mom has a crush on her too. Maybe that's why she left."

"Haw!" Coralee slapped her thigh. "Nobody loves men more than your mama."

France had no idea what to say to this. She'd never have thought of her mother as loving men. She certainly didn't flirt, not that France could remember. She'd been too busy trying to keep North's attention. One evening, when North was speaking to a singles' group at church, Grendy appeared in the doorway of the room on a bicycle, wearing short shorts, claiming she'd locked herself out of their house and needed North's key. France, who heard about this from a friend, knew better. Her mother was desperate to make herself known, while at the same time sizing up her competition.

Theo crawled into the water and began rolling around in the shallows. He sat up and yelled to France, "I'm a water cat!"

France smiled and waved. "Theo's been telling me about Mom's trucker friend, Wayne Purdy," she said. "They went out for ice cream once. The three of them."

Coralee stared at France. She seemed stunned. "That guy was Wayne? Are you sure?"

"According to Theo."

She'd already recovered. "He sure has changed. Used to be such a fox."

"I wonder if he and Mom . . ."

"God no," Coralee said. "Wayne's a real jerk."

"But Theo said she was saying what a great guy he was."

"She says that about everybody," Coralee said. "You can cross him off your list. Believe me." She sighed. "I better get going. Got a million errands to run." But she didn't move.

France sat sideways in her chair, her butt stretching out the plastic. She was cold to the bone. She would never be warm again. "Why are you doing this?" she asked Coralee. "Training me? When you're so busy."

"Grendy would've wanted me to," Coralee said. "She would've loved your being in the show."

"You're talking like she's dead."

"Oh no!" said Coralee. "She's just fine, wherever she is."

"But you don't know where that could be."

"I wish I did. She's my best friend. But I don't."

"You can't tell me anything else?"

Coralee sat up. "I shouldn't," she said, "but I will. This is just between us." Coralee spoke slowly and distinctly. "Lydia never slept with Elvis." She lifted her sunglasses and leaned toward France, widening her brown eyes as if she expected some big reaction.

"Oh," France said. She thought, How about telling me something relevant?

Coralee did a zipping-her-lips motion. Theo was crawling up the beach toward them.

"So," Coralee said to France. "Think you want to be a mermaid?"

"I really don't know," France said, not meeting Coralee's eyes. She decided to be honest. "Don't think I could if I wanted to."

"Nonsense!" Coralee said. "It's in your genes! We'll continue your training day after tomorrow. Every other day for the next two weeks, and then every day till the show. Get Brett to baby-sit Theo." She mentioned that the older mermaids were practicing *Mermaids on the Moon* that afternoon, if she and Theo wanted to come and watch. "Lydia's going to do the part of the astronaut, so you can see what you'll be doing. You'll see how much we need you. Lydia'd rather be a pig than an astronaut!"

Eight

France, wanting a break from child care as much as anything, arranged for Brett to baby-sit for Theo the following afternoon, and he was thrilled. He insisted on going to the Mermaid Springs Gift Shop to buy Brett a present with the three dollars he'd saved. He walked up and down the aisles of the shop, studying the stationery and paperweights and mermaid dolls and T-shirts. There were bins of stuffed animals and shelves stocked with magnets, lamps, wind chimes, videos, even flatware with mermaid handles. France could see he was getting more and more frustrated, and she did not want to deal with another tantrum. "I can't decide," he said, his face flooded with anxiety. He was working himself up again.

France crouched down beside him. "What does she like?"

His face relaxed. "Jewelry," he said. "She really likes jewelry."

"Let's go see what they've got."

A young woman with a crew cut, wearing a halter top, stepped behind the counter and showed them some cheap-looking neck-laces and bracelets and rings with mermaid charms on them. But the price was not cheap. Theo pointed to a necklace with an enamel mermaid hanging on it. It cost ten dollars. "She'd love this. Is this three dollars?"

The young woman behind the counter gave France an expec-tant smile. Was she going to be a nice mom, or a mean mom? "I'm not his mother," France told her. "I'm his aunt."

The young woman gave an even bigger smile, raising her eye-brows. Aunts always spoiled their nephews.

France told Theo that three dollars should cover it exactly.

Later that afternoon Theo and France went to see the older mer-maids practice *Mermaids on the Moon*. The only other person sit-ting in the theater was the short, gray-haired man wearing the cowboy hat who'd been in the canteen the day before. Ace. He gave them an uncurious wave. Theo sat down directly in front of the glass window, but France sat back a few rows.

Suddenly Ace got up and dashed off to the control booth. "Blue Danube," the theme song from *2001: A Space Odyssey* blared out over the loudspeakers. A white plastic replica of a spaceship that said Florida, USA, on the side, wobbled up from the deep. The music changed: Tony Bennett singing "Fly Me to the Moon." One of Grendy's favorite songs. An astronaut emerged from the spaceship—Lydia!—dressed in a green tank suit, not a spacesuit, looking only slightly haggard. She carried a black bag and a small American flag.

"Cool!" yelled Theo.

Lydia did some dives and flips and turns, and zipped up and down like an elevator, free from gravity. Wheee! Her shag haircut stood up in little spikes. France pictured Grendy in this part, wishing she'd been able to see her mother in action instead of only in photos.

Lydia frog-legged over and stuck the flag in the sand, then shook her fist in a victory cheer. She cruised around, exploring, picking up gold-painted rocks that had been strewn about, and examining them with great excitement. She picked up one and reared back as if she were going to hurl it through the glass. France and Theo both flinched, but she dropped the rock, smiling—it was a joke! You can't throw a rock in the water! She bent down and continued collecting gold rocks, tucking them into the black bag she carried with her.

Then the music changed: *"Bompity-bomp, dangity-dang, dingity-ding dong. Blue Moon. You saw me standing alone."* Up swam the alien mermaids, Coralee and Rose, also dressed in green one-piece suits. It was a shock to see their bulges and waxy faces, but after a few seconds the shock wore off, and France focused on how strong and graceful they were.

They circled the astronaut, who dropped her bag in surprise. One of the alien mermaids—Rose—picked up the black bag, opened it, and emptied out all the gold rocks. Tsk tsk! She scolded the astronaut. The astronaut began lunging at the aliens, presumably wanting to stick one of them in her bag, but they all evaded her. Finally, Coralee pushed the astronaut down on her butt, near the statue, to watch the mermaids do some back dolphins, which they did beautifully. "Moon River," sung by Andy Williams, began to play. Grendy disliked Andy Williams. Somebody else must've picked the last two songs.

Rose, by waving flirtatiously, coaxed the astronaut into joining them in some synchronized moves. They tried sitting on each other's shoulders to make a tower, but Lydia, who was on the top, kept pulling the other two upward. The three of them tried to form a square, which, of course, came off like a triangle. Then they all just wriggled around in the water, knocking into each other.

"This isn't very good," Theo announced.

"Shhh." France wanted to sneak out, but she didn't want them to see her leave, so she sat tight.

Suddenly, Lydia hurled herself toward the surface of the water. She swam over, stuck her head into a porthole at the top of the theater, and glared down at France—looking like a sea witch with her white face and wild hair. "Where is your mother?" she yelled at France. "It's all turning to shit without her. It's her fault."

The alien mermaids slunk off the underwater stage, swimming away in their humping, inchworm way, disappearing under the air lock. "Moon River" stopped. Ace tiptoed out of the control booth and left by a side door.

"Is it the end already?" said Theo.

"It is for today," said Lydia. "We need a real astronaut. But I'm not having one of those young things in the show. Come on, France, help us out here!"

France's heart began pounding and she felt excited in spite of herself. Perhaps she would do it. She wouldn't be doing it just for herself. She'd be helping out her mother's best friends. She would be showing her mother how much she loved and missed her by trying to do the thing her mother cared about most. She would make her mother proud of her. This was absurd, she knew—her mother could be in another country by now. But at least she'd be doing something down here besides asking questions. She'd figure out later how to handle Bruno's doll show. "I'll do it," she said.

Lydia didn't hesitate. "We'll get you trained quick," she decreed from her porthole. "We'll have to skip the scuba diving certification. It's gotta be hush-hush, or they'll kick us out of here."

"What about me?" yelled Theo.

"You can help Ace in the control booth." Lydia slammed the porthole cover.

Theo began whooping and leaping about the theater, and France watched him, feeling better than she had in weeks. People who knew her back home would think she'd lost her mind. Naomi would probably think she'd been brainwashed and should be committed. Or she'd accuse France of selling out. Bruno would find it hilarious. He'd want to come down and watch and he'd miss his own gallery show. She'd tell Naomi that it was simply a way to find out more about her mother, and she'd tell Bruno that he couldn't come down. Period.

France and Theo had dinner that evening with Lydia, Coralee, and Rose at Applebee's restaurant, which was packed with people. Where had they all come from? Three TVs blared in the bar. Faux Tiffany lamps hung over the tables. The wall beside France was covered with pictures of the Tampa Bay Buccaneers. Coralee and Rose ordered burgers. Lydia ordered a fried chicken salad with no dressing and a hot fudge sundae, to be served at the same time. Theo and France ordered a small cheese pizza to split. Theo went off to the bathroom to wash his hands.

"I still can't figure out where she is," France said. "Or why she's hiding."

"Could she be . . ." Rose bit her lip.

"Think about this," Lydia said. She leaned close, straining her already skintight shirt, which she must've bought in the kids' section. She said in a stage whisper, "Did you ever wonder if your dad did her in? He could've forced Grendy to write that note and then killed her and dumped her body somewhere. You think?"

France felt like giggling. "It's not like this is some TV show," she said, echoing what her father had said to her when she'd brought up abduction. "This is my own father you're talking about." She noticed them all staring at her, eyes full of pity and fear. Had they discussed this before? "He'd never do such a thing," France said, and added lamely, "He loves her." She didn't want to admit it, but *murder* had drifted into her mind more than once. If her mother'd discovered him having an affair, and they got into a fight and he lost control . . . or maybe he hired some thug to kidnap her. But she couldn't go any farther. She just couldn't. Right before her own divorce she'd caught herself hoping, a few times, that Ray would meet an untimely death so that she'd be spared the shame of a divorce. Those thoughts made her realize how bad things had gotten.

"Everyone's capable of murder," Rose said emphatically, "if the circumstances are right." She was wearing a terry cloth one-piece shorts outfit, kelly green, with little anchors on the buttons, an outfit that signaled, like sweatpants, that you'd given up on style. France's overall shorts, which she was wearing again today, fell into that same category. They allowed her to go braless, which was the death of style altogether.

The waiter, a bald young man with a goatee who looked as if he'd been trucked in from New York, delivered their food in a big flurry, bringing with him the smell of meat and tomato sauce and grease. France began to saw a piece of pizza into small bites, the way Theo liked it.

Lydia dug into her hot fudge sundae and licked her spoon like a lollipop. "If Grendy doesn't show up soon, maybe we should go to the police."

"She left of her own free will," France said, wanting it to be true. "The police would laugh us out of the station." Theo pushed his way into the booth and pressed against her, his elbows digging into her thigh. "Besides, Theo was right there and saw his grandma write the note," France said. "Right, Theo?"

"No," Theo said. "I didn't see her write it." He was studying his pizza, not seeming inclined to eat it. Was it France's duty to cajole him and get him to eat? She didn't have the energy right now. She wanted to cover her ears to block out the TV noise. "Why would the police laugh?" Theo asked.

"Nothing," France said. "Never mind." She had to get them off this subject. "I'm really excited about being a mermaid," she said.

"Well, technically, you won't really be a mermaid," Lydia said. "Since you won't be wearing a tail. You'll be in the spacesuit."

"You're full of it, Lydia." Rose was salting her french fries to beat the band.

Coralee slapped her water glass down on the table. For some reason she'd pulled her hair back with a jewel-encrusted headband, baring her pale forehead, usually hidden beneath her bangs. It was an unnerving sight, almost as unnerving as her cleavage had been. "France will too be a mermaid," Coralee said. "She'll be doing everything we do."

"Almost everything," Lydia said. "And she doesn't have to do it as well as we do, 'cause she's just learning the moves from the alien mermaids. But you can *call* yourself a mermaid, sure. Being a mermaid is so special. We do things ordinary people can't do!"

"They could if they had training," Theo said. "Brett says that a monkey could do it." He fell sideways into France's lap and she pushed him upright again.

"Eat," she told him.

"Meow meow meow," he said. He hissed at her. "That means Winky's not hungry."

"I don't give a damn about Winky," France heard herself saying. "If you don't eat, I'll . . ." She'll what?

Theo hissed at her again.

"Cool it, Winks," Rose said, shaking her fork at him.

Theo hissed and showed his claws.

"It takes a special kind of person to be a *good* mermaid," Lydia broke in brightly. "You have to be a beauty queen and an athlete and a sex kitten all rolled into one."

"Maybe back then," Rose said, plucking her terry cloth playsuit. "Now we're the merhags."

"Speak for yourself," Lydia said. "I prefer the word mermalum." She displayed a spoon full of goodies so they could all appreciate it. "This is a great sundae, by the way. I can eat anything and never gain."

"What's a sex kitten?" Theo asked France.

"Never mind."

"How come she gets a sundae?" Theo asked. "I want one."

France sighed. "Lydia gets whatever she wants." The pizza was bland and greasy, and Theo wasn't going to eat it. Next time she'd order something *she* liked. But that wasn't a guarantee it would taste any better. There didn't seem to be any good places to eat in Mermaid City.

"I'm very sensitive about the age stuff," Lydia said. "I stayed at Mermaid Springs the longest any mermaid ever has. I was thirty-two when I left here the first time. By then I wasn't the lead anymore. I got stuck in the back. The day I decided to quit, they were introducing us all at the end, and they said I was the world's oldest living mermaid! The audience laughed. For years I had nightmares about that moment. Now it feels like an honor to be an old mermaid."

"When I wasn't a mermaid I used to dream about it all the time," Coralee said, her forehead glowing. "I dreamed I was swimming underwater and could breathe without a hose and I never had to come up." She was attempting to twist her straw into a pretzel shape.

"I have a better mermaid dream," Lydia said. "I dream that I'm swimming in the springs and I swim up into that little castle, and it becomes a big castle. And it's all furnished with velvet and gold. In the last room I come to, there's a man on a couch, with his back to me. A dark-haired man. He's watching the news on TV. And I think—there he is! That must be Elvis. He's come back for me. He can breathe underwater too. It's the greatest feeling. But I always wake up before he turns around, so I never know for sure."

"Didn't Del have dark hair?" Coralee asked, smoothing out her straw.

"It's not Del," Lydia snapped. "I should know. It's my dream."

"Maybe it's an African American man," Theo said. "How come there aren't any African American mermaids?"

"Good question." Rose nodded approvingly. "There should be." She resumed gobbling up her fries. There was something too urgent about the way she ate, as if she feared she'd never have access to food again.

"A black mermaid?" Lydia said. "That's ridiculous. How would an afro look on a mermaid?"

Rose didn't glance up from her feast. "Probably better than a hacked-up shag," she said.

Lydia, for once, was struck silent. Her features twitched anxiously as she searched for the right comeback.

"You want your salad?" Coralee asked her.

Lydia didn't reply.

"Rose, do you have a mermaid dream?" France said, hoping to restore peace.

"I don't dream. Period."

How could a psychic not dream? But she'd supposedly lost her powers. France would have to ask her about it.

"If you don't dream, you're mentally ill," Theo said, resting his chin on the table. "I saw that on my Eyewitness video."

Rose shrugged. Lydia brayed with laughter. Coralee smiled. She was surreptitiously helping herself to the fried chicken on Lydia's salad.

"I have a recurring dream," France said. "It's not about mermaids. I'll be having an ordinary dream about something, like working at the gallery, and suddenly a customer I've been waiting on, some strange woman or man will turn to me and say, 'I'm your sister. I never died in that accident.' At first I'm scared, and then I'm relieved and happy, and then I wake up."

There was an uncomfortable silence. They all began eating in earnest, all except Theo, who was staring up at her as if she were the moon. She was just as insensitive as Lydia. Theo had so many emotional overreactions that she'd numbed herself to all of his feelings. Her mother was missing, but his own mother was dead. She had to remember that. She brushed her hand through his short bristly hair. He gave her one of his sweetest smiles, and then his elbow shot out, knocking over her iced tea. He screamed and cried until Lydia offered him the rest of her sundae.

"Are you bonkers?" her father said on the phone when she told him about deciding to be in the mermaid show. "Why would you want to do a fool thing like that?"

"What's wrong with it?" France said, squirming in the kitchen chair. The chair cushion shot out from under her and onto the floor—none of the cushions could be tied to the chairs anymore, so they wouldn't stay on. The kitchen was a small red box.

"You're spending too much time with those idiots," her father said. "If you're not careful you'll be as bad as your mother."

"Do you even want Mom to come back?"

"Of course."

"Do you still love her?" She had a hard time asking her father questions like this.

He didn't have a hard time answering. "I've loved her since the day I met her. She was carefree and happy and made me feel like that's what life was all about."

This sounded good, but was it the whole truth? France told herself that she and Ray got married because they had no confidence that they could live on their own. It was a nice theory, anyway. Ray, too, seemed carefree at first, but France had put the quietus to that.

"I don't remember Mom being carefree," France told her father. "And what was with those crime novels she used to read?" For years Grendy was addicted to paperback crime books. She would send France and Beauvais to the drugstore and tell them to buy any book with a knife, gun, or blood dripping from a dead person on the cover. Then they were supposed to hide the books somewhere in the house, which would ensure that she parceled them out. She'd quickly find the ones France hid and yell at France for not hiding them well enough. She never found all the ones Beauvais hid, and Beauvais later confessed to Grendy that she'd taken most of them to school and sold them.

Now, on the phone, her father said, "It's my fault."

France perked up. Now they were getting somewhere. "What's your fault?" she said.

"I should've taken those books away from her. Those books got her all stirred up. And now she's got Theo hooked on the Hardy Boys."

He wasn't going to admit to anything important. But France now saw why she'd brought up the topic of crime novels. "You didn't do her in, did you?" she said, trying to make it sound like a joke, which it was, mostly. "You didn't kill her."

"If I did," he said, "I've blocked it out of my mind. A repressed memory."

Was this the way an innocent man would answer that question?

North jumped in before she could say anything else. "How're you and Theo getting along? How's he acting? Is he asking you to play Candy Land all the time? I got so sick of Candy Land."

Theo was lying on the living room floor, inspecting a book

about aquatic life. He had the whole thing memorized, and she'd only read it to him once. When he wasn't exploding or doing pratfalls, he could be a delight.

"He's fine," France said. "He's never even mentioned Candy Land."

After she hung up, Theo spoke. "He didn't kill Grandma. I saw her drive away." He was still staring down at his book.

"Where did you say she was going again?" France asked, hoping to trick him.

"I told you already. She didn't say. She just said she was sorry, and that she had to go. Want to play Candy Land?"

In Chapter VIII of *The Mystery of Cabin Island*, the Hardy boys and their buddies heard faint calls for help coming from the darkness outside their cabin. Donning coats and boots, they tromped around in the snow until they discovered a strange man trapped beneath a fallen pine tree. When they asked him what he was doing there, he only mumbled unintelligibly. The gang carried him into their warm cabin and they all settled in. Later that night, Joe, who was doing guard duty, heard another spooky noise, this time coming from somewhere in the house!

"The wailing noise came again with a kind of taunting quality.

"Owoooooooo-oo!"

"Hey, what's going on?" Joe called out.

There was no response.

Nine

France and Theo pulled into Rose's driveway, their tires crunching on the oyster shells. Rose had a gorgeous house—a new, cracker-style house on stilts with a wraparound porch that offered a view of the gray marsh, and beyond that, the Gulf. Earlier that day, Rose had called and invited them to dinner.

"Have you been here before?" France asked Theo, but he leaped out of the car and began striding back and forth, twiddling his fingers, off in Theo land. Although it was seven o'clock, the air was hot and still and had a suspended quality, as if it were waiting for something. Theo had insisted on wearing a long-sleeved shirt and jeans, even though France told him he'd burn up if they sat outside. France hadn't changed from her overall shorts and Grendy's flip-flops, and wondered if she should've dressed up. At least she'd put on a bra. Now she was the one wearing the same clothes all the time. How quickly she'd lost all sense of decorum!

Rose met them at the door and ushered them in. She was very pale, with spots of red on her cheeks. She still wore the light blue eye shadow, but she'd arranged her white-blond hair in a low knot and, despite her boxy white shirt and khaki skirt, seemed more sophisticated and subdued than she did among the mermaids.

France apologized for her appearance and presented the wine she'd bought at Publix, and then Rose led them through a large room that was crammed waist-high with stuff. It was so overwhelming that France couldn't take it all in, but she got the impression of unopened boxes, piles of books and magazines and videos, baskets of unfolded laundry. Boxes were stacked on all the furniture, and boxes blocked the view from the bay window. Bruno's house was also full of junk, but he displayed it so you could sit and admire it. This room had been transformed into storage space.

The kitchen wasn't much better. The counters and table were covered with cans of soup, six packs of Coke, notebooks and loose paper, stacks of newspapers, and table linens. Where would they eat?

A tall woman with shoulder-length dark hair was stirring something wonderfully garlicky on the stove.

"Donna, France, France, Donna," Rose said, blinking rapidly. She must be embarrassed about the state of her house. "And you know Theo."

"Greetings, Winky," Donna said in a theatrical voice.

"Meow," Theo said.

Donna stepped forward to shake France's hand. She had a striking face but looked worn out—there were dark circles under her eyes. She wore a sand-colored sleeveless sweater. "Let's get drinks and sit on the porch." She turned off the stove with a flourish. "What'll you have?"

The women wanted wine, and Theo got a Coke. When Donna opened the back door, Theo said, "Meow meow meow meow meow? That means could I sit in here?" Why would he want to do that? France wondered. Maybe he felt at home with all the chaos. His room would look this way eventually.

"Oh come on out and sit in Aunt Donna's lap."

Aunt Donna?

France braced herself for an outburst, but Theo remained calm. They all trooped outside onto the back porch and positioned themselves in white wicker chairs, except for Theo, who clambered up in a rocking chair. He'd apparently decided against Aunt Donna's lap.

They exchanged pleasantries for a while—Donna talked about being a dentist and some of the new technologies they used, like panoramic X rays and ultrasound plaque removal. She was younger than Rose—late forties, France decided. There was a long healed scar on one of her cheeks.

France spoke enthusiastically about WomenSpace, aware that part of her hoped to seem politically correct to two lesbians. As she talked, describing some of the art, she found herself missing the place even more. Had Naomi discovered wonderful new art since she'd been gone?

She told them about the upcoming doll show, and without mentioning Bruno, described Peanut and Baby Tangerine. "And Wilma," Theo added. She told them how upset Naomi would be that she wasn't going to make it back for the doll show, since she'd decided to stay for *Mermaids on the Moon*.

"Sounds like you should go back," Rose said. She was wearing the little glittery earrings. "You might lose your job."

"I don't think so," France said, not really wanting to think about it. She would have to tell Naomi and Bruno as soon as possible that she wouldn't be back till after Labor Day. Then, in an attempt to entertain, she told Rose and Donna about the problem with Bruno making the dolls, and the lie she'd told Naomi. As she talked she glanced over at Theo, who was staring at her openmouthed. His aunt telling lies! He wouldn't trust her again. She stopped talking, her face burning. What the hell was the matter with her?

Donna yawned. "Sorry," she said. "Long night." Her face was the bleached-out color of her sweater.

Rose said, "And this is the gallery you want to buy into? You should straighten things out."

"I will," France said, wishing she'd never brought it up. Maybe she *should* chuck the mermaid show and go back for the doll show. Which was more important? It was all too confusing. She slapped at her leg. She was getting eaten alive by mosquitoes.

"Don't you just love Clinton?" Donna said. "I wish he could be President forever. I don't care who he fooled around with." She was stretched out in a lounge chair, her long mauve skirt tucked between her legs. She sighed. "Gore's so boring."

The Democratic Convention was wrapping up tomorrow in Los Angeles. If she'd been in Indiana, France would've watched it on TV, but here she'd satisfied herself with reading snippets about it in the *St. Petersburg Times* while she was grocery shopping at Publix.

Rose said, "At least he's not led around by his you-know-what." She held up her glass and said, "To our next President."

"To Al Gore," France said, raising her glass. "Better than the alternative."

"Clinton is a bad man," said Theo. "He's a big fat liar." He wouldn't meet France's eyes.

Donna took a sip of wine and then announced, in her dramatic voice, "The Russians said there are no signs of life on the *Kursk*. The knocking inside has stopped. Isn't it terrible?"

Oh no. France turned to Theo, steeling herself. With a look of intense concentration, Theo tipped his glass slowly till some of his Coke dribbled onto the porch. "They're all drowned," he said in a voice that was scarier than his eruptions. He allowed more of his Coke to slosh out.

"Theo," France said. "Be careful."

"I am being careful," he said in the same flat voice, but he stopped spilling his Coke.

"Don't you just love it out here?" Donna said. "It's my favorite place to sit." She gestured to the view in front of them—a neat, weedless lawn stretching back to some shrubbery and a brick wall.

"We practically live out here," Rose said. "So much more private than out front, with the road."

But the Gulf is out there with the road, France thought. Rose and Donna didn't seem to be bothered by mosquitoes. They'd probably coated themselves with bug spray. Theo didn't seem to be bothered either. Maybe this was why he'd worn long sleeves and pants. He could have let her know.

France slapped her leg again. "Were you really an underwater wrestler?" she asked Rose.

"You tell her, dear," Donna said. "Tell her all about it." She clambered up from her chair. "I'm going in to check on dinner. Hope you like eggplant!"

"Sure do," France said. She glanced at Theo, who was swinging his legs and scowling. He wouldn't eat a bite of eggplant.

When Donna left, Rose sat up straight and came to life. Her eyes looked sapphire blue. "When I was a kid I saw people underwater wrestling. They had a big glass tank full of water and two men dove in and went at it, and then two women. I told the mermaid trainer I'd done it so she'd let me stay."

"It's wrong to tell lies," Theo said. "You'll go to hell."

"Not for a little lie like that," France said. She scratched her bites and addressed Rose. "They must've believed you, about the wrestling."

"I started mermaid training right away. After the first week I was ready to quit, but Grendy talked me into staying. 'The mermaids are a sisterhood,' she said. I liked the sound of that, being an only child."

Theo leaped up and pointed. "A cat!"

A white cat with black splotches sat in the middle of the lawn, gazing at them.

"That's Sisterwoman," Rose said. "We got her from a friend in Cassadaga last weekend. Donna's allergic to cats, so the poor kitty has to stay outside."

Theo set his glass on a table and tiptoed down the steps and into the backyard, as if he were sneaking up on Sisterwoman, even though she was watching his every move.

"She's real friendly," Rose called to Theo. "But she does have her claws!"

Theo didn't turn around. He crouched down beside the cat and they stared at each other. Sisterwoman's tail twitched. Don't scratch him, France silently begged the cat.

Donna banged out the back door swinging a wine bottle. Neither the cat nor Theo moved. She poured wine in everyone's glass and sat back down. "Has she been telling you about mermaids in their youth?"

Rose said sharply, "I'm getting there." She turned to France. "My family used to come down here on vacations and I loved it, so I decided to go to UF."

"Her family owns a bunch of car dealerships in Michigan," Donna said. "Rich, rich, rich. I come from trailer park trash."

"I'm sorry," France said, and then wished she hadn't. She was going to have to say she wanted to go inside, even though there was nowhere to sit in there. The mosquitoes were fierce and so small she couldn't see them.

Theo squatted beside the cat, scratching the top of her head.

"Don't crowd her!" Rose yelled.

Theo sat down hard and Sisterwoman darted off, scrambling behind the hedge. Theo watched her. Please don't have a tantrum, France thought. Please. She broke out in a sweat.

"Being a mermaid is the only thing Rose ever stuck with," Donna said. "Except me."

They exchanged a meaningful smile.

"Why didn't you stick with being a psychic?" France asked.

Silence.

"Coralee told me. You lived in Cassadaga."

"Ghost Town," Donna said, lifting her walnut-colored hair from her neck. "That's what people around there call it."

"You saw ghosts?" France asked Rose.

Rose shook her head. "They don't really have materializations anymore. Just spirit messages and readings. I lived there for five years. Had to go through three years of training to be a medium. That's how I met Donna."

"I went to Rose for a reading," Donna said. "It was love at first sight, even though she didn't tell me anything useful! She told me that a spirit, a short elderly man named John, had a message for me. Never drive when you're sleepy, that was his message. But I never knew any short John."

"You do have a history of falling asleep at the wheel," Rose pointed out. "That's how she got the scar on her cheek."

Sisterwoman had slunk back to Theo and lay on her side while Theo stroked her. France knew she couldn't even imagine how happy he felt. She clasped her hands to keep from scratching her rashy, bitten-up legs. "Could you give me a reading?" she asked Rose.

"She lost her ability to commune with spirits," Donna said. "Got too full of herself." She snickered.

Rose went somber, and Donna reached over and patted her leg. "Rose here used to be quite the knockout. Still is! Did you know she was Miss Chicken of the Sea? But soon as the cans with her picture came out, she lost her focus. Left Cassadaga and went up to Atlanta and got a part in an awful Turner soap opera. It was canceled in less than a year. By then she'd closed herself off to the spirits."

"Maybe they'll come back," France said. "The spirits." France told people she didn't believe in psychics, but she'd been to one once, wanting to believe.

Rose shrugged. "I didn't really like knowing more than everyone else," she said. "It was exhausting."

France drank some of her wine, parsing it out. She wished Bruno were here. He'd know where to go with this topic. "Miss Chicken of the Sea," she said. "That's neat."

"Lydia's always bragging about her piddly commercials," Donna said. "Rose here is too modest to tell people about hers." She drained her glass of wine. "I'll never understand why Rose didn't get the lead parts in those mermaid shows."

"Maybe I put out dyke signals."

"Nonsense." Donna squinted dubiously at France. "So you're going to take your mother's place in the show?"

"I'm going to try."

Donna swung the wine bottle back and forth. "You have to be in great shape. Are you in great shape?"

"I walk every day." Whoopee. Who was she kidding? When were they going to eat? Sisterwoman was trotting across the yard, and Theo trotted after her. He was going to scare her away. France managed not to yell anything at him.

"Grendy was always the star," Donna said. "She was just more of a showoff than Rose. I bet she's just hiding now, wanting everyone to miss her. Wanting Rose to miss her."

"Donna," Rose said. "Is the sauce still on the stove?"

"Oops. I see. I've overstayed my welcome." Donna rose from her chair, carrying the wine bottle and her glass, and pulled the back door open with a yank.

"Sorry about, you know," said Rose. She bowed her head. "She promised to be on her best behavior."

"It's okay," France said, scratching her ankle. "She's proud of you, that's all."

Theo came staggering up the steps and leaned against France. "I can't find Sisterwoman."

"Could we go in?" France said to Rose. "I'm getting eaten alive."

"The West Nile virus has claimed four lives in Florida this summer alone," Theo said. "Children and old people are most vulnerable."

Rose gestured with her head. "Go ahead in if you want to," she said, but Theo didn't move. He didn't want to be alone with Donna, and France couldn't blame him. France stood up, and Rose did too, but Rose wasn't done with the subject. "Grendy comes out here and talks about the old days. Donna gets jealous."

"That's too bad," said France. What was she to make of this tangle of emotions and relationships? All she wanted was a clear, straightforward answer to her question. She said it aloud. "Where is my mother?"

"Your mom's fine," Rose said, squeezing her arm. "She'll be back soon."

"You've heard from her?"

Rose hesitated and formed her words carefully. "I haven't gotten any news of her," she said, and France found this an odd way to put it. "I thought she left because of the stalker," Rose said. "But I'm thinking now it was something else."

France couldn't help herself. "Did a spirit tell you this?"

"Hard to know. I still get these feelings."

Theo had straddled the porch railing. "Grandma heard Grandpa talking to someone in his office at church," he said. "That's why she left."

France took a deep breath. She decided not to get angry at Theo for withholding information. "Who was it?"

"I don't know."

"I bet it was nothing." Rose pulled Theo to his feet as if she wanted to herd him into the kitchen.

"Sure you don't know?" France said again.

He shook his head. "She said Grandpa would take care of me for a while. She didn't say anything about you." His face crumpled and he began to wail. France tried to hold him and comfort him, and this time he allowed her to, but he was stiff in her arms.

At Beauvais's funeral, she'd volunteered to take care of Theo during the service so her parents wouldn't have to do it, and she was glad for the distraction. She didn't realize that an eighteen-month-old couldn't stay still. She had to take him out of the sanctuary, where an old friend of North's was officiating, and let him loose in the narthex. He ran around, wearing an idiotic bow tie, trying to climb up and down stairs, and she followed him, trying to keep him from killing himself. This frantic activity kept her from feeling sad—from feeling almost anything except fear. But the whole time she kept thinking, I'm missing my sister's funeral. She and Theo seemed destined to try to comfort each other as best they could.

Theo wailed louder, sounding like a tornado siren. "I love Sisterwoman," he yelled. "I want a cat. My heart is breaking!"

"We'll get you a cat," France said, and decided she would. It was the least she could do for him.

"I want Sisterwoman!"

Donna stuck her head out the door, releasing the spicy smell. "You can have the cat," she said. "Please take her. You'd be doing us a favor."

Ten

"Sisterwoman's a special cat," France told Theo. "She used to live in Cassadaga."

The three of them were on the screened porch, taking the morning air. The cat lay like a sphinx on the little rag rug. Up close, her black spots were tabby-colored, and she had a raccoon-like mask of tabby on her face. Her eyes were green. She was quite fat. Theo, in his pjs, sat beside her, grinning. Except when he went to bed last night, he hadn't left the cat's side.

"Talk quietly," Theo said. "She's resting."

France and Ray had had a cat called Burt, a big marmalade cat, who came with Ray when they married and went with him when they divorced, but France still remembered the basics of cat care. She and Theo had stopped at Wal-Mart for a litter box and litter, a pooper-scooper, and dry cat food. She'd decided that Sister-woman would be a house cat, because she didn't want to risk her

running off. Theo didn't need another loss. France had no idea
how her parents would feel about Theo's having a cat, but she figured that Grendy, being such an animal lover, wouldn't care too
much. North was another story. He was probably the reason Theo
didn't already have one.

France drained her coffee. She wanted more but was too lazy
to go inside and get it. She propped her bare feet on the seat of a
metal chair. It was so pleasant out here. How did anyone ever get
anything done in Florida? A whisper of a breeze lifted the napkin
under her cup. The sun shone down in a column through the
branches of the live oak tree, the way God would appear if he had
a mind to. Or a spirit. "I wish I were a medium," France said
dreamily.

Theo pounced on this. "What's a medium?"

That would teach her to babble without thinking. "Mediums
can communicate with the spirits of dead people and give messages.
At least they say they can. Everyone in Cassadaga is a medium."

"Even the animals?"

"Well. I don't know about that."

"Sisterwoman might be medium."

"She might be."

Sisterwoman puffed herself up and closed her eyes.

"How could you tell if she was?" Theo asked.

"I guess she'd let us know. She'd start sending us messages."

"How would she send messages?"

He wasn't going to let this drop. France rousted herself and sat
down on the cool wooden floor beside the cat. She began to stroke
Sisterwoman, whose fur was unusually soft, like a rabbit's. She
had an alarmingly loud purr.

"Is she sending a message now?" Theo said.

"She might be." France scratched Sisterwoman's forehead. "I think she's got a third eye."

"Where?"

"You can't see it. It's invisible. It's right in the middle of her forehead. When I rub it, I can tell what she's thinking."

"Can I do it?"

"Let me do it," France said. "You have to know how to translate her message." How far would she sink to entertain a child? Pretty far, evidently.

Theo sat expectantly beside her. What sort of message would a cat send? What did Theo need to hear?

He answered the question for her. "Is she sending a message from a dead person?" He was fascinated by the idea—she could tell by the wild glint in his eye. "From Grandma?"

"No, no. She's not dead."

Sisterwoman laid down her head and seemed to melt onto the floor, fat stomach spreading. France continued to scratch her head.

Theo whispered, "From my mother?"

Oh dear. "Let me see." Beauvais. It was too hard thinking of her as an adult. France wasn't around her much then, and Beauvais was unhappy most of the time. Beauvais as a child. "Your mom wants me to tell you about something that happened when she was little. She loved animals too."

Theo ogled Sisterwoman as if she were a rare and exotic creature. "She did? As much as I do?"

"Just as much. She tried to save an elephant's life once, when everyone else was scared and ran away from it."

"An elephant?"

So France told Theo the story about the elephant, describing only the surface story and leaving out the underneath. But she remembered the underneath all too well.

A few weeks after North's confession and before he was transferred to the church in Indiana, the family had stopped by Sears for a new window fan and stumbled upon a traveling elephant show in the parking lot. A handful of people stood beneath a ring of flapping pennants watching a small elephant perform.

Two people stood inside the circle, wearing short-sleeved black shirts, loose black pants, and black sunglasses. "I'm a Believer" by the Monkees blasted from inside the elephant's trailer. The woman trainer tapped the elephant on its hind leg with a long silver stick and the elephant, whose arched back had bits of hay scattered all over it, stuck out her left front foot and right rear foot, and then the opposite feet. The crowd clapped, and France and Grendy and Beauvais clapped too, but not North, who was standing between France and Beauvais. France could tell by his body posture—arms folded, legs spread—that he was itching for a fight. He'd gotten angrier and angrier since his confession about Tammy, but he hadn't come across anyone to really fight with. France didn't understand why he was so angry. Tammy Vickers had left town. Everybody from church was avoiding him. Grendy was playing the forgiving martyr. He should've been grateful.

"What do you think of this setup?" North asked them.

France shrugged. She'd planned to be at Mary Lou's house by this time.

"I feel sorry for the elephant," Beauvais said. She was wearing France's red pucker shirt, getting it all stinky.

"Well I don't like it," he said. "Animal cruelty." He peered over at Grendy, who stood on the other side of France. "I'm surprised you're not having a fit."

"It doesn't bother me," Grendy said, refusing to meet his eyes.

What was going on between them? France wondered.

"Watch Jezebel play catch," shouted the man.

The woman prodded Jezebel up onto a little stool and then up onto her hind legs. The man threw a rainbow-colored plastic ball to Jezebel and she caught it with her trunk. The woman poked Jezebel, who tossed the ball up into the air and caught it, again, and again. Suddenly she spun the ball out into the crowd, toward France, but her father reached up and snatched it.

He tossed the ball from hand to hand and addressed the trainers. "Perhaps I need to remind you that pachyderms do not perspire."

France's knees felt weak, and she glanced at her mother. Grendy just stood there, staring at Jezebel, who still balanced on her hind legs, waiting for the ball. Nobody knows he's my father, France thought.

"Would you be so kind," said her father, "as to tell me when this elephant last had a drink of water? It must be a hundred degrees out here."

"Please throw the ball to Jezebel," said the woman trainer, smiling.

"Throw it," said an old man behind them.

"Elephants drink gallons of water a day in their natural habitat," North said. "I don't see a watering trough anywhere. Does anyone else see one?" Her father was a born performer. Couldn't even share the stage with an elephant.

"Give her the goddamned ball," somebody said.

"Honey," said Grendy, "don't do this." She spoke softly, with no urgency. France knew he wouldn't listen.

"My question has not been answered." North began rolling the ball around on his arm, bouncing it off his bicep and catching it.

Jezebel clambered down off the stool. The woman prodded her, but she stepped back, away from the stool. The trainer man marched over and stood in front of North. "We take good care of our elephant," he said. "She gets plenty of hay and water. Okay?"

The trainer woman yelled sharply at Jezebel and poked her with the stick. Jezebel balked and rolled her eyes.

"What's your friend doing there?" her father asked the man trainer. "If that's not maltreatment?"

"You're making it worse," Grendy told him. "It's just a show."

North made a spitting sound. "Is this any kind of life for an elephant? It's barbaric. Probably against the law," he said, and a few people muttered agreement.

Her father was right, France knew, so why did she want so badly to shut him up? She must have sensed, even then, that this had nothing to do with the elephant.

The man trainer was sweating—there were rings of sweat around his neck. "Jezebel has to know who's boss," he said.

North stuck out his arm and spun the ball on his index finger. "I'm going to take Jezebel off your hands," he said.

France pictured them pulling into the driveway, towing Jezebel's trailer behind them. Did her father think this was making up for Tammy Vickers in some way?

"We don't need an elephant," Beauvais said.

"Would you stop the theatrics?" Grendy said, and to France's dismay, Grendy's eyes filled with tears. Her father didn't need tears. He needed a firm hand. He was the one, France thought, who needed to be shown who was boss.

"How much for the elephant?" North yelled to the trainers.

The woman trainer scowled and poked Jezebel, who backed into the crowd.

"Show's over," said the trainer man.

North placed the ball in Beauvais's arms. "Hold on to this," he said. "I'm going to get your mother that elephant."

"I don't want the elephant," Grendy said, and giggled nervously.

Both trainers were now prodding Jezebel with poles, trying to get her back into her trailer. She lurched sideways, stamping her feet.

Beauvais stepped into the circle holding the ball. She tossed it toward Jezebel, but it rolled off down the parking lot.

North grabbed Beauvais's arm.

"Let me throw the ball again," Beauvais yelled. "She wants the ball."

Jezebel reared up and gave a loud bellow. She lunged toward them.

Grendy said, "Girls! Go get in the car," but France couldn't move.

Beauvais planted herself in front of Jezebel. "Do not be afraid," she said. Who was she talking to? Who did she think she was, standing there with her pigtails, only eight years old?

"Get the gun!" yelled the woman trainer, and the man started sprinting across the parking lot.

"Oh my God," said Grendy, a perfectly appropriate thing to say under the circumstances, but it struck France as wrong, somehow, and it seemed as if Grendy was almost enjoying this, as if the whole thing had become some sort of little mating dance. France didn't want to see it, didn't want to know about it. It made her sick. And look what they'd done to the elephant.

"So what happened to the elephant?" Theo asked. "Is she okay?" He had that whiny tone in his voice, that pre-meltdown tone.

Why hadn't she considered how Theo would react to the end of the story? North had swung Beauvais up in his arms and carried her, kicking and screaming, toward the car. The next morning, the headlines in the local paper said, ELEPHANT GOES BERSERK: SHOT BY TRAINER. As if North'd had nothing to do with it. They never discussed the elephant, and they never spoke of Tammy Vickers again either, because, oddly enough, North's encounter with the elephant had somehow wiped his slate clean.

Sisterwoman rolled to her feet, stretched and yawned. She strolled over to the glider, leaped up, and began to lick her front paw. Session over. This was another example of why she shouldn't be a parent. A parent wouldn't lie to her child the way she was about to lie to Theo. "Beauvais threw the ball to Jezebel," France said. "And she caught it. She calmed right down. After that she was just fine."

"Yay!" Theo leaped to his feet, startling Sisterwoman, who flung herself onto the floor and streaked into the house. "That was a great message!"

France basked in Theo's jubilation, feeling only slightly ashamed.

"Is the cat really a medium?" Bruno asked her on the phone.

"What do you think?"

"I mean, where'd you get the idea to tell Theo that story? Maybe it *was* a message from Beauvais."

"I hope she sends me a more important message next time. Like telling me where Mom is. One good thing, Theo's stopped acting like a cat now that he's got a real one."

"Listen," Bruno said. "I just read about something that happened in Orlando. Did you hear about the glowing orbs?"

"Orbs?"

"Balls of electromagnetic energy, floating over the roads. They were thought to be caused by marsh gas. Now scientists have determined they're Native American spirits."

This must be another tidbit from the *Weekly World News*, France decided. She told Bruno about her chance to be in *Mermaids on the Moon*, and he, of course, thought it was wonderful and made perfect sense, but he didn't say he wanted to come down and see it. He was all caught up in his own show. "I'm doing the Rose doll next," he said.

"How will you get the dolls to Naomi?"

"Take them myself."

France felt panicky. "Maybe I should come back to deliver them."

"Don't you want to be in the mermaid show?"

France sighed. In her mind she had already become the astronaut, planting the flag in the sand. "I'll call Naomi and tell her that

I won't be back and that you'll be helping me out by delivering the dolls," France said. "I'll tell her not to discuss the dolls with you, because you're very sensitive about them. They remind you of some awful childhood memory. Your mom forced you to play with dolls. If she pesters you about who made them, or says anything about them, it will stir up hurtful feelings. She thinks you still work at Mr. Donut, by the way."

"Hurtful feelings?"

That did sound stupid. "Or maybe I'll get someone else to deliver them," she said. Trouble was, most of her close friends worked at the gallery. She'd lost touch with many high school and college friends, and friends from her social work days.

"I'll deliver them myself," Bruno said. "They're my dolls." She could tell by his voice that he'd made up his mind.

"Just let *me* tell her the truth," France said. "I'll call her. Promise."

But she decided not to call Naomi just yet. She had to come up with the right thing to say. She still had time.

At the end of Chapter X, the Hardy Boys and their friends were examining a photograph taken with Joe's newfangled self-developing camera. The photo showed a man called Hanleigh, one of their most persistent tormenters, poking the chimney of their cabin with a stick, searching for the missing treasure. Caught red-handed! But wait. Hanleigh was not alone in the photo!

"Some distance behind him, partially hidden among the trees, was another figure. The stranger was dark and slim and was dressed in a long, flowing white robe. A turban covered his head!"

Eleven

Brett wore her streaked brown hair pulled back in a big plastic hair gripper, a long chunk of her bangs left loose to frame her face. She sat down on the velour couch across from France. Her shoes were open-toed platforms, her toenails painted white. Theo kept running in circles around Brett. "I got a cat, I got a cat," he kept yelling. "Here, kitty. Here, Sisterwoman." Sisterwoman, sensibly, had hidden somewhere.

"You two really look alike," Brett told them. "Your eyebrows are exactly the same. They almost connect in the middle." Not a flattering description, but France was pleased that Brett had noticed this link between them. Theo couldn't have cared less.

"Sisterwoman sends messages from dead people," Theo said. "She told me how my mom saved an elephant's life."

Brett's eyes widened. "Really," she said, glancing at France, who was sitting in the red chair across from her.

France wondered if she could get in trouble with Child Protective Services if Brett should report her. She remembered some regulation about involving a child in the occult. "Why don't you go get Brett's present?" France suggested.

"I forgot to make her a card!" Theo raced off for his bedroom, where he kept his coffee can of crayon stubs.

"Theo's got a vivid imagination," France said.

"You got that right." Brett had a pleasant, gravelly voice.

"He thinks you're a real mermaid."

Brett twisted up her lips in a tough way that reminded France of Beauvais. "Sucky job."

"You don't like being a mermaid?"

"Granny talked me into doing it," Brett said. "Pay's lousy. I'm always getting colds and ear infections. My hair's like straw. Water's too fricking cold. We have to pick up trash and wash the windows. We do the same stupid things over and over. Weirdos harass us. Other than that, it's just great." She sighed, sighed again, and then started blinking and sniffling.

"What's the problem?" France said, alarmed. "Is it that bad?"

"No. It's just . . . guy trouble," Brett said.

"Oh," France said, in a way that she hoped would discourage further revelations.

"My boyfriend, Ross. He wants me to drop out of school and marry him. I only have one more year at UF. I'm a folklore major. Anyway, he says he's moving out West, with or without me." Brett patted her eyes. Theo was right—she did like jewelry. She had turquoise rings on three fingers, and silver and turquoise bracelets on her arm. "He went out with Rachel last night," she went on.

"Just to make me jealous. She thinks she's so hot because she's the Little fricking Mermaid. Last year she was an octopus."

"Do you want to marry him?"

Brett heaved herself back in the chair. "I don't know. He's so skewed."

France couldn't help asking. "Skewed?"

"He showed up at one of our *Little Mermaid* shows, back in June, and never left. He doesn't have a life. He moved into a disgusting little trailer. Then he starts, you know, hanging around with the other mermaids and drinking beer with them and talking about stuff he doesn't know crap about, like Armageddon. It's disgusting."

"So break up with him," France said, hoping this would be the end of it.

"The real problem is," Brett said, and lowered her voice melodramatically, "I'm in love with someone else."

"Oh," France said. "Why are you telling *me* this?"

Brett seemed not to have heard her. "The guy I'm really in love with, he started getting mean," she said. "Making nasty comments about me. In public. Like, 'Doesn't Brett look like a bag lady?' Just because my purse is full of stuff."

France glanced down at the floor, hoping to see Brett's purse.

"I threw it away. A hundred-fifty-dollar purse from the Limited. Don't you think that's mean?"

France felt herself falling back into the role of social worker, a role she came to despise when she did it for a living. "It's too easy," she said, "to get caught up in the details of these situations, too easy to lose track of the big picture."

Brett nodded but obviously wasn't listening. "One time he told me that my skirt looked like an Amish woman's. This skirt here!" She stretched out her leg to display her pink, knee-length skirt with lace around the hem. "Does this look like an Amish woman's skirt to you?"

France tried to picture the Amish women she'd seen in Indiana. "They don't wear pink."

Brett waved her hand. "The point is, I'm getting insulted and I'm hanging on by my fingernails." She stuck out her tongue. "Talk about pathetic."

"If you're unhappy, do something about it."

"I'm beyond unhappy," she said. "I'm wretched." She laughed. "I keep waiting for him to come to his senses and start treating me right. The way he did at first. Oh, and get this." She hooked her loose bangs behind her ear. "He's always trying to make me jealous in these weird ways. Like we're talking on the phone and somebody comes into his office, some woman, and he says to her, 'You look great.' Was that necessary? He's trying to torment me. I asked him, 'Do you drool often?' and he just laughs."

France was determined to escape the social worker role, even if it meant being rude. "You need to talk to someone. A counselor."

"He is a counselor, sort of. That's how I met him."

France felt herself descend to another level of irritation. But Brett was Coralee's granddaughter. And she was just a child, really. "Are you going to be okay?" France asked her.

"Sure," Brett said, and took a deep breath. She called Theo's name, and he came running in, bearing her present and a card he'd been drawing. He held it out and gazed lovingly at her.

Brett opened the box and squealed. "Oh, thank you, Theo," she said, giving him a big hug. "You dear thing. It's gorgeous!" She examined his card. "Now tell me what all these things are."

Theo proceeded to explain his drawing, which appeared to be a bunch of scribbles. He pointed out fish, a turtle, a manatee. And the bay, and the sky, and the palm trees. And Brett, the real mermaid. And Theo, the scuba diver. And Grandpa, sitting on a picnic table. And Sisterwoman, his new cat. France was slightly hurt that he hadn't drawn her, but told herself she was being silly. And where was Grandma? Brett listened with rapt attention that wasn't put on, asking him questions, praising his every effort. No wonder Theo loved her so much.

France slipped out the door to go to practice.

Feeling like Francie Pants crashing *The Little Mermaid Show*, France ventured into the mermaid dressing room. She passed through an entryway where costumes hung on pegs, including the gold dress and tiara the Little Mermaid wore when she danced with her prince on land. She turned the corner, walked past a row of flippers hanging on drying racks and saw Coralee and Rose in the locker room. They both said hello. Rose, leaning against the lockers, wore plaid shorts and a shirt with matching plaid trim. Coralee, who sat on the bench pulling on her flippers, had already squeezed into her green alien bathing suit, which appeared to have an amazing amount of spandex in it. With her makeup and long hair, Coralee was downright glamorous. France wondered how Coralee had looked in 1961, when she and Lydia and Grendy and

Rose had changed clothes in this very dressing room for their un-derwater picnic. Coralee, the oldest, would've been twenty-six. Old for a young mermaid, but still a knockout.

France didn't want anyone evaluating her thirty-eight-year-old body. She wasn't fat, but she was flabby. She wasn't glamorous and never had been. Beauvais had had the glamour. Her sixth grade class elected her Snow Princess and in eleventh grade she was Prom Queen. Even when her hard living began to show on her face, she still turned heads. France tugged on the seat of the turquoise and black bathing suit she wore beneath her shorts and T-shirt. She must get another bathing suit soon, one with lots of spandex.

Coralee told her that Lydia was already down in the water waiting for them. "Rose's gonna be in the control booth so she can give you directions," Coralee said. She explained that Rose would be talking into a microphone that only the mermaids, swimming near the theater, could hear. They could also hear the music un-derwater, but they wouldn't be using music today. Rose was silent while Coralee talked.

"You get to keep your face mask on, since you're the astronaut! Lucky you. You'll work with the air hose today," Coralee said, "and learn how to regulate your depth so you can stay down at the right level. Now I'll explain about the chute." Coralee led her over to a metal chute that stuck up out of the floor like a big tin can, the opening about as wide around as Theo's wading pool. It was full of dark water. A skinny ladder went down the side. At the bottom the chute turned so the mermaids could swim out into the spring. Coralee perched on the edge of the chute, dangling her flippers in the water. "It's a little dark down there, but you have the light from up here." She pointed to the fluorescent light in the ceiling. "Then when the chute turns, you can see the sunlight in the spring. There's an air hose down there, where it turns."

"I can't go down there," France said. "I'll get claustrophobia."

Rose spoke up for the first time. "You have to, to be in the show," she said.

"I can't," France said. She felt her chest contract just thinking about it.

"She doesn't *have* to," Coralee said. "She could dive down from outside, before the curtain goes up, and wait in the air lock."

"Nobody's done that," Rose said sternly, "in all the years I've been here."

"Not that you know of," Coralee said.

"It's mermaid tradition," Rose said. "She has to use the chute."

What was with Rose? France wondered. Why'd she turned snippy all of a sudden? "Well," said France, "maybe I can work up to it."

Coralee flicked her flippers, splashing the water. "We'll tackle the chute later. You can dive in from above today. Long as nobody from management sees you. Their office is over on the other side, but you never know."

"They walk down this way," Rose said. "They'll see you sooner or later. And if they don't, Ace will tell them."

Coralee climbed into the chute and clung to the top rung of the ladder. "What's your problem?" she asked Rose. "We'll deal with Ace. Now go on, get out of here."

Rose sniffed. "Don't come crying to me when they cancel our show."

Maybe Rose was angry about having to give up Sisterwoman,

even though she'd graciously echoed Donna and offered her to Theo. "Thanks so much for giving us Sisterwoman," France told Rose now. "Theo's in heaven. And thank Donna for the great dinner. We had so much fun." The dinner had been great, and the evening had gotten better. They'd eaten at a table outside, but by that time France had coated herself in bug spray. And Donna had mellowed as the evening progressed.

Rose turned and stomped toward the dressing room door. "I wasn't attached to that cat anyway," she said.

Coralee bobbed underwater and came back up sleek. "Don't pay her any attention."

France didn't want Coralee to go down yet. She wanted to postpone the moment when she herself had to go outside, alone, and dive in. "Did you know Brett's in a bad relationship?" she asked Coralee. "She's really upset about it."

Coralee drew a sharp breath. "I thought something like that might be going on. I was hoping she'd open up to you. Maybe you can talk her out of it. She won't listen to me. You're more her age."

"Can you talk people out of things like that? I don't think so."

"Brett's had it rough," Coralee said. "She needs a friend. I can only do so much."

France had a pang of conscience. Coralee was helping her, taking time to train her to be a mermaid. She could try and be a friend to Brett. What would it hurt? "I'll talk to her," she told Coralee, who gave her a little wave and dropped down into the chute.

Outside in the sun, France stood at the edge of the water in her sad-sack turquoise bathing suit, wearing her mask and flippers, her legs trembling, feeling like a huge fraud. She could never do this in a million years. And why was she even trying? What was she trying to prove? Before she could bolt, her stomach knotted with fear, she dove into the frigid water and began swimming slowly down toward the stage. There was the overflowing treasure chest, the statue, and Coralee and Lydia, hovering there in the water, the good fairy and the bad fairy. Grendy should be here, France thought. Grendy should be teaching her how to be a mermaid. She opened her mouth and emitted a watery roar. Where is my mother? Her ears popped and she slowed down, trying to let them equalize. But now her eyes were on the air hose. It felt all wrong to be swimming down instead of up when she needed air, but she kept going. Lydia waved the air hose at her, and she finally grabbed it. The hose blasted air into her mouth like she was sticking her head out the window of a speeding car. She began floating upward. Rose's voice came over the intercom, eerie and disembodied. "Let out some air."

She did, and sank back down. Try to relax, she told herself. She glanced over at the glass where she could see Rose, in the control booth, watching her. "Girls, show her the back dolphin." Coralee and Lydia, side by side, flipped slowly over backward, moving perfectly in synch, arching and peddling around in a full circle. It was a move France had seen often in *The Little Mermaid Show*. "France," said Rose. "Drop your hose and do one." She sounded like a marine sergeant.

Rose didn't want her to be a mermaid. She thought France couldn't do it. Don't underestimate me, France thought. She took some more air, dropped her hose, and flung herself into a back dolphin, using her arms to pull her through it, blowing air out her nose, then raced down to snatch up the hose where it rested on the stage floor. The air rushed into her mouth, scratching her throat. She couldn't get a good breath. Up. She had to go up. She pushed off the stage, fleeing to the surface, where she greedily gulped the air.

She lifted her mask. Over on the swimming beach, sunbathers lolled and swimmers yelped and cavorted under the cloudy sky, oblivious to the drama going on below. How had Grendy managed to conquer her fear? France's legs were tired from dog-paddling. She would have to swim to the bank or dive back down. Replacing the mask, she took a deep breath and dove back down to the stage, letting her air out slowly. She'd try one more time.

"Welcome back," said Rose's echoing voice. To France it sounded sarcastic. Coralee gave her a thumbs-up sign. Then she saw Lydia motioning at her to go down under the stage, into the air lock. France turned to see someone else in the theater. The man wearing the cowboy hat. Ace.

France plunged down under the stage. She popped up in the pocket of air, the sound of her breathing echoing off the fiberglass walls. She remembered Linda Huddle, and the bad air, and her heart began to pound.

Coralee sprang up beside her. "It's all right," she said, breathing heavily. "He didn't see you close up."

"I can't pretend to be Mom. He knows Mom's gone. Everyone knows Mom's gone."

"If anyone asks, we'll say we've been hiding her." She giggled.

"Are you?" France said. "Hiding her?"

"Of course not," said Coralee.

"You never know," France said. And of course, that was the

whole problem. "Besides," she added. "I can't use the chute. Or the hose."

"Don't worry about the hose," Coralee said. "Everyone almost quits because of the hose. It'll get easier."

France could only breathe in and out, appreciating the experience as she never had before.

Rose's voice came over the sound system. "Please exit the water," she intoned, sounding like a robot. "Lightning has been spotted in the vicinity."

In the dressing room, their skin covered with goose bumps, France, Coralee, and Lydia sloshed across the wet tile floor and stood underneath hot showers. While they were dressing, Rose came barging in. "Ace knows what's up!" she said. "He asked who the fourth swimmer was and I said Grendy, and I'm sure he didn't believe me."

"That little monkey," Lydia said. She was wrapped in a huge pink towel, her jaggedy hair plastered to the sides of her face. "He can't prove it," she said.

"He's doing our music," Rose said. "He'll find out sooner or later."

Outside, thunder rumbled. France rubbed lotion into her legs—strawberry-smelling lotion that her mother had left behind in her locker. "Maybe I better not be in the show," France said, feeling a surprising letdown.

"Let's bite the bullet," Lydia said. "Get him on our side."

Rose dropped down on one of the gray benches. "You really

want to take the risk?" she asked Lydia. "Anyway, I don't think she really wants to do it. You guys just talked her into it."

"Let France speak for herself," said Coralee, hooking up her sexy black bra. She knew what France was going to say.

"I do want to do it," France said. She was attempting to rub lotion on her stomach and back without removing her towel. "I really want to."

"She sucks," Lydia said, "but she's the only thing we've got."

Coralee spoke without turning around. "You sucked too, Lydia, when you first started. She's coming along fine. And, Rose. Remember how Grendy gave you pep talks so you wouldn't quit?"

"It was our job," Rose said. "We were committed to it. It was our calling."

"I'm committed to it too," France said, and decided that she was.

There was a big clap of thunder. Too close. Rose folded her arms on her chest. "I'm just trying to save us all from a big disaster," she said.

Coralee twisted a tank dress over her head. "Well, stop trying so hard."

Lydia removed her towel, standing naked before them. She was flat-chested and had a flat stomach, but her thighs resembled ham hocks. She attacked her hair with the towel. "You're going to have to get your butt in gear," she told France. "You better practice like the devil, or you'll never make it. And then we'll have to cancel the show anyway."

At least she doesn't assume I can't do it, France thought. "I will," she said. "I'll practice."

"I'll send Ace to you, Lydia," Rose said. "Next time he comes snooping around."

Rose had definitely changed her attitude toward France. Had she done something to offend Rose? Or said something? Maybe it was Donna's influence. Donna disliked Grendy, so it was logical that she wouldn't like France. But Rose loved Grendy. So she said.

"I'll work on Ace," Lydia said, snapping at Rose with her towel. "Leave him to me."

Twelve

On Saturday morning Theo asked if they could go to the flea market.

"Uggh, I hate those things," France said. "All that dust gives me a headache."

"Grandma and I went every Saturday," Theo said.

"What about Grandpa?"

"He only likes new things."

"No wonder your room is so full of junk," France told Theo, and his face began to crumple. Another storm brewing. No ordinary pouting for him.

"It's not junk."

"Okay, okay," she said. Why couldn't he take a joke? "We'll go."

The flea market was held in a field on the outskirts of Mermaid City. Rows of vendors were set up under long narrow buildings with tin roofs and no walls, but even so the place smelled of dust and sweat. France found herself scanning the scene for Grendy, as she did everywhere she went. Many of the other customers seemed drunk or depraved, or maybe they were just disintegrating in the heat. There were white trashy families sorting through the clothes and wealthy, slightly bored-looking women, the kind who came into WomenSpace, searching for treasures.

Theo stopped and held out his hand. "Grandma always gives me five dollars to spend."

France smiled and gave him a few bucks.

Most of the stuff for sale was pure schlock—happy meal toys, cheap cosmetics, marbles, driftwood clocks, posters of tractors in plastic frames. Live puppies and kittens panted in their cages— France steered Theo away from those. Some vendors were trying to sell jelly jars and dirty stuffed animals and other odds and ends that belonged in the dump. There were some tempting displays of glittering costume jewelry locked in little cases, but France forced herself to walk past them.

She followed Theo as he pawed through the jumble of items spread out on wooden tables. He found a yellow sombrero ashtray for fifty cents, a little orange Buddha for one dollar, an iron monkey wearing a fez for two dollars. Four juice glasses that said FLORIDA SUNSHINE! in faded green print for three dollars. He also wanted a poster of a tiger and a collar with rhinestones on it for Sisterwoman, so France gave him the extra money. She could imagine her father shaking his head in disgust.

Just as they were ready to go, France saw a plate on a table, a souvenir plate from the state of Kansas. She picked it up and rubbed at the dust. There were pictures of cattle, wheat fields, sunflowers, and Eisenhower's boyhood home in Abilene. The town of Lymon was not on the map. Neither was the town of Brookville, where their family had once stopped for dinner on a trip to see the Grand Canyon. They ate at a restaurant on the main street that served food family-style—fried chicken, home-made biscuits, carrots with ginger, peppers, and corn, and apple pie. "This is fabulous!" Grendy had said. She didn't even pretend to be on her diet. "What heavenly food! Let's stop on the way back." North had grumbled about the food being standard Mid-western fare, but he'd eaten every bite. Beauvais and France ate and ate and didn't fight, and France was relieved to be eating and even more relieved that they were all getting along and thought that Brookville must be a magical place. But they hadn't stopped in Brookville on the way home. They hadn't even gone through Kansas. The plate cost five dollars. She decided to buy it.

Theo carried his treasures in plastic bags that banged against his legs as they made their way, under the glaring sun, toward the car.

"Did I tell you that your mom and I visited every state in the U.S.?"

"Can we do that?"

"Who? You and me?"

"Yes. You can take me."

Had he already decided that he was going to live with her? That they weren't going to find his grandma? "We can *all* go," France said. "Grandma and Grandpa too."

"And Bruno?"

"Right." Actually, it was hard to get Bruno to go around the block.

At home, instead of calling Naomi like she should've, she collapsed on the couch, flat on her back. Sisterwoman sprang up and lay on her chest like a man's fat necktie. France scratched her underneath the new collar. She'd missed having a cat. Why hadn't she gotten another one after Ray and Burt left?

"Maybe she'll send us another message," Theo said. He sat on the carpet a few feet away, lining up his new purchases and admiring them.

"Maybe," France said. Silently she asked the cat, "Where is my mother?" France closed her eyes and tried to be receptive. Nothing. "She can't send messages all the time," France said. "It tires her out. Let's go swimming at Mermaid Springs. Want to?"

"Please," Theo said. "Please please. One more message. I'll never ask again."

France glanced over at the coffee table, where her dirty Kansas plate lay. Something about one of their trips. Beauvais was always better away from home. She began rubbing Sisterwoman's forehead. "I'm getting something," she said, closing her eyes. "A story your mom wants to tell you."

"Another story when she rescued someone?"

Surely she could think of something. The little German girl, in Arizona.

She told Theo about camping in Monument Valley. They'd driven there through a dust storm and then a thunderstorm, past towns called Ship Rock and Red Mesa, past Indian children on ponies herding sheep, past rock formations jutting up out of the flat red earth like monster teeth.

France, who was twelve, felt suddenly and acutely homesick, as if she'd just landed on the moon. At the campground on the Navajo reservation they ate their yucky supper—tuna something—and watched the sun set on the formations behind their campsite, the rock face turning pink and then purple and then red. Beauvais kept saying. "Can we move here?" North and Grendy were quiet, but France could tell they were awestruck.

Suddenly they heard a soft whimpering. "Is that an animal?" Beauvais said. She got up from the picnic table to investigate. It was a little girl around five or six, sobbing. She could only shake her head when they asked her questions, then finally she let out a torrent of German. None of them spoke German. North had been too young to fight in World War II.

"She must be lost," Beauvais decided. She got a flashlight from the car. "I'll walk around with her to find her parents." No one else volunteered to help. North and Grendy busied themselves putting the food away, and France began unloading sleeping bags from the car. The truth was, none of the rest of them wanted to deal with the girl. They were exhausted. And they knew Beauvais would do it.

Nearly an hour later, Beauvais came back. She'd taken the girl to nearly every campsite before they found her parents, who were calmly waiting in their tent. They didn't speak much English either, but they'd invited her in for some cookies and hot cocoa, which she said was delicious. They'd given her some German coins. The whole campground was full of Germans, she said. What were they doing here, out in the middle of nowhere? Could they go to Germany next summer? She regarded it all as a big adventure. She said it was her favorite part of the trip.

"She liked to help people," Theo said. "Did she ever help you?"

"Sure," France said. "Of course." But the only time she could remember was when she'd had the affair with Mr. Quackenberry, and she could never tell Theo about that. "Sisterwoman's finished for today," she said. "Go get your bathing suit on. I'll be right behind you."

Theo ran off to his bedroom, but France lay lethargically on the couch, rubbing Sisterwoman's head. Was Beauvais's spirit causing her to remember Mr. Quackenberry?

She began having sex with Rudy Quackenberry the summer she was fifteen. France and two of her friends were spending the night in a mobile home belonging to the sociology teacher, Jamie Blau, a first-year teacher who still wanted to be buddies with the teenagers. She'd gone out of town to visit her boyfriend and had given France the key to her trailer, telling her she could invite only one friend over and that she should never tell anyone about it. At 1 A.M. a man began pounding on the trailer door and yelling, "Jamie. Let me in!"

When France opened the door, she saw Mr. Quackenberry, who appeared to be drunk. He was just as shocked to see her as she was to see him. They stared at each other for a few seconds, registering what they were actually seeing, the wrongness of it, and then Mr. Quackenberry turned and wobbled off to his pickup truck. Her friends, Joanna, Laurie, Lisa, and Michelle asked who it was, and for some reason she said, "Just some man."

Then she was assigned to Rudy for driver's ed. From their first day, there was a charge between them because of their secret encounter at the trailer. France had never considered Mr. Quackenberry attractive, the way she and all the other girls did Mr. Hall, the algebra teacher, who had a chiseled movie-star face. Bearlike Mr. Quackenberry had dark hair, layered over his ears and parted in the middle, and a trim mustache that was a bit uneven. But he had an air of confidence and a sense of humor that made him a popular chemistry teacher and swim coach.

Nothing happened between them until the day they practiced merging onto I-65. When it was her turn, France could not make herself merge. Rudy, in his coach persona, began hollering at her. "Pull out. What are you waiting for? A personal invitation?" She'd stopped the car on the shoulder, humiliated and frozen with fear. Finally he came around and removed her from the car. Debbie, another student, took over, merging flawlessly between semis, all the while cracking her gum. Back at the high school parking lot, he pulled France aside. "Maybe you need some private lessons," he said kindly, and she burst into tears.

Every afternoon after driver's ed class she drove off with Rudy and they came back two hours later from a remote cornfield France knew about from her corn detassling days. It was also the place where she and Bruno made out, and whenever she was parked there with one of them she kept remembering being there with the other one, and she imagined she was in some sort of X-rated comedy. She was surprised to find that her relationship with an older man progressed as most high school relationships did—teasing and complimenting, kissing, fondling, focused fiddling, and then the actual deed. Rudy was so paranoid he had to watch out the window while they did it, which somewhat curtailed their enjoyment. France was a virgin but didn't tell him. She didn't want either one of them to have to pretend that what they were doing had any real weight or meaning.

France had so far refused to go all the way with Bruno, worried that if she gave in he'd dump her and tell all the other guys and they'd think she was a slut. All the magazines said this would

happen. At first she couldn't figure out why she'd given in so easily to Rudy, but then she decided it was because they were totally
different kinds of relationships. Rudy would never tell—she
promised every time that she'd never tell either—and he gave no
indication that he was losing interest in her. Besides, France had
been on the verge of caving in to Bruno, and so, with a teenager's
twisted logic, told herself that screwing Rudy would help her keep
Bruno at bay.

Perhaps she subconsciously hoped her parents would put a
stop to her private lessons, but they never seemed to think them
odd, mostly because they were too busy wringing their hands over
Beauvais. After driver's ed ended, Rudy and France switched to
his pickup truck and kept up the private lessons into the fall, returning to the cornfield until it was harvested. During that school
year, her junior year, and the summer afterward, she and Rudy
continued to sneak off occasionally to a Travel Inn—where they
had much more satisfying sex—in between her dates with Bruno
and parties and dances and track practice and her job at Foxmoor
Casuals. She had no problem keeping her two lives separate, and
had no desire to tell her friends about Rudy. Back then she was
proud of her ability to compartmentalize, thinking it indicated
how strong she was, not knowing what a self-defeating habit it
might become. It was a habit she'd picked up, without even knowing it, from North.

October of her senior year, despite Rudy's use of condoms, she
got pregnant. Rudy met her in the hardware section of Kmart,
gave her money for an abortion, and with tears in his eyes, told her
their "thing" was over. France drove right home—she was now an
excellent driver—and was so freaked out that she told Beauvais

everything. Beauvais, then a sophomore, didn't even seem surprised. "Mr. Quack? What a creep!" was all she said. Beauvais knew someone who'd had an abortion, so she took over. She scheduled an appointment for France at an abortion clinic in Indianapolis, since there wasn't one in Cedar Valley. She arranged for one of her friends, a hoody girl who'd already dropped out of school, to take them to the clinic, and then, when the day came, she called the school pretending to be Grendy, and said that neither France nor Beauvais would be in that day due to illness. The hoody girl drove a van full of other hoods, and everybody but France smoked pot all the way down to Indianapolis. France would've smoked too, but she was afraid the doctor would see that she was high and send her away. What she mostly remembered about the trip, besides the surprisingly painful and sad procedure, was the drive there and back. The hoody girl, whose name was Wally, drove exclusively in the left lane on I-65 and was such a serious tailgater that France felt they were all going to die at any second. France kept imagining what Rudy would say: "This isn't a train here. Are you trying to hook up to their bumper?"

France had never told Bruno anything about this experience. By the time she got pregnant they'd officially started seeing other people, and soon after her abortion she stopped seeing Bruno altogether because she'd decided that she wouldn't have sex again till she was married and didn't want to be tempted. She knew now that she'd totally misjudged Bruno. He wouldn't have dumped her or told his friends, and Mr. Quack ended up doing both. One day someone passed a note to France in the hallway. "There's a place in France where Rudy likes to dance."

France scratched Sisterwoman under the chin, noticing little black dots, like blackheads, on her muzzle. France had tucked this ugly memory away because it didn't fit in with the rest of her life, but something about coming to Florida, becoming a mermaid, and spending time with Theo and Sisterwoman had brought it back. Sisterwoman. She was the real culprit. France pressed Sisterwoman's ears flat on her head so that she looked like a rat, but it didn't phase her a bit. She purred on, sure of her own identity.

The next day was Sunday. France forced herself to call Naomi around nine, hoping Naomi would still be in bed and she could leave a message telling her she wouldn't be back till after Labor Day—and by the way, *Mr. Donut* is the dollmaker! But no, Naomi and Roger were up reading the *New York Times* and drinking coffee. She was so happy to talk to France that France couldn't bring herself to spill the beans. Instead, she made a story of the dinner at Rose's, talking about the mermaid rivalry and their acquisition of Sisterwoman.

"You should go to that town, with all the mediums," Naomi said. "Get a reading with someone. Maybe you'll find out something about your mom."

"I don't believe in that stuff, really," France said. But she had actually started thinking that Sisterwoman was clairvoyant. This was the way it all started, she decided. Next stop—séances. She'd better leap off at this station, or who knows where she'd end up? "It's a bunch of hooey," she added.

Although she didn't feel like it, she decided to take Theo to her parents' church, Mermaid Springs Methodist. Grendy's trail was growing cold, and perhaps she could find out something from

someone at church. France had stopped going to church years earlier, soon after Beauvais ran away from home. Her parents saw
France's straying from the church as a sort of adolescent rebellion,
a shunning of their values, but the real reason she quit going to
church was not a lack of faith or a rejection of Christianity. She
could no longer stand to see her father up there in the pulpit. She
couldn't see him there without remembering the fight he'd had
with Beauvais the night before she ran away. Beauvais had been
caught in a lie—she'd spent the night with her no-good boyfriend
instead of at Wally's house. She'd sat at the kitchen table and
sobbed while her mother paced and her father threw words at her:
slut, lying bitch, useless piece of shit. France had known even then that
her father was at the end of his rope with Beauvais, and that he
didn't really mean those words, but nonetheless, she couldn't forget the fact that he'd used them. He would've hurled them at
France if he'd known about Mr. Quack.

As far as she knew he'd never apologized for calling Beauvais
names, even after Beauvais later apologized to her parents for
causing them so much heartache.

Mermaid Springs Methodist, a brick building with white pillars,
was much larger than France had expected it to be. She dropped
Theo off at a Play-Doh–smelling Sunday-school classroom and
he stood there, lumpishly, in his little plaid shirt and khakis, till
one of the teachers, a quick little bird of a woman, whisked him
toward a table where a group of kids clustered, gluing seeds to paper plates, worshiping the Lord with arts and crafts. Theo'd been
here before, so he knew the score. France asked the woman if she'd

heard from Grendy, and the woman gave her a vacant, distracted smile. France patted Theo's shoulder and sneaked out.

She decided to sit up in the balcony so that she'd have a better view, took a program, and padded up the carpeted stairs in her mules. At their church in Cedar Valley, the stairs to the balcony had been uncarpeted, and anyone walking up or down was heard by everyone in the congregation. A friend of France's, Jimmy Kondas, had once tried to creep down the stairs during a prayer but slipped and fell, clattering all the way to the bottom, laughing like a hyena. The balcony was declared off limits to teenagers for a month.

Here, the balcony was nearly full. France sat down in the center behind a row of teenagers, mostly girls wearing thin, tight shirts. In back of France sat twin boys in sailor suits, coloring in coloring books. The Cedar Valley church had dark wood and blood-red carpet and brilliant stained glass. In contrast, this sanctuary looked pale and apologetic, with its white columns and walls, celery-green pew cushions, and clear glass windows. The air conditioning wasn't doing its job. She removed the cotton sweater she'd put on over her sleeveless rayon dress, thankful that she was wearing a bra. Looking down, she saw lots of gray heads and brightly colored clothing. The minister, in his white robe, sat up on the rostrum, surrounded by baskets of peach-colored flowers, waiting for the Bach prelude to end.

There were the prayers, in which the tragedy of the *Kursk* was mentioned, and the hymns, which brought nostalgic tears to France's eyes—"God of Ages" and "How Great Thou Art." The red-robed choir, which had been sitting on the right side of the rostrum, rose to sing an anthem entitled "I Believe," which had lines in it about hearing a newborn baby cry, touching the leaf and seeing the sky. It could've been an Andy Williams song. France wondered how her father had stood this kind of music, being the purist snob he was.

The minister, Reverend Drake Boles, who had blow-dried, Clintonesque hair, spoke about Andrew, the very first disciple, who'd never got much press. He'd had integrity and character and brought many people to Christ, Reverend Boles said, but was always known simply as Simon Peter's brother. And it never seemed to bother him! Not the way it would most of us power-hungry types today, as evidenced in the self-help book *The Peter Principle*. Not the way it had bothered France, who was often referred to, although not in a positive way, as Beauvais's sister.

Reverend Boles bounced as he spoke, gesturing, and his voice rose higher when he wanted to emphasize a point. He let out blurts of laughter. France liked his style, but couldn't help comparing it with her father's. She pictured her father standing up there, as he must've often done, a tall, thin, handsome man with trim white hair. He had a much quieter, more serious manner, and a rich, sonorous voice. He quoted philosophers and theologians— Tillich, Bonhoeffer. France sometimes listened only to the sound of his voice, finding it strangely soothing.

After their wedding, Ray had asked her, "Did you hear what your dad said in the prayer? About how I would be the leader in the home? I couldn't believe it." France, stung with belated embarrassment—what had their friends thought?—realized that she hadn't heard a word of it.

"We've seen things done in the name of Christ that are bleah!"

Reverend Boles said. Amen, France thought. She fanned herself
with the program. Her mind wandered. A few rows down sat a
man with a marvelous nest of curly hair on his neck and a tidy
woman wearing a gold blazer and claret-colored scarf. Beside her,
a little girl in a black velvet dress and Mary Janes threw down her
baby-doll. A blissed-out teenage couple sat with their sides
pressed together, the way France and Andrew McLoud used to
sit, feeling as though they were on a date and were getting away
with something.

Then the choir rose again to sing the benediction. There
was Lydia, in the soprano section. Lydia! She was the last person France had expected to see here. Suddenly, the scene around
France went from benign to sinister. Why hadn't Lydia mentioned the fact that she belonged to this church? Was she someone North had been counseling? France knew she was wildly
casting about, but she had no idea what was possible and what
wasn't, and the uncertainty terrified her. She sat in the balcony till
the postlude was over and the last straggler disappeared, and then
she thought of Theo waiting with the arts-and-crafts lady and
bolted downstairs.

Coralee, in a knee-length black dress, stood at the bottom of
the stairs, with some older man, and Brett. They all three turned
to greet her. Did everyone go to this church?

Coralee waved her over and hugged her with one arm. "This is
my husband, Ken. And you know Brett."

Ken was slightly taller than Coralee, and he wore a baggy seer-
sucker suit. He had graying blond hair and a sunburned nose.
"Charmed," he said, with a heavy Southern accent.

Brett wore a demure white skirt and a lavender top. She seemed embarrassed to be caught at church. She turned away and mumbled hello.

"I didn't know you all went to church here," France said.

"Small town," Ken said.

Just then Theo burst through the milling crowd. France held out her arms, but he went directly to Brett. He hugged Brett tightly and then pulled back. He stared up at her chest. "That's not the necklace I gave you," he said, pointing at her silver cross with turquoise beads strung above it. Brett flushed, turned, and walked off.

"Bye!" Theo called after her. He began to trot back and forth, twiddling his fingers. He did this, France had realized, when he was thinking especially hard.

"Girl's got no manners," Ken said.

"France and Theo," Coralee said. "Won't you have lunch with us? We're headed to Applebee's."

"Thanks, but maybe another time. I want to talk to Reverend Boles and the choir director. See if they have any idea where Mom could be."

Theo was silent all the way home, and when France tried to get him to talk, he turned his head and stared fixedly out the window, frowning. Both the minister and choir director had seemed kind but hassled and said they were sorry but they couldn't help her. In the house she kicked off her sandals and dove onto the sofa, thanking God for air conditioning that worked.

"Aunt Frances," Theo called her from her parents' bedroom. "Can you come here?"

He stood in front of a framed photo hung on the wall, a photo of Grendy and North in front of their new Florida home. "That's the necklace Brett had on," Theo said, and sure enough, the necklaces looked identical.

"Can't be the same one," France said.

"Grandma hardly ever wore it," Theo said. "I don't think she liked it." He raced over to Grendy's dresser, snatched up her pink satin jewelry box and set it on the bed, then rooted around in it, pulling out clumps of necklaces and bracelets. "It's not here," he whined.

"Maybe Grandma took it with her," France said, her mouth dry.

"Did Brett steal it?"

"I don't know," France said.

He gave her a pained, bewildered look. His beloved Brett a thief?

"Probably not. There must be some explanation."

Thirteen

The next day, France called Brett and asked her to meet them at Mermaid Springs so she could watch Theo during mermaid practice. She didn't want to leave Brett alone in the house. What else might she steal? What else had she already stolen? She didn't feel ready to confront Brett about it yet. She didn't know where it might lead. And she didn't want to hurt Coralee. Or Theo.

At the previous practice, on Saturday, France had again refused the chute. She'd worked on regulating the air in her lungs so she could stay down at the right level, just above the stage. That day she'd done much better with the air hose, and today she dove into the springs with a new confidence.

She swam down, waved to Lydia and Coralee, and picked up her air hose. But someone had set the dial on the air hose too low, and breathing through it was like breathing through a straw. She took a few sucks, dropped the hose, and held on to the edge of the stage. "Do a back dolphin," Rose ordered from the control booth. France couldn't move. She felt the way she had when Mr. Quack had ordered her to merge. "Do you want to get out?" Rose asked. France nodded. "Okay, get out." France dropped the hose and catapulted toward the surface. This time she took a few deep breaths and dove right back down. When she picked up the hose again, one of them had adjusted it. "Just play around with the hose for a while," Rose said from the booth. "I'm coming in."

While the three mermaids perfected their moves for *Mermaids on the Moon*, France experimented with the air hose, taking in and letting out just the right amount of air, swimming around with it, dropping it for longer and longer periods of time. It was strangely liberating to be able to stay underwater for so long. At one point she felt so loose that she attempted a back dolphin and actually managed to pull herself neatly around, her legs only flopping at the end. Hoping that Theo and Brett were watching her progress, she swam up and peered through the window into the theater, but it was empty. Where were they? She'd asked them to stay in the theater.

After practice, France walked shivering into the dressing room, her sun-warmed towel wrapped around her. She thought she'd be the first one in, but when she opened the door she heard voices. Theo was sitting on a bench, crying, but trying to stop. Brett had her arm around him. France asked what the matter was.

"I can't tell you," Theo said. "My heart is breaking."

"What's going on?"

Brett shrugged sheepishly. "I thought I'd give him a tour of the place. He'd never been in the dressing room."

"She showed me her tail!" Theo burst out.

Puzzled, France said, "What's wrong with that?"

"He thought I had a real tail," Brett said. "I forgot."

"You said you were a real mermaid."

"I'm really sorry, Theo," Brett said.

Something about her voice sounded insincere. Had she upset Theo on purpose? Surely she wouldn't be so mean. Theo continued to cry as if his heart were indeed breaking. France couldn't stand it anymore. "Why don't you and Theo go get some ice cream?" Before she began taking care of Theo, she'd scoffed at this sort of parental bribery. She gave Brett some money, and she and Theo left just as Rose emerged from the chute, waterlogged and blue-skinned. France asked Rose if she'd mind staying to talk, and Rose agreed.

After the others had showered, dressed, and left, France, warm and cozy in her mother's Mermaid Springs sweatshirt, gathered her courage. "Why are you trying to discourage me from being a mermaid?" she asked Rose.

Rose, dressed in a purple warm-up suit, unwrapping her white-blond hair from its turban, didn't try to deny it. "I guess I'm still counting on your mom coming back in time to swim in the show."

"Better not count on that," France said. She had to say it. "Did you set my air hose too low on purpose?"

"Of course not!" Rose stopped combing her hair, which covered her face. "I just think it would be better if you went on home to Indiana. She might not come back if you're here."

"Why wouldn't she?"

Rose parted her hair and revealed her flushed face. "I don't know," she said. "That's what a spirit told me."

Was she serious? With Rose, it was hard to tell. France decided to be honest. "I don't want to go back till I find out where Mom went. Theo can't live with me. My life's just not set up for him." She realized that she sounded like her father.

Rose clutched her floral makeup bag in both hands. "Why don't you leave Theo here with me and Donna? That way you can get back to your gallery and your boyfriend. And then when Grendy shows up again, he'll be right here."

Rose must be out of her mind. Why would she put Theo at the mercy of Donna? And that cluttered house! But she'd just told Rose she didn't want him. "Thanks, but I'd rather Theo stay with me till I find Mom," she said.

"He feels very much at home down here," Rose pointed out, which was true. "It was just a thought."

"I understand," France said. She stuffed her wet towel and suit into her tote bag, wondering what had become of Theo and Brett.

Rose peered at herself in the mottled mirror, rubbing base makeup onto her face. "How's Sisterwoman?" she asked France.

"Great."

"I forgot to tell you," Rose said. She clicked open her box of blue eye shadow and began stroking it on. How many of those boxes had she already used up? "Did you know Sisterwoman's psychic?" Rose said. "My friend Lynn, the one who gave her to me, is an animal intuitive consultant. She communicates spiritually with animals. But I guess Sisterwoman communicated too much for Lynn. She got too chatty."

Her father was right—the mermaids were all wacky. But she and Theo had decided that Sisterwoman had a third eye, so what did that say about them? "We've already discovered her psychic ability," France said. "She won't tell me where Mom is, though."

"Can't force the spirits," Rose said. "Maybe you're not ready to know."

That evening, after dinner, France couldn't stand the thought of sitting around the house and she didn't feel like taking her usual walk, so she and Theo went for a drive. "Where do you want to go?" she asked him, and he said he wanted to go over to the Gulf. He told her which road to turn down, and they followed it for a few miles through the woods, passing mobile homes and shacks, neat little cottages and an occasional large new house, like Rose and Donna's.

The road ended at a little inlet where there were shelters with picnic tables and wooden piers lined with people fishing, dark figures against the orange sky. They parked and walked down to the water. France sat gingerly on a splintery picnic table, and Theo squatted in an apron of sand in front of her, digging with an oyster shell. The air smelled like fish and gasoline. Little islands, sprouting sawgrass and palm trees, led like stepping-stones into the Gulf. France soaked up the view, realizing that she hadn't enjoyed a distant view since she left Indiana, since the day she'd stood in the drizzle outside Bruno's studio gazing at the cornfields. This part of Florida was so heavily wooded that the farthest she could usually see was across the street.

"We used to come out here a lot," Theo said.

"You and Grandma?"

"Me and Brett."

"Oh. Nice." France waved a deer fly away from her face.

"And Grandpa."

"Grandpa? Wasn't Brett baby-sitting?"

"Yeah." A seagull pranced near Theo, scolding shrilly.

"So why did Grandpa come with you?"

Theo tipped over and rolled around on his back, grinding sand into his hair, but France didn't want to stop him from talking. Finally he sat up, raining sand. "Grandpa came with me and Brett a lot."

"Where was Grandma?"

"Mermaid practice."

They watched a small fishing boat as it puttered between the channel markers.

"Why did Brett show me her tail?" he asked.

How much could you say to a kid Theo's age? And Theo wasn't an ordinary kid. She wondered if she should make excuses for Brett. Try to smooth the whole thing over. "I don't know why she did it," France said. "I think it was a little mean of her."

"Why would she be mean to me? We're true friends."

"Maybe she's angry about something else and took it out on you. People do that sometimes." France really didn't want to know, but she had to ask. "What else did you and Brett and Grandpa do together?"

"Went to the aquarium. Went to the Reptile Show."

That sounded harmless enough. Though why North would want to hang around with Theo and his paid baby-sitter she couldn't imagine. But, of course, she could imagine.

Theo went on. "Sometimes we just stayed at home and I watched TV and they went in another room and talked."

France felt the hope drain from her body. Surely her father wasn't the counselor who'd been treating Brett badly. Would he really be so stupid? Had he given Grendy's necklace to Brett?

France told herself it was time to go, but her body felt too limp and heavy to move. Now that she had this information, it was her duty to call her father and confront him. She dreaded it for many reasons, but mostly because, from experience, she knew how good he was at talking himself out of any bad situation he found himself in. Three years of divinity school and many more of preaching had taught him how to talk. She didn't know how many times her mother had confronted him, but France had only seen her do it once.

At the time France was still married, miserable, and in denial about her misery. Grendy had asked her to drop by one afternoon, so she did, reluctantly, not liking the breathless melodramatic quality of her mother's voice. Grendy was mulching the parsonage garden. She stood up when she saw France coming. "Can we talk a minute?" Grendy asked, gesturing at the screen porch. The parsonage was a beautiful brick arts-and-crafts house with a large yard that Grendy had landscaped beautifully, but it had never felt like home to France.

"If it's about the money," France said, "Ray started at State Farm today. We're getting back on our feet."

"It's not about money." Grendy dropped the mulch and headed for the porch. Back then she kept her dark hair very short, her skin was still beautiful, and she moved with an elegant grace, even though she was a size eighteen. France lumbered after her, heart pounding, wondering what her mother could possibly have to say. The two of them hadn't talked in weeks. Three new Great Danes sprawled on the screened porch. They didn't even rise when France walked in, just lifted their heads and stopped panting for a second while they gave her the once-over, then laid their heads down and resumed panting, huge tongues lolling.

Back then, Grendy was on a Great Dane rescue mission. She drove all over the state to rescue Great Danes from shelters and had enlisted France's help in putting out the word to dog lovers around the country, and she usually managed to get them adopted. Ray and France had Burt the cat, who hated dogs, so France couldn't take in any of the orphans, but her mother kept Hinky, Dinky, and Parley-vous till they died. Grendy loved to tell people about the time Beauvais, tired of hearing her father disparage the dogs, dressed Dinky up in a dress and wig and took him to church, where he sat beside her in the balcony. Her father had to preach his entire sermon, about sheltering and feeding the homeless, under Dinky's mournful gaze.

France made for the porch swing and Grendy settled in the rocker across from her, peeling off her gardening gloves. She began scratching the head of the beast at her feet. He had a white circle around one eye.

"Do you know Daphne Fox?" Grendy blurted out. "She's very troubled. Your father's counseling her." She wouldn't meet France's eyes.

"I don't know her," France said slowly, wishing she could plug up her ears. She felt a wave of nausea. Why hadn't she told Grendy she couldn't come by today?

As if sensing that France was about to bolt, Grendy spoke

quickly. "Laura Lowe invited me to coffee last week to tell me she'd seen Dad at the 500, with a woman. She thought it might be Daphne."

"He doesn't even like the 500!"

"You think Laura was lying?"

"Maybe she's mistaken."

"Maybe she's a two-headed Martian," Grendy said. "Maybe I'm purple and you're pink."

"Just what is it you want from me?" France asked her mother.

The dog licked Grendy's wrist, slowly and deliberately, as though he was trying to comfort her. Grendy looked at France reproachfully. At least someone loves me, her eyes said. "I want you to come with me to talk to him," she said.

Grendy picked France up at noon the following day, punctual as always. She sat out in her Volvo, beeping her horn every few seconds as if it was an accident.

"It's supposed to get up to ninety-five today," France said when she slid into the front seat and saw that Grendy was wearing a long-sleeved linen dress. France wore a pair of Ray's boxer shorts, damned if she was going to treat this as a formal occasion. She'd called in sick to work for the past three days. She didn't feel well, but she was also trying to avoid her coworker Dennis, tall, blond, and a bit goofy, whom everybody at social services called The Menace. Last week they'd all gone out to TGIF for happy hour, and somehow she and Dennis had ended up at his apartment. She didn't get home till midnight, but fortunately Ray still wasn't back from his pool tournament in South Bend.

Grendy backed out of the driveway too fast, barely missing the oak tree and the front bumper of Ray's BMW. "You're sure you want to do this?" Grendy asked.

"Of course I don't want to do it," France snapped. Grendy'd decided to give North the chance to tell his side of the story. She'd set up an appointment with him, telling him only that they had some business to discuss, and that she'd asked France to come with her. France couldn't stop a phrase from running through her head. *I had sex with The Menace.* And here she was going to point the finger at her father.

"Keep out of it," Ray'd advised her. He'd been on his way to work, dressed like a model from *GQ* magazine. He only lasted six months at State Farm. His boss caught him making off with a huge box of office supplies and two brass lamps. France had rousted him out of pool halls and berated him for buying yet another cashmere sweater, but looked the other way when he brought home stolen office furniture and useful doodads—until he got caught.

"Mom begged me to go," France told Ray. "And I want to see Dad clear things up."

"Are you so sure she's wrong?" Ray said.

"I want her to be wrong," France said. *I had sex with The Menace.* She left the room before Ray could see her face.

Grendy's hands, gripping the steering wheel, were too white. "I went back and checked the Visa bills," she said. "There's all this strange stuff on there. Dinners at Chez Pierre. Rooms at the Hilton in Chicago."

"What do you expect? He travels a lot," France said, irritated by Grendy's sudden fervor.

When they walked into the church office they were greeted by the secretary, Velma Best. Velma was in her forties, laughed a lot, loudly, always wore running shoes, and Grendy loved her because she was ugly, and because her husband was a car salesman with one arm. She waggled her fingers at them from behind her cluttered desk. "Welcome to the morgue!" she said. The place was unusually quiet.

"Where's Dad?" France said. "He's expecting us."

"Oh dear." Velma slapped her hand over her mouth. "He got sick! I rescheduled all his afternoon appointments. He didn't tell me you were coming."

So he'd ducked out on them. "How long ago did he leave?" France said.

"He's just now leaving. Maybe you can catch him."

They found him sitting on the edge of his desk with his suit coat on, rummaging through his briefcase.

"What's the problem?" Grendy said.

"The problem?" He dropped his briefcase on the desk.

"You're sick?" France prompted.

"It's my back." He grimaced. "I did something to it."

"Do you have a minute?" said Grendy.

"If it can't wait." He grimaced again.

"France has something to say," Grendy said.

France's heart began to trip along, faster and faster, like a car engine catching. She lowered herself into a studded, brown leather chair. Grendy, perhaps thinking this was part of a strategy, sat down too. France stared at Grendy, raising her eyebrows, refusing to take over.

"Well, I . . ." Grendy stared down at her cheery straw purse.

Don't cry, France thought. Whatever you do, don't cry. "That tie!" Grendy said suddenly. "Where'd you get that tie?"

"This tie?" He peered down at his paisley tie.

"Not that one. You know the one I mean. With the fire hydrants and dogs." She bought all of North's clothes. "Who gave you the dog tie?"

He frowned, clearly spooked. "I can't remember," he said slowly.

"She wants to know if Daphne gave it to you," France said.

"Who?"

"Daphne."

Grendy waved her hand to shush France. She spoke in a loud, stage voice, working hard to make her lines convincing. "Daphne. I know you took her to the 500. Why the 500? You don't even like the 500."

"I have been to the 500 a few times over the years," North said, slowly and patiently, as if they were retarded. "When I went with Daphne there were seven, no, eight of us there, including her husband. They had tickets and invited me. I knew you wouldn't want to go." He proceeded to tick off the names of the other people.

We could check up on that, France thought. Surely he wouldn't lie about it. Maybe he wasn't guilty. Suddenly France wanted nothing more than to lie down on the ugly brown carpet and go to sleep. *I had sex with The Menace.* "Ask him about the Visa bills," she told Grendy.

He had ready explanations for each item Grendy dejectedly brought up, each dinner or room charge or suspicious purchase. Chupps's Jewelry Store? A surprise for their upcoming anniversary, and now she'd spoiled it. The Hilton in Chicago, when he was supposed to be staying with his cousin Daniel? Daniel's wife had gotten the flu, and North had thoughtfully taken a hotel room.

When Grendy finished, he went over and squatted down before her. "I can't believe you don't trust me. It really hurts. I gotta tell you."

Grendy finally burst into tears. "I'm sorry," she said. "It was France's idea. Coming here."

"That's not true," France said, but her words got lost in the drama of their reconnection. She watched him kneeling there, in front of Grendy, clasping her hands as though he were proposing to her. "Doesn't that hurt your back?" France said.

He didn't respond. "Let's pray," he said. Grendy closed her eyes. "Our Father," he said, "keep us from vain imaginings."

France got up and left the room.

On the way home, Grendy talked maniacally. "I'm so stupid," she said. "Always jumping to conclusions. I'm such a fool!"

"At least this time an elephant doesn't have to die for his sins," France said.

"What?" Grendy said, as if she had no idea what France was talking about.

"Never mind." They passed a day care playground, and France saw a blond child in a sunsuit whack another child with a stick. Her fling with Dennis would turn into a short-lived affair, and Ray would begin spying on her, finally following her to Dennis's apartment and waiting till she came out so he could confront her. This breach in the etiquette of their relationship gave it new life, but only for a week or so. "What about the tie?" France asked her mother. "He never said where he got the tie."

Grendy giggled. "That tie's a goner. I gave it to the paper boy." She made a raspberry noise. "Now I'll have to get it back. Serves me right." She swerved to avoid a pothole. Her voice went down an octave. "You believed him, didn't you?"

"Sure I did," France said, her mind and body numb. She'd just remembered that Ray had given the fire hydrant tie to North as a Christmas present. France leaned back against the seat, riding out another wave of nausea. "Why'd you say the whole thing was my idea? Thanks a lot."

"I knew you wouldn't mind," Grendy said, and the truth was, France really didn't. Part of her was happy that she and her mother felt close, even though it wouldn't last. Beauvais was gone, touring again with Mumbo Jumbo, but Grendy pined after her and worried about her and talked about her—she was still the center of Grendy's life.

France suddenly wanted to pour out her problems to her mother, tell her the state of her own marriage. But she couldn't do it. Grendy thought of France as the good daughter, the one who didn't need any help, and France couldn't bring herself to shatter that illusion.

"I think Beauvais could've gotten the truth out of him," Grendy said, and France knew that Grendy hadn't believed him either.

When France and Theo got back from the Gulf, France called North before she lost her nerve. Theo played with Sisterwoman and a sock on the screen porch.

"Now let me get this straight," North said. "This mentally disturbed kid is wearing your mother's necklace and you think I gave it to her?"

"She's not mentally disturbed," France said.

"She's been in a mental institution. A treatment center. I shouldn't be telling you this stuff."

"You let her baby-sit for Theo?"

"Your mother felt sorry for her. And she wanted to do Coralee a favor."

Her mother did have a penchant for rescuing. France wanted, so much, to believe in his innocence. It was so much easier that way.

"So you didn't give her the necklace?"

"Why would I do a fool thing like that?"

"She stole it. She's a thief."

"How would I know? Maybe it's not even your mother's necklace."

This was going nowhere. And the necklace really was beside the point. She took a deep breath and told him what Theo had said.

"That's true. I did hang out with them a bit," he said. "When I found out about Brett's past, I was uneasy."

"Is this why mother left? Because of you and Brett?"

"Your mother knew I was concerned about Theo's welfare. And Brett's, because I was counseling her at church. That's all there was to it."

France felt crushed by his denial, but there was still anger in her, and it leaped out. "I'm going to find out where Mom went. And I'll find out the truth about you and Brett, if it's the last thing I do."

"You and Theo should come home," her father said. "You're barking up the wrong tree down there. You're not doing anybody any good."

"I'm not doing you any good, you mean," France said, surprising herself. She'd sounded just like Beauvais.

After she hung up she called Bruno. He still hadn't finished the last mermaid doll. He listened to the evidence against North. "Guilty as sin," Bruno said, as she knew he would. "He gave that necklace to Brett. But don't take my word for it. Ask the cat."

"She's not saying," France said. She'd already asked Sisterwoman, but got nothing. Sisterwoman, so far, only wanted to communicate with Theo about the past. "Should I come home?" she asked Bruno. "I miss you. And my real life. Maybe I should come home."

"Only if you want to," he said. "Do you want to?"

"I don't want to," France said. Things were always clearer when she talked with Bruno.

She called Naomi and blurted out that she was going to miss the doll show.

"But you have to be here! After all the work you put into it! Plus, I need your help. I'm doing up new ads. And people keep coming in to show me new stuff. I really depend on your judgment. Some woman came in who only does cowgirls. Great stuff. I'm already sending out invites for the Black-and-White show. It's nuts around here."

"I miss that kind of nuts," France said. She couldn't bring herself to tell Naomi about swimming in *Mermaids on the Moon*. She was sure she'd lose all credibility. "You're doing that instead of coming back here to help?" Naomi would say. She told Naomi that Mr. Donut, who also knew the artist, would be delivering more dolls for the show.

"Your dolls, you mean," Naomi said, and France didn't bother to correct her.

Frank and Joe's friend Chet, a fat, good-natured, but not very brave fellow, was assigned watch duty at the end of Chapter XIII. The gang was expecting another visit from the ghost. Chet fought to stay awake, but the cabin's warmth and stillness caused him to doze off in a big soft chair.

"Suddenly a loud bang jolted him awake. For a moment he was speechless, then a yell of fright burst from his lips. Before his chair hulked a dark figure!"

Fourteen

The following afternoon France went to mermaid practice early, bringing Theo with her so he could sit in the theater and watch. They'd just been to the Homosassa Library, where he'd checked out a slew of new science and animal books, and he brought some of them with him to Mermaid Springs—hopefully enough to keep him entertained. He promised not to leave the theater. Brett, she'd decided, was never coming near Theo again.

In the water she worked mostly with Coralee, practicing back dolphins without the air hose, dropping it before and picking it up after. Coralee spotted her. France could feel herself becoming a bit more graceful, and she was in awe of the feeling. Finding herself enjoying and getting good at doing something she'd never imagined she would do was strangely satisfying. She should give more things a try. Live a bolder life.

She felt so connected to Coralee that when they took a break in the air lock underneath the stage, she found herself telling Coralee about Brett and the necklace and her possible affair with North. "If it's true, I'm really sorry," France said. It was ridiculous to apologize for her father, but someone had to do it.

Coralee's ever-present smile dimmed. "Oh dear. Brett's been in trouble so many times. All my other grandchildren are model citizens, but this one . . ."

"Takes up all your time and energy?" France was thinking of Beauvais.

"Something like that."

"I don't know for sure," France said. "It could be nothing."

"That slimy bastard," Coralee said. "I'd see them together, Brett and North and Theo, and things didn't look right. Why didn't I say something?" She slapped at the water. "Kenny wants me to just stay out of it. Let her mother handle it. But her mother won't do anything. Says that Brett's twenty-two and she's got to learn from her mistakes."

"Did my mom know about it?" France asked. "Is that why she left?"

"I don't think she noticed. Or maybe she was just acting like she didn't notice. Maybe she's just so used to it that she doesn't care."

"How could she not care?"

Coralee smoothed some wet hair out of her eyes. "If he did it a lot," she said, "she might tell herself she didn't care. If she wanted to stay married bad enough. She was hell bent on being with North. She could've had her pick."

France didn't want to hash over the past again. "What should we do about Brett?"

"You don't need to do anything, honey," Coralee said. "I'll take care of it. That's what I'm here for. Good old Granny. I'll figure out something."

Suddenly Lydia emerged from the water world. "Break's over, merhags," she said, and must've noticed France's puzzled expression. "I've decided to claim my hagdom," she said. "I'm now an official merhag. Ready to get back to work?"

She called me a merhag! Me! France felt elated and silly about it at the same time.

The next morning Brett came to see France and Theo in a torrential rainstorm. It had been pouring since the previous afternoon and showed no signs of stopping. "Surprised to see me?" Brett asked. She peeled off her raincoat and handed it to France.

"I am," France said. She considered asking her to leave, but part of her felt obligated to find out anything she could. Anything that might lead to her mother's return. She hung up Brett's coat and sat in a cushionless kitchen chair. Theo came over to stand next to France.

Brett sat down across from them, a drop of water running down her nose. She brushed aside France's offer of a towel.

Theo was staring at Brett. "Why are your hands shaking?"

"Lack of booze," Brett said, holding her hand in front of her, making it flutter. All her rings and bracelets were missing. "Just kidding," she added. "I'm cold."

France suggested that Theo draw a picture for the refrigerator, and he shuffled off, leaving waves of uneasiness behind him.

Brett leaned back, her face twisted up in the tough sneer. "Just came by to thank you for telling Granny about me and North."

France heard Theo's video come on, the one about parrots. "Did you take my mother's necklace?"

"What?"

"You were wearing Mom's necklace. At church."

Brett shook her head violently. "Theo gave it to me."

"You expect me to believe that?" France said, shaking with anger. "Even if he did give it to you, why would you accept such an expensive necklace?"

"Expensive! Ha!"

"Do you know what all this is doing to Theo?"

"Theo's okay," Brett said.

"Why'd you show him your tail? He loved believing you were a real mermaid."

"Theo lives in a dream world. Somebody needs to straighten him out."

"You're the one in a dream world," France said. "Fooling around with a married man." France realized, even as she said these things, that it was her father who needed to be called on the carpet. She remembered how she'd felt about Mr. Quackenberry, how she'd gradually convinced herself that he was her true love.

Brett had tears in her eyes. As if she could read France's mind, she said, "He promised we'd be together. He said he'd marry me." She pushed her chair back, stood up and hulked over France.

It was the same old pathetic story, but now, at least, France knew what had happened. "Good luck trying to get my father to love you. He doesn't really love anybody."

Brett snatched up her coat and slammed out of the house. France watched her run through the rain to a little black sports car.

"Aunt Frances?" said Theo. He stood in the doorway. "There's an exotic bird show at the fairgrounds. Can we go?"

Everything was about to go up in smoke, and Theo wanted to go see birds.

"Let me call Grandpa first," France said.

He picked up the phone after screening the call. Before she could even tell him about Brett's visit, he said, "I think I need to talk to someone."

"Yes?" France kept her voice neutral, indicating a willingness to listen to anything reasonable.

"I'm having a real problem with Brett," he said. "I just didn't feel I could tell you about it earlier."

France heard the UPS truck rumbling down the street, the squeal of brakes, the idling of the engine while the driver delivered a package to the house next door, then the truck roaring off again. France held on to the kitchen counter and wished she'd ordered something from a catalog.

"Would you have a problem helping your old father out?"

"With what?"

"Brett thinks there's something going on between us."

"Is there?"

"Not really," he said. "Not now."

"There was something. You *were* having an affair."

"It might appear that way. To some people."

France forced herself to say nothing.

"I let myself get too involved with her. She's very needy and unstable. She thinks we're having an affair. So yes. You could call it that."

"You could call it that," France repeated, and wanted to laugh. He wouldn't come out and admit to anything. The mental energy it must take. "Brett just sat in this kitchen and called it that. You could've at least bought her a new necklace."

"No," he said. "I had nothing to do with the necklace. Listen. I need you to talk some sense into her. Tell her to stop hounding me day and night. She's got to get herself under control." There was a tinge of pleasure in his voice. He was delighting in the havoc he'd created. The same way he'd delighted in tormenting the elephant. That's what drove France over the edge.

"She's your problem," she said. "Deal with her." She'd never hung up on her father before. She'd never had such an angry conversation with him. She felt like the spirit of Beauvais possessed her. Sisterwoman sat beside her chair, gazing up at her. Sisterwoman was just an ordinary cat, for God's sake.

"I'm taking the dolls up tomorrow," Bruno told her on the phone.

"Tell her you're also the artist's friend, helping us out."

"I won't tell her anything. Unless she asks. Then I'll tell her the truth."

France wanted to fly through the phone and strangle him. "Why are you doing this to me? I'm going to lose my job."

"If she fires you, she's not worth working for. She shouldn't have assumed that only a woman would make dolls. You're so up in arms about your father telling his lies."

"That's totally different," France said.

At the next mermaid practice, Lydia said, "We've only got a week left, girls. We gotta get this show together."

France still couldn't bring herself to use the chute, but again dove down from above, down to the air lock underneath the stage. Today they were going to go through the entire show. Lydia had supposedly sweet-talked Ace, who was in the control booth, and he'd agreed not to say anything. "Blue Danube" started up, surprisingly loud. For the first time ever France swam into the lightweight plastic space capsule, which was the size of a small domed tent, and pushed it up till it was above the stage. The music changed for her entry. *"Fly me to the Moon and let me play among the stars."* Clutching her air hose and the flag and the bag, France tumbled out the door of the space capsule. She swooped up and down as if she were enjoying weightlessness for the first time, then threw herself into a few loopty-loops. She planted the flag beside the statue of David and then began collecting moon rocks. *"Moon moon moon blue moon."* She turned to see the alien mermaids circling her, interrupting her moon rock collecting. *"You saw me standing alone."* It was a rush to see them. Rose scolded her, almost too realistically, and emptied France's bag of moon rocks. She sat down to watch the three of them perform. *"Without a love of my own."*

Rose beckoned, and she zipped up to join them. *"Moon River, wider than a mile."* They all did a couple of back dolphins in a line, then formed a tower, with France on top, then a square, with France on the bottom, and then linked arms for the cancan. France lagged a bit behind, her moves raggedy and sloppy compared to theirs, but she was doing it! And as the astronaut, she reminded herself, she was supposed to be a bit clumsy and out of her element.

She was especially frightened of their last move, the Ferris wheel, when they dropped their air hoses and held on to each other's tails— or legs, because they weren't wearing tails today. France was always

afraid she was going to panic and need air. But she gamely gripped
Rose's ankles while Coralee held on to her ankles, and rolled through
an entire rotation. When they finished she heard Theo clapping in
the control booth. "Good job, Aunt Frances," he cheered.

France swam over and peered into the theater, almost expecting to see her mother sitting there. She didn't see a soul. Why
couldn't she get it through her head that her mother could be anywhere? Canada. Mexico. Africa. She might be sick, or hurt, and all
alone. She might be dead.

France turned and let herself float slowly up to the surface.
The other mermaids had already retreated into the chute. All the
sunlight in the water was gone. Up in the real world, it must be
raining again. She dreaded getting out of the spring. Maybe she
and Theo should be out on the open road, searching for her
mother. But where would they start? Nobody had given them any
solid leads. Not even Sisterwoman, who'd refused to cooperate.
Or Rose, whose ability to speak with spirits came and went.

France broke through the water into the rain. Across the river,
the beach was deserted. She began to paddle toward the water's
edge. Maybe, like Naomi said, what they needed was a human
medium. There was a whole town of them not too far away. Perhaps Beauvais would speak through a professional medium, tell
her where Grendy'd gone. What would it hurt to try?

"Aunt Frances!" Theo stood on the bank, waving at her. "Lightning has been spotted. Please evacuate the water."

Later that evening, when Theo and France were watching *101
Dalmatians*, Brett came to the door again. France didn't want to let

her in, but then she thought of Coralee. Brett was drunk. She walked in, lurching a little, and sat down in a kitchen chair. She wore blue jeans with the knees ripped. She closed one eye and studied France with the other. Her hair shimmered on her shoulders.

"How'd you get out here?" France asked her. She didn't see a car in the driveway.

"Walked all the way from Homosassa. It's a hell of a long way. Could you drive me somewhere? Lost my license. DUIs."

France decided not to mention the little black sports car Brett had shown up in the day before. "Theo's here," she told Brett.

"He can come too," Brett said. Then she yelled, "Come on, boy!" When she stood up, France didn't stand with her. "If you don't drive me," she said, "I'll have to keep walking. And I'm not in any condition to walk. You owe me one."

France got up and slung her backpack over her shoulder. Brett was right, she shouldn't be out by herself. She really hated for Theo to see Brett like this. He erupted in a temper tantrum when she told him they had to turn off the movie, but a few minutes later he sat quietly in the backseat of the rental car, nursing the lollipop she'd bribed him with. He wore a T-shirt that said, "New Dog, Old Tricks," one that Bruno got him.

"Just tell me where we're going," France said. It was a cloudy night, and the highway was dark, the lights from the gas stations and houses too sporadic to make a difference.

"It's a little place next to the Winn-Dixie," Brett said.

"Why are we going there?" Theo said.

"So I can get me a little bitty drink. To tide me over, till I can get a great big drink." She turned to face France. "This'll be weird," she said. "I haven't been in a liquor store in ages." She gave France a wide-eyed look. "I used to be such a bad kid. Two years in the Girls' Reform."

France glanced back at Theo, whose mouth hung open. He would never forget this.

"Haven't touched a drop in over two years," she said. "Not till this morning. Right after Granny told my mom about North."

"She would've found out one way or another," France said. I will not feel responsible for her starting to drink, France thought. France felt she should've learned something over the years about how to deal with people in Brett's state, but all she wanted to do was get away from her. She pulled into the Winn-Dixie parking lot and into a space in front of Jubil's Liquor. "Theo and I will stay in the car."

"No you won't!" Brett drew herself up, then switched to a pleading, whining voice. "I don't trust myself in there," she said.

"You're not going to shoplift?"

"Course not! I've got baby-sitting money!"

Inside, Brett stood swaying in front of a row of vodka bottles. "This'll show him," she said. "Mr. Minister." She reached up and grabbed two fifths of Smirnoff. "They're shipping me off to a crazy hospital tomorrow. No more baby-sitting for me!" She slapped France on the back.

This might be her last chance to talk to Brett. "Tell me something. Were you in my dad's office the night my mother left?"

"Must've been another one of his gal pals. Your mother is better off without him." Brett fixed France in a red-eyed stare. "She's happier now."

"Where is she?" France grabbed Brett's shoulders.

"Butt. Out." Brett lurched away from France. "She's paying for these," Brett yelled to the store clerk. As she was sidestepping out of the store she glanced back at Theo, a nakedly sad look on her face, and France thought she was going to say good-bye, but she didn't. She body-slammed the door open and ran across the parking lot. France couldn't bring herself to run after her.

"What the hell?" said the man behind the counter.

"Aunt Frances," said Theo, tugging on her shirt.

"Yeah?"

He leaned against her. "A bird's respiratory system is sensitive to many kinds of household fumes. You should never let a pet bird fly around in your kitchen."

France squatted down beside him. He stared at the door, terrified. "Thank you for telling me that, Theo." He allowed her to give him a hug before he stiffened up and stepped away.

France wrote a check for the vodka. She called her father from a pay phone while Theo waited in the car. Brett stood in the far corner of the parking lot, leaning against an oak tree, sipping from one of her bottles. She appeared to be watching France.

"Your girlfriend," France told North. "She's flipped out. She's drunk and she stole vodka and left me to pay for it."

He grunted. "She's always pulling stunts like this. Couldn't you stop her?"

Theo honked the car horn.

"So it's my fault," France said.

"No, it's *my* fault," he said loudly. "Everything is all *my* fault. We should never have moved down to that hellhole. If we'd stayed here none of this would've happened."

For the second time, France hung up on him. She called Coralee and asked her to go get Brett from the parking lot.

The exotic bird fair was held at the fairground in one of the long low buildings used for 4-H exhibits. It was air conditioned, unlike the buildings at the county fairground in Indiana, where France used to display outfits she'd sewn, "matching ensembles"—bell bottoms and bubble shirts—that Beauvais had drawn the patterns for. France had never even considered giving Beauvais any credit for her contribution.

The room smelled of musty wet newspaper. It was early in the morning, but lines of people filed past the rows of cages, pointing and cooing at the birds, asking the owners if they could hold one. Some of the birds sat on small plastic trees outside their cages, shifting back and forth on limbs hung with ropes and brightly colored wooden beads and plastic toys. There were hand-lettered signs in front of the birds—Sun Conures, Blue Indian Ringnecks, Senegals.

Theo stopped next to a blue-and-gold macaw sitting on a man's shoulder and stared in fascination. The bird was as big as Sisterwoman. The man was tall, rotund, and bearded. "Birds make better pets than dogs do," he told them. "Rusty's much more affectionate than a dog." He kissed the bird on the beak. "I've hand-fed mine since they were babies. My African Gray"—he nodded toward a big gray bird on a perch beside him—"talks real good. He can imitate my wife's voice perfectly. When I'm out back he calls me into the house and then when I come in he laughs and laughs at me."

And you like that? France thought. "Where are these birds from?" she asked him.

Theo answered. "South America and Mexico."

"Right you are." The man turned to France. "Can your son hold Rusty?" France didn't bother correcting people anymore.

Theo looked eagerly at her, and she nodded, but she felt anxious. Suppose the bird nipped Theo and he dropped him and screamed and the bird flapped away and pandemonium ensued? But no, the bird hopped right up on Theo's arm, clinging with his long, dexterous talons, his head twitching mechanically.

"Hello, friend," Theo said to the bird. He stood still and brave.

France declined the man's offer to hold the bird, but reached over and smoothed its oily feathers.

"I want a bird," Theo told her as they walked away. "I really want a bird. I don't want a dog. A bird's more affectionate. Please can I?"

"What about Sisterwoman?" France said. "She'd eat it."

"I could get a small bird and keep it in a cage. Please please please."

"I thought you wanted a goat."

"I want a bird. Please. A cat and fish just aren't enough."

"We'll see," said France, hating herself for falling back on such a tired response. If Theo did come and live with her, these sorts of situations would come up all the time. It was the first time she'd let herself think about Theo actually living with her. She really didn't like the idea of birds in her apartment. Sisterwoman and his fish were enough.

He'd stopped again in front of a cage full of lovebirds, pale yellow, with green heads and red faces. Their cage floor was littered with grapes, apples, carrots, and peanuts. "I want one like this," he said. "Aren't they pretty?"

France agreed, and then decided to talk to him about Brett and what had happened. It was easier to get him to reveal things when he was occupied with something else, she'd found. In the car, she'd try to explain that Brett had a problem, and that she wasn't really mad at them, she was angry at Grandpa, and that she was going to get help, and that France knew Theo was sad about it and that was okay. She'd thought this was pretty good parentspeak, but Theo had stared out the window, refusing to respond. Now, while he watched the lovebirds, she tried to talk to him again about Brett. "Brett and Grandpa were friends and Grandma didn't like it. It was Brett that you and Grandma heard that night in Grandpa's office, wasn't it?"

"No it wasn't," Theo said. "It wasn't Brett. It was someone else."

"Are you sure?"

"I'm sure."

Was Theo just trying to let Brett off the hook? "Who was it?" she said quietly.

He shrugged. "A lady. Some other lady."

"So when she heard this lady's voice your grandma got very angry."

"She wasn't angry," Theo said. "She was scared. Very scared." He moved on to the next set of cages that were full of peach front conures.

Her mother was scared. Hiding somewhere, scared.

Fifteen

France calculated correctly that they could drive to Cassadaga in two hours, but once they got close they couldn't find the right county road. For nearly an hour they passed the same gas stations and strip malls over and over again. France felt as if they'd be mired forever in Orlando's suburban sprawl. They stopped to ask directions at two gas stations, but both employees had just moved to the area and had never heard of Cassadaga.

Finally, just by chance, they stumbled upon the right road, which took them through wooded, slightly hilly countryside with no evidence of the development they'd just left behind. At the edge of the town some small houses and stores were clustered, many with huge signs—PSYCHIC ON PREMISES! . . . TAROT READINGS! When they were eating dinner at Rose and Donna's, Rose had mentioned these hangers-on—they weren't connected with the real Cassadaga. They weren't the real thing.

A sign at the entrance to the town said CASSADAGA SPIRITU-
ALIST CAMP. Rose had also told her that the founders came from
a spiritualist community in upstate New York in the late 1800s
and established this place as their summer camp, but now members of the Spiritualist Association lived here year round. One
main street ran through the center of town. A large buff-colored
building with a wraparound porch, The Lost in Time Hotel,
stood on one side of the street, and on the other corner was a
metaphysical bookstore with a few Harley-Davidson motorcycles
parked in front of it. "Inquire here about readings," said a sedate
sign in the window.

The bookstore was stocked with the usual new age fare, and
no motorcycle riders were evident. A bookstore employee, a
woman with a bowl haircut, wearing a T-shirt that said Cracker
Barrel on the front, led France and Theo back to a bulletin board,
where the mediums had posted their business cards, and pointed
out a phone she could use to make an appointment. France tried
to remember the name of the medium Rose had mentioned, the
one who'd given her Sisterwoman. Lynn somebody. She might be
a good medium, even if she didn't like Sisterwoman. France found
a card for a Lynn Bolsterly, who turned out to be a man, but she
went ahead and scheduled a reading with him in ten minutes.

She and Theo strolled down the main street toward Lynn's
house, which he'd told them was at the bottom of the street, beside Spirit Pond. It was as hot and muggy as ever, but the oaks
made a canopy over them. The street was lined with frame houses
built around the turn of the century, and even though the houses
roosted under palm trees, they could've been transplanted from
the Midwest. They were tidy, newly painted, with well-tended

flower gardens, picket fences, and lawn ornaments. The ordinariness of the place only made it seem even more bizarre. The sole indication that this wasn't any old town was the small wooden signs hanging in front of the houses—MARY BRADFORD WHITE, MEDIUM. ROMAN ALBANESE, SPIRITUAL ADVISER.

Theo grabbed France's hand. He had chattered constantly in the car about seeing spirits and what they would say and look like and how they would be friendly, but now he'd gone quiet, his shoulders hunched in apprehension. Two women in their eighties, both in skirts and stockings, hobbled past them. "What do mediums look like?" Theo asked.

"Like anyone," France said. "Like regular people." She and Theo were the ones who looked weird—Theo in a huge tie-dyed T-shirt, jeans, and work boots, an outfit he'd picked out himself, and France in Grendy's favorite sundress, which was so loose she'd tied the straps together in back with a shoelace and gathered the waist up with one of Theo's cowboy belts, which was almost too small. In a moment of softheadedness she'd decided that the outfit would send Grendy vibes into the universe.

They stopped in front of the Colby Temple, a large white Spanish-style building. A little breeze, fluttering through the palm trees, came from the direction of Spirit Pond, a few hundred yards away, where the Harley riders appeared to be picnicking on a blanket. Theo darted off to a gazebo-shaped hut labeled HEALING CENTER to pet a black cat who was lounging in the shade. France studied the bulletin board in front of the Temple. An official-looking newsletter announced that along with the regular Sunday services and candlelight healing services, speakers would offer programs about Paranormal Investigations, Photographing Spirits,

and Animal Spirituality. What the hell was she doing here? She
wanted to get her reading and get out. As long as Lynn wasn't a
blatant fraud, she'd be satisfied.

Once, back in Cedar Valley, she and Grendy had been shopping at the mall for a baby swing for Theo, and coming home
they'd noticed a new sign in an old house on Seventh Street. PSY-
CHIC READINGS. LEARN THE TRUTH. Grendy pulled into the
driveway. "I've never done this before and nobody's going to stop
me," she said. The house had hardly any furniture in it. Two
women, one younger and one older, who looked like gypsies, answered the door. A swarthy man sat in a backroom with a couple
of children who were watching TV. France was whisked into another room by the younger woman and told a pack of formulaic
lies, culminating in a request for more money. "You have a curse on
your life," said the young woman, in her beguiling accent. "I can remove this curse, if you come to see me twice a week. I will light
candles for you. But it will cost you money."

One hundred dollars per candle, it turned out. Part of France's
mind was shrieking and chortling, and part of her was thinking,
"Hmm. Lighting candles. Couldn't hurt any." Maybe she was
cursed. She'd been divorced for years and still hadn't met the right
man.

Grendy'd had an equally unsatisfying session with the older
woman, who'd asked what sort of job she had. Grendy told her she
had no job and no money, but the woman didn't believe her. The
woman said, "You are a very generous person. People do not appreciate this about you. But I do."

"Generous my ass!" Grendy'd said to France. France had never heard her say ass before. Grendy went on, "Does she think I'm that stupid? She says, 'You will have trouble with appliances this week,' and then she says, 'Your husband loves you, but not as much as you think he should.' What a bunch of gobbledygook." That last part was true, of course.

Underneath all the hilarity, France knew, she and Grendy had been disappointed. Had they really expected someone to tell their fortunes? Of course they wanted to hear good things, but they might have been told about Beauvais's imminent death. And to-day—did she really want to find out what had happened to Grendy? If she and Theo hadn't driven all this way, and searched for an hour to find the place, she'd have hightailed it right out of there.

Lynn lived in a stucco house with stone lions on either side of the gate, and sunflowers tilting over the front steps. His white hair was so thick and curly it looked like a wig. He wore a polyester golf shirt. There should be a rule against mediums wearing poly-ester, France thought. His living room was lovely, with antique furniture, hardwood floors, and a fireplace made of pink marble. Native American figures sat on the mantel. "My wife's a healer," Lynn told them in a nasal, Midwestern voice. "She's got a Native American spirit guide."

The room smelled like animals. Sure enough, Lynn intro-duced them to two greyhounds and a thin white cat named Casper. Theo knelt to pet the cat, and France could see the anxi-ety leave his body.

"Lynn!" a woman called from another room. "Would you come here please?"

Lynn excused himself and left the room. The woman began talking in an angry, complaining tone, and France strained to listen. "That settles it," the woman said. "We're getting out of here."

"We'll talk about this later," Lynn said cheerfully.

"We're moving. Period."

Lynn mumbled something to her and returned to the living room, a placid expression on his face. Great, France thought. This reading was costing her thirty bucks. She should get a discount for his being distracted.

He escorted France, Theo, and Casper onto a sunporch, where the air was a tad stuffy. The room was painted such bright colors that it reminded France of the parrots. A picture of a praying Jesus hung on the orange wall. Theo sat on a couch with Casper, so involved with the cat he didn't seem to know, or care, where he was. France and Lynn sat down across from each other in chairs covered by dusty white bedspreads. Lynn rubbed his hands briskly together, then they joined hands and he said a prayer, asking the spirits to guide them. France was unable to take her eyes off his teeth. They didn't look like dentures, but they were very prominent and unnaturally white.

After the prayer, Lynn leaned back and closed his eyes. He breathed deeply through his pointed, aristocratic nose. Theo stroked Casper. The windowsills were lined with stuffed animals, mostly teddy bears. Why? To make child spirits feel at home? Creepy. France's chair felt lumpy and too soft. Lynn was still breathing deeply. Had he fallen asleep? Just when she was starting to get worried, he opened his eyes.

"The place you live is very comfortable," he said. "But you're going to move again."

Was he talking about her parents' house, or her apartment in Indianapolis? Either way, it sounded like a standard psychic line.

He closed his eyes again. At this rate, France thought, she'd be lucky to find out three things before her thirty minutes were up. But this time he didn't wait so long. "You're an artist," he said. "Why aren't you teaching art?" He smiled.

"I don't know," France said, her eyes drawn again to his teeth. They seemed too big for his mouth. "I've never taught anything," she said. And I've never had any desire to, she added silently.

"I see you teaching art in the future. Lots of teaching."

Uggh, thought France.

Lynn began nodding and gazed off to the side of France. "There's someone," he said. "A woman. I see her baking bread. I see her tending a garden. A garden in a northern climate. She's tending irises."

This sounded exactly like Grendy. "Is this person a spirit?" France said, her throat closing. She glanced at Theo, who was still in a cat trance. "Is she dead?"

"No. She's alive, and very troubled."

"Thank God," France said, collapsing back in the chair. "That she's alive, I mean. It sounds like my mom." You weren't supposed to volunteer information to these people, France knew, but she had come about a specific subject, and she didn't want to waste time. "Why's she upset?" she asked Lynn. Without even thinking about it she unbuckled the cowboy belt around her waist and yanked it off. Much better.

Lynn closed his eyes and folded his hands. "I'm not getting anything about that." His eyes popped open. "You have a question," he said. "About your mother."

"My grandmother," Theo piped up.

"You are mother and son?"

Why couldn't he tell? "He's my sister's son."

"Your sister has passed on."

"She's dead," Theo said. He dumped Casper out of his lap. "It scratched me," he whined, and Lynn said that she probably hadn't meant to. Theo peeked over at the stuffed animals. "Can I play with a bear?" Lynn said sure, so Theo gathered up three of them, all different sizes, and sat back down.

"My mother's disappeared," France said. "We want to know where she is."

"She's gone to be with your sister. Her daughter."

France suddenly felt near tears. This was too much. Why was she doing this to herself? Worse yet, why was she subjecting Theo to it? He sat there hugging the bears but staring at Lynn, rapt. "I thought you said she wasn't dead," France said.

"No, no," Lynn boomed. "She's not. She wanted to go be with your sister's spirit. She feels very bad about your sister's death. She feels responsible. I see a car accident."

"I was there," Theo said. "In the car."

"Your mother is happy where she is now," Lynn told Theo. "She watches over you from the spirit world."

"Like an angel," Theo said.

"But your grandmother doesn't know she's happy. She wants to spend time in her daughter's presence. And be forgiven. What's your sister's name?"

"Beauvais. And my mother's name is Grendy." France felt an unexpected jolt of jealousy. Her mother was still closer to Beauvais than she was to France. "Where is my mom?" France asked him.

"I see her in a safe, special place. The only danger to her comes from within."

To her embarrassment, France began to cry. "My father drove her away," she said.

"He took up with someone half his age," Theo put in. Where had he heard that?

Lynn handed France a box of tissues in a crocheted holder. She helped herself. Lynn's small hazel eyes were warm and kind. She decided she liked him.

"Grendy was not driven away by her husband." Lynn twisted up his face. He looked past France and spoke as if he were Grendy. "I've got to get away. I've got to sort things out. Make sense of things."

"Is she alone?" France asked.

"She walks with spirits. With Beauvais, and . . . do you have a relative named Nan? Nanna?"

France couldn't think of anyone.

Lynn closed his eyes. His upper lip slid upward, gradually revealing the teeth. "And I see a gentleman who keeps looking at his pocket watch. George, his name is. He wants me to tell you that you're letting things get away from you. Important things."

France was getting impatient. Who were these people he was talking about? She'd never heard of them. "When will my mother come back?"

Lynn squinted into the distance. "Not for a long time. She's very disturbed."

"We're all disturbed," France said. This "long time" crap wasn't going to fly. She had a life, and a job to get back to. "Where is she?"

"Right now she doesn't want to be found."

"Oh." Too bad, France thought. For the first time, she felt really angry at her mother for leaving. "Can't you give me a clearer picture of where she is?"

"When you look up, you'll see her."

"She's in the sky?" said Theo, without turning around.

"You'll also see her down below," Lynn said. "It's strange, but that's what I'm getting." He pulled his upper lip down over his teeth.

"She's everywhere," France said, and remembered a sappy poem she'd read once. "I am the wind that blows through the tree. I am the wave that breaks in the sea." She couldn't help giggling.

"She's not everywhere," Lynn corrected her sternly. "I'm getting something else. About someone close to you."

France raised her eyebrows, pressing her lips together. Now her own teeth felt funny. She hadn't been to the dentist in over a year.

"Cliffhangers," Lynn said. "This person loves cliffhangers. His entire life feels like a cliffhanger. He never knows what's going to happen next." Lynn began to wriggle around in his chair. "I feel frustrated," he said, evidently speaking in the person's voice. "I'm in a box." He held up his hands, boxing himself in. "I can't communicate."

Theo. It was an amazingly accurate description of Theo. Theo was kneeling on the floor, arranging his bears on the couch, muttering to them. He had to be read a chapter of a Hardy Boys book every night. His whole life *had* been a cliffhanger. And whatever was wrong with him only made it worse. She was saddened by this description of Theo's feelings. She'd known he got frustrated, but she'd just assumed that deep down he felt okay.

"He'll learn," Lynn told her. "It'll be a slow process. He'll exceed everybody's expectations." Was a spirit telling him these things, or had he simply been observing Theo's behavior? It didn't really matter.

Suddenly Lynn stood up, took Theo's hand, and led him over beside France, then joined their hands. "Treat each other well," Lynn told them. "Your bond is stronger than any other." His teeth gleamed.

France shrank inside. How corny. Was it true? It was true. Why did it take a strange little man with big white teeth to point this out to her? France gazed at Theo's smooth, guileless face. His face had become familiar and dear. She could never again get along without him.

Theo drew back from her gaze. He dropped her hand. "I have a cat," he told Lynn. "Sisterwoman. She used to live in Cassadaga. She's a medium too."

"Ah yes," Lynn said. "Sisterwoman scares *some people*, but you don't need to be afraid." He obviously disapproved of the other Lynn. "Sisterwoman only wants to help you. She's a real treasure."

Lynn allowed Theo to choose a bear to take home with him. When France handed him a check, she said, "I hope you don't have to move. I heard your wife."

He stared at her, and she wondered what had gotten into her. It wasn't any of her business, of course, but somehow the fact that Lynn knew so much about her life made her feel she could stick her nose into his. He finally shook his head ruefully. "The competition among the mediums is tough," he said. "Three other mediums have Native guides. My wife wants to move back to Cleveland."

Sixteen

When France and Theo got back to Conch Court late that afternoon, there was a strange car in the driveway. A midsize Chrysler so nondescript that it had to be a rental car. North was sitting at the kitchen table, dressed in nylon shorts and a T-shirt, tying his running shoes. He didn't get up when they walked in. He had a queer expression on his face, like he'd just taken a wrong turn and didn't know where he was, but was trying to hide his confusion. "I thought I'd better come back down," he said. "Things sounded out of control. And I needed to get some more of my things."

Go away, France wanted to yell at him. You don't belong here.

Theo ran and gave him a big hug and then leaned back against his legs. "Guess what? We went to see a real medium. I got a cat now. Sisterwoman. She's a medium too. She speaks to spirits. I petted a macaw! At the bird fair. I got to hold it. Aunt Frances said I could get one tomorrow."

"I didn't say that." The last person she wanted to see, besides Brett, was her father.

"I noticed you have a cat. She and I have gotten ourselves acquainted." Sisterwoman sat in the doorway, twitching her tail. She didn't like him. North went on. "I don't know how your grandma will feel about the cat, but we'll deal with that later, okay?" He looked up at France. "What's all this about going to a medium?"

She forced herself to speak calmly. "Theo and I went to Cassadaga." She quickly described the town. "It was just for fun."

"That's against biblical teaching," North began, ready to launch into a lecture.

Unlike committing adultery, France thought. She interrupted him. "Why didn't you tell me you were coming?"

"I just decided at the last minute," he said. "Some getup you have on," he added, referring to Grendy's sundress.

"Glad you like it," France said, resisting the pull to explain herself. Now that he was here, she would take the opportunity to really let him have it. She said, in a chipper voice, "How about we have a talk?"

"Later. I'm headed out for a run."

"You don't run."

"I'm taking it up." He slapped his taut stomach.

"Wait just a minute." France got everyone a glass of water. "Why don't you go read awhile in your room?" she told Theo.

"Brett's going in the hospital," Theo told North. "She's sick."

North glanced at France, speechless for a moment.

France nodded.

"That's too bad," he said. He patted Theo's head. "She'll be better soon. Hey. How's about you and me go to the carnival down by Wal-Mart?"

"Can I? Can I?" Theo asked France. He now saw her as the one in charge. This pleased her. She said maybe, but he needed to go to his room right now.

After Theo left, North drank down the entire glass of water. "I've got to run," he said, staring into the empty glass.

"It's still a hundred degrees," France said. "Why not wait till it cools off?"

"When will that be? October?"

"Brett acted like she knows where Mom is," France said.

North swished some nonexistent water around in his glass. "If she does, it's news to me."

Why wasn't she standing up to him? Accusing him? Ranting and raving? She'd forgotten the effect her father had on people. Being around him was like injecting a dose of false well-being into your system. You wanted to see the world the way he saw it, because he seemed so sure of himself, so convincing—everything would be better if you'd only see the world through his eyes. What do you need your own eyes for, anyway? No wonder Grendy had to leave in order to think straight. She found herself resorting to his tactics. "That sweatband is so seventies," she told him.

He yanked it off his head and threw it on the floor.

France wasn't going to be amused by his antics. "Mom overheard you and some woman talking in your office. That's why she left." She told him what Theo had said.

"Let's take a walk," he said, jumping up. "I'll explain as we go. That way I'll still get my thirty minutes in."

France went to check on Theo, who'd gone directly to his

room. He was lining stuffed animals up on his bed, including the bear he'd brought back from Cassadaga. Sisterwoman lay curled at the end of the bed, as if she were guarding the lot of them. "I'm going to give my stuffed animals a reading," Theo said. "They want to know where their mother is. She's up in the sky, in an airplane. That's what I'm going to tell them."

"Sounds good," France said. "Listen. Please don't tell Grandpa anything more about going to see Lynn. Or about Sisterwoman being a medium. He just doesn't understand."

Theo's switch flicked on. "I'm sorry I'm sorry I'm sorry," he said, sobbing. "Oh. I didn't mean to. I'm sorry."

"It's okay," she told him. "Theo. It's okay. Really." She kept saying it till he finally wound down.

He didn't want to go on the walk, and only agreed to let France go if she walked in the middle of the street, away from the drain. He didn't say anything about his grandfather staying away from the drain.

France and North started down the shady street. The houses and trees appeared to be flat and far away, like pictures in a book, and France wished that some of the neighbors were out.

"This is such a tacky little place," North said. They were passing a house with a row of plywood women gardeners bending over, displaying their backsides.

"I kind of like it," France said. She took a step away from the drainage ditch, which seemed to be exerting a magnetic pull.

"Florida is full of tacky stuff," North said. "Mermaids. An entire town of mediums. Alligator wrestling."

"Oh, and Roselawn's not tacky?" France asked. Roselawn was a nudist colony an hour north of Cedar Valley. "And how about the world's largest ball of twine? And the butter cow at the state fair? And the dead mafia guys in the cornfields?"

"All right, all right," North said amiably. "You've made your point."

They were getting too comfortable. "Who were you talking to that night in your office?"

North scratched his head. "She should've just knocked on the door."

"You're having another affair."

He quickened his step. "Oh, come on."

"So who were you with?"

He stared straight ahead. "Lydia."

"Lydia?" She grabbed his wrist. "Were you fooling around with her too?"

He stopped and stared down at her hand on his wrist. She let go. "What a joke," he said.

"What was Lydia doing there? She doesn't even like you. She said she wouldn't touch you with a ten-foot pole."

"The feeling's mutual." He put his hands on his hips. "She came to tell me something."

"What?"

North shook his head. "She scheduled an appointment, but when she showed up she had nothing to say." Was this another ploy? But she could easily check this out with Lydia.

France said, "I think she did tell you something, but you're not going to tell me."

"She just babbled awhile about the church and then said she'd changed her mind and didn't really want to talk. I have no idea what she was going to say."

France realized she was standing right beside the drain. Her father had backed her up against it. She jumped away.

"You're as bad as Theo," North said.

France remembered what Lynn had said. *I feel like I'm in a box.* "Theo needs help," she told her father.

"I agree," her father said. "Poor little guy."

There was something phony about the way he said it. Ultimately, he cared only about himself.

"At least this means that nothing bad happened to your mother," he said. "She apparently thought she had a reason to leave. Even if it wasn't a real reason."

"It was a real reason to her. Your viewpoint isn't the only one in the world. I bet you know the reason she ran off the first time, too."

Her father scowled.

"It's really sad to me," France said, "that you continue with the lies. How can you live with yourself?" She'd never been so direct with him before, and her voice sounded strong and sure. "Preying on someone Brett's age. That's really low."

He turned and jogged off down the street.

Seventeen

Mermaid practice was scheduled every afternoon the final week before the show. On Monday, when France arrived in the dressing room, Rose, Lydia, and Coralee were sitting on the benches, fully dressed.

Coralee wore black square glasses that France had never seen before. "I'm sorry," she told France.

"I'm off the team?" France asked her.

"Somebody told management about you," Coralee said. "I'm thinking it was Brett." Coralee wouldn't look at France. Was she angry at France because of North's behavior? France wouldn't blame her if she was.

"They're assholes over there," Lydia said. "Ace got in trouble too. A written warning."

"It's probably for the best," Rose said, calmly crossing her legs.

"The *best?*" shrieked Lydia. She jumped up and began hopping about in a rage, the edge of her wraparound skirt flapping open. "You know how stupid our show's gonna be with no astronaut? I'm not going to do it. I will *not* be an astronaut. Especially with no astronaut costume." She kicked a locker for emphasis. "Ouch," she said.

"I'm really sorry." Coralee held her head in her hands. "Everybody. I'll be the astronaut. I'll make up a costume somehow."

"*I'm* sorry," France said. "If my father hadn't . . ." She couldn't bring herself to say it. "Isn't there anything we can do?"

Rose was concentrating on dangling her Dr. Scholl's sandal from her foot. "You couldn't use the chute anyway," she said.

"I was going to," France said. "I was working up to it."

"You tried," Rose said. "That's what counts. But don't feel like you need to hang around down here anymore on our account."

"I'm doing it on my account," France said. It felt essential that she swim with the mermaids. And Theo would be so disappointed—now he probably wouldn't be allowed to help in the control booth. "There's no way around it?" she said. "Can't you give me a crash course in scuba diving?"

"We don't do the scuba diving stuff," Rose said. "The trainer's not here right now. She only comes when they hire new mermaids."

In the end, she had to leave. When she got back to the house, Theo was taking a nap and North sat on the couch reading a book about medieval cathedrals. He didn't acknowledge her, and she walked by him without speaking. She wondered how long he was going to stay, but she didn't want to ask him. It was his house, after all. She was now sleeping on that couch, so she had no place to retreat to. In the kitchen, Sisterwoman was perched on top of the refrigerator like a vulture, watching her. "Hey, Sis," she said. She took the phone outside, called Lydia's house, and left a message, telling her that she'd be over to see her that evening. Since France wasn't in the mermaid show anymore, she figured she could be more direct with Lydia. She'd get the truth out of someone.

That evening, she left her father and Theo playing Candy Land and drove out to Lydia's condo, which resembled a Southwestern cliff dwelling. France was taken aback by how large Lydia's great room was—a vaulted ceiling and a huge picture window out of which France could see the dark golf course and beyond it the brightly lit driving range.

They sat across from each other on mission-style chairs. Lydia wore navy blue pjs covered with white stars. Her hair was pulled back in a clip and she wore no makeup. Like Rose, she seemed totally different in her own home. France still wore Grendy's sundress, and wondered if Lydia recognized it, but she made no comment.

If Grendy's bedroom was a mermaid shrine, Lydia's entire house appeared to be one. She had mermaid everything—pillows, lamps, a blue rug with a big mermaid in the center, and a mermaid clock on the wall. She had the same black-and-white photos that Grendy had, along with a color photo of mermaids in yellow bathing suits, with wings strapped to their backs. Only the mermaid in the middle, Lydia, wore a psychedelic-looking tail. Grendy wasn't in that picture. "If you're here about getting back into the show," Lydia said, "I've been racking my brains. I'm stumped." She sipped her iced tea. Andy Williams music was coming from the other room. "Days of Wine and Roses."

"You went to see my dad," France said. "The night Mom left." She told Lydia Theo's version of what happened.

Lydia took another sip of tea. "Would you like water? Juice?" She rose. "You really should drink something."

"Water's fine."

She walked across the beige carpet and turned the corner, disappearing into the room where Andy was singing. Lydia's sudden solicitousness unnerved France. She remembered the time one of her clients, when she was a social worker, baked her a big chocolate cake and brought it to the office. They'd all eaten a piece, even though they'd been warned never to accept food from clients. Nobody got sick, but later, the client was arrested for welfare fraud. France heard the sound of running water, ice tinkling.

Over the fireplace hung a big poster—an enlarged photo of Lydia underwater in Mermaid Springs, wearing a red tank suit, kneeling in the eelgrass, holding bread for the swarming fishies in one hand and her air hose, like a torch, in the other. Her dark hair floated up behind her and she pouted at the camera. It was a stunning picture.

Lydia was back, holding out a glass.

France took a drink of the icy, chemical-tasting water. She had to ask. She owed it to her mom. "Are you and Dad involved?"

"God no!" Lydia shook her head. "I thought your father ought to know something. Your mother wouldn't tell him." Lydia sat back down in her chair.

"So you told him."

"I chickened out."

"You might as well tell me," France said.

"I can tell you what it has to do with," Lydia said. She tucked her legs underneath her. "The stars on my pajamas glow in the dark," she added.

"What does it have to do with?" France asked her.

"Elvis."

"Not him again." France felt like she was a dog chasing her tail. "What about Elvis?"

"Well, only your mom knew what really happened between me and Elvis. But then she told Coralee, and Coralee told Rose, so now all the merhags know. And you're a merhag. You might as well know too."

France smiled in spite of herself. "Was a merhag. Almost."

"You still are one, in here." Lydia patted her heart. She was not being ironic.

"Right," France said. "Go ahead."

Lydia told her about the night, back in 1961, that Elvis stayed at the Holiday Times Motel across the road. At eight o'clock Lydia knocked on the door of room 203, as he'd asked her to do after the show. A stunningly average middle-aged man answered the door, bald with a gut, and Lydia saw that the hotel room was full of such middle-aged men. Was it some kind of party for dull men only? Elvis was sitting on the bed, talking on the phone. He glanced up and saw her and all the men disappeared. Elvis never even introduced them. Act like a mermaid, Lydia kept telling herself. He likes mermaids. She smiled mysteriously, the way she did underwater. He pointed at a chair and offered her a Coke—there were a bunch of bottles on ice in the sink. He wasn't drinking anything. The next thing he did was check his watch, which she took to be a bad sign. His arms were very hairy. Then he asked her what it was like to be a mermaid. What it felt like. He spoke with a hillbilly accent, the same accent she'd worked so hard to get rid of. Leaning forward in her chair, she told him about their mermaid shows, and her parts in them, and then she started babbling about having grown up on a cattle farm in the mountains of West Virginia, aware that she was slipping back into her hillbilly accent, and she explained how she'd had to work in her mother's craft store when she was just a child, and then Elvis interrupted her. "I asked what it feels like to be a mermaid. How does it feel to be down there like that, wearing a tail, breathing underwater?"

Lydia began to get really nervous, because she had no idea how to answer that question. She wasn't the touchy-feely type. She wasn't a deep thinker. Elvis just sat there—Elvis!—and she realized he was in his underwear. He had on a white undershirt and boxer shorts and he leered at her as if he knew he was making her uncomfortable. "What's your name?" he asked her, and she told him, for the second time.

"Lydia," he said, "you could tell me all about your girlfriends and Mommy and Daddy but I don't want to hear that bullshit. Listen. I don't want to screw. I don't even want to touch you. I just want to know what it feels like to be a mermaid. You understand?"

"Yeah." Lydia twisted the hoop in her ear. Why was he saying he didn't want to screw? Was that what he thought she wanted? *Was* it what she wanted—to lose her virginity to Elvis? She was shocked and then mad at herself for being shocked. Why had she expected him to be a nice guy? Finally she took a swallow of Coke (which she'd never been able to drink since) and said, "Wet. It feels wet."

He burst out with a laugh. "That the best you can do?"

By then she was getting mad and was determined not to play his little game. "How's it feel to be a rock and roll star?" she asked him, thinking she was being clever and that he might appreciate that.

He sneered. "That's a real boring subject." He glanced at his watch again. "Finish your Coke."

She forced herself to drink and drink, tears coming to her eyes, and the phone rang and he answered it and said, "Hey, baby," and waved to her, bye-bye! And she was out the door, being led along by one of those middle-aged men who magically appeared again. As she was crossing the highway back to Mermaid Springs, she realized that she'd lost one of Rose's earrings, the big silver hoops she'd borrowed without permission, because Rose refused to lend her jewelry to Lydia for this very reason. So she figured she'd better come up with a damn good story. She sat on a bench in the shadows beside the Mermaid Canteen for forty-five minutes, figuring that was long enough. The whole time she kept picturing herself and Elvis rolling around on his bed, naked, his hairy arms holding her tightly—since she was a virgin she couldn't conjure up many specific details—but it was all very loving and romantic and by the time she went back to the cottage she'd almost convinced herself it was true.

"So you didn't really have sex with Elvis," France said. "I'm sorry." What else could she say?

Lydia's face was pale and her hand shook when she picked up her iced tea from the coffee table. "It was the most humiliating experience of my life. I decided right then to marry a nice, ugly man who would treat me like a queen. And I got me a rich one, too."

"You were going to tell me something about my mom."

"Well." Lydia adjusted her pajama top, peeking down into it, to see if she was all there. "When the mermaids got back together in '97, for the reunion, the four of us were out for drinks one night, and Coralee let it slip."

"Let what slip?"

"That Grendy also went to Elvis's room later that night. And Elvis told Grendy the truth about what happened between him and me. I was so mad. And embarrassed. Plus, I couldn't believe Grendy'd throw herself at Elvis. She was engaged to your father at the time!"

What was one fling when compared to North's years of catting around? "Can you blame her?" France asked Lydia.

Lydia pursed her lips.

If France started laughing now, she might never stop. From the other room she could hear Andy singing the song from *West Side Story* about Maria. She'd always hated that song. Andy was such a wimp. No wonder his wife left him for Spider Sabich. France asked Lydia, "So you went to see Dad that night to tell him about Mom and Elvis?"

Lydia drew herself up self-righteously. "I told her she ought to tell him. That he ought to know."

"Why? That was over thirty years ago."

"There's more to it," Lydia said. "I've told you too much already. She'll have to tell you the rest. She'll be grateful to me, one day, that this has come out. I've started the ball rolling."

The music had stopped. No more insipid crooning. "Mom might not ever come back," France said. "She could be dead. You said so yourself. Dad might've killed her. Or maybe she killed herself. You'd be glad, because you want to rule the roost around here."

"What kind of monster do you think I am?"

France just raised her eyebrows.

Lydia unfolded her legs and swiveled to face France. "Just don't tell Coralee or Rose I went to see North," she pleaded. "I promised them I wouldn't."

France had the advantage and she decided to use it. "Okay. Here's the deal," she said. Lydia frowned, but France kept talking. "You and I, we'll sneak into the springs after hours. You help me with that chute. We won't tell the other two. They obviously can't keep a secret. Then the day of the dress rehearsal, I'll just show up ready to be in it. Until then you can be the astronaut. During the show I'll never take off my helmet, so people watching won't know who it is. We can fool management, and you won't have to be the astronaut."

"You really want to do it that bad?"

"I want to be the astronaut."

Lydia shook some ice into her mouth and crunched it. "Sounds like a plan," she said. Suddenly she popped up off the sofa and darted around the room turning out the lights. In the dark she glided back to stand in front of France, the white stars on her pajamas glowing. She twirled around, a universe unto herself. "These used to be my husband's," she said. "Aren't they the greatest?"

When she walked into her parents' house, North and Theo were eating popcorn and watching a rerun of "The Man from U.N.C.L.E." on TV Land.

"Hi, Aunt Frances," Theo said. "I won two games of Candy Land."

Her father stood up. When she saw him standing there in the dim light, she felt slightly afraid of him. "Can I have a word?" he said.

In the kitchen, France turned on the fluorescent light, even though she hated it, and they sat down. France glanced around for Sisterwoman but didn't see her.

North had that expression on his face again, as though he didn't know where he was. His mask of certainty was gone. "I went back to church yesterday. People weren't friendly. Drake wasn't friendly. Then I drove all the way to Tampa to visit Brett in the hospital, but the nurse wouldn't let me see her." His voice was full of self-pity.

"Don't you think you're focusing on the wrong thing?" France said. It was raining again, drops hitting the windows insistently, like maddening little requests.

North picked up the salt and pepper shakers, which were shaped like Florida oranges, turned them upside down, and shook them, making a little pile. He stirred a finger around in the little mess.

"Don't you feel at all bad about what happened?" France said.

He nodded, looking sure of himself again. "I'm sad, yes," he said. "I'm sad about a lot of things. I think the hospital is the best place for Brett right now."

Theo called from the other room, "Grandpa! Come watch with me."

"In a minute." He smeared the salt and pepper across the table.

France felt like shaking her father. Or hitting him over the head with the skillet. "How would you feel," she said, "if I told you that I'd had an affair with a teacher in high school? For over a year." Waiting for his reaction she felt nauseous, as if she were sixteen again.

Her father looked even more vulnerable and scared than she was. Don't do this to me, his eyes said. He was ill-equipped for being a parent, for really comforting someone, even though he could go through the motions with his eyes closed. "You should've told us," he said in a pained voice, as if he'd been the one wronged. "Who was it?"

"Never mind that," France said. She didn't like the impulse she had to protect Mr. Quack, but she didn't want her father to get off track. "I got pregnant and had an abortion." She was shaking with emotion, but she didn't know which one.

He returned to stirring his salt and pepper mess. She could tell by his face that he'd shut down completely. "Why are you telling me this now?" he said. "What do you want me to do? I'm very sorry, of course."

France reached over and swept his mess onto the red linoleum floor. "He was much older," she said. "Do you blame me in that situation, or him?" She hadn't wanted to believe he would be this cold.

He folded his arms on his white cotton bathrobe and stared at the mess on the floor. "I wasn't there," he said. "Blame isn't useful. And one situation is not like another."

"It was his fault. And this is *your* fault." Once she'd started speaking this way to him, it was hard to stop. "*Your fault*," she repeated. "Tell me. Why is it that you went into the ministry? Ego? Power? What?"

"I see we aren't getting anywhere here," North said, leaning back in his chair. "I wanted to tell you I'm going back to Indiana day after tomorrow. Maybe Theo should go back with me."

She had to act reasonable. "You can't handle him. You said so yourself."

"I don't think it's good for him down here. He needs a more stable environment. Away from old women who think they're mermaids."

France tried to stay calm and read between the lines. He wanted Theo away from here—but what was the real reason? Was he afraid Theo had more secrets to tell? Or was he just trying to punish Grendy? Or her? "Theo's staying here," France said. "We're doing fine."

"I didn't think you really wanted him."

"I've changed my mind." Theo was not going back with North. Who knew what North was capable of doing, now that he'd been found out? "He's still having those temper tantrums," France told her father. "And acting strange. You're too old to take care of him."

North reached over and patted her knee, using his minister's voice. "Your mother and I do have legal custody of him," he said. "Let's just remember that."

"Aunt Frances!" Theo yelled from the next room. "Where's Sisterwoman? I can't find Sisterwoman!"

"I let her out," North called to him. "She wanted to go out."

Theo began to scream. "She's gone! She's gone! I'll never see her again." He ran out of the house, stumbled and tripped over the rug on the screened porch, got up and banged out the door. "Sisterwoman!" he yelled.

"Why'd you do that?" France asked her father. She stood up. "She's not supposed to go outside!"

North widened his eyes and shrugged. "How was I to know? You never told me."

France glared at him. He was right, she hadn't told him.

"She'll turn up," he said.

"You let her out on purpose. Hoping to get rid of her."

"You're off your rocker. Why would I do that?"

Outside, Theo was wandering around the house, calling and sobbing in a voice that would scare any animal away.

"Where is she?" France asked her father. "What did you do with her?"

He leaned his chin in his hand. "You're not thinking straight. You're blaming me for everything." His voice, as usual, gave noth-

ing away, and it held no hint of empathy. "Would you like me to
help you search the neighborhood?"

"No way," she said. Was he jealous of the cat? Or was he just
trying to hurt her and Theo? "Theo will be devastated if she
doesn't come back," she said.

"I'll take him somewhere for a treat. The carnival."

"Don't you get it? One thing does not make up for the other."

France and Theo went out in the dark to try and find Sisterwoman. They didn't have a flashlight, so they didn't go but a few
steps into the woods. France squatted beside the drainage ditch
and called. They combed the immediate neighborhood, searching
people's yards and carports, grateful for their security lights, peeking under vehicles and bushes and reaching between boxes and
behind garbage cans. France told Theo to use a calm voice, but he
couldn't do it. He sobbed and yelled so loudly that a few neighbors came out to help them search, including the woman France
had seen pulling vines, and the bare-chested jogging man, who
was still bare-chested. But they had no luck.

Finally she and Theo drove around the entire Star of the Sea
subdivision, calling for Sisterwoman out the windows. When they
started for home, Theo turned on himself. "I'm stupid." He
bounced around in the backseat, hitting himself in the head. "I'm
so stupid. It's all my fault."

"You're not stupid. It's not your fault. Don't hit yourself! She'll
be back." She was yelling, out of control. No wonder he didn't listen to her.

It wasn't till they parked the car and saw Sisterwoman,
stretched out on the top porch step, that France decided her father could live.

Theo cradled Sisterwoman and carried her into the house like his baby.

"Oh good," North said, glancing up from the TV. "You found her."

France went in to kiss Theo good night, picking her way through piles of stuff—his new bear, his Hardy Boys books, Candy Land, Sisterwoman's rubber mouse. Even though she still abhorred the mess, she felt some affection toward the things, because they belonged to him. He was lying on top of the covers, staring at the ceiling. Sisterwoman lay beside him. France sat down on the other side of him and smoothed back his hair. The light from his aquarium was the only light in the room. She couldn't see his face clearly, but she knew he had something to say.

"I think Sisterwoman just wanted a breath of fresh air. She would never run away. She loves me. Did my mom grow up to be a bad person?"

France felt her heart contract. "Of course not. Why would you say that?"

"Grandpa told me. He said she was just like Brett. That she was a holic. What's a holic?"

"Let me tell you something," France said. She reached for his floppy little hand and held it. "Your mom came to visit Grandma and Grandpa right after you were born, because she wanted to show you off. You were just three weeks old."

"I was little?"

"This little." She showed him. "I've never seen anyone happier than she was about being a mother. She carried you around day and night like you were the most precious thing on earth. You had on a little yellow romper thing. She talked to you, sang to you, silly songs, Beatles songs, and Christmas carols. She'd gotten a really good job, working as office manager at the University of Kansas. She hadn't had anything holic to drink in two years. She looked great. Her face was so relaxed and happy. She knew you were the best thing in the world."

"Then she died," Theo said in a flat voice. "And I lived."

France bent down to hug him, and for once, he hugged her back, a fierce hug that pulled her down so she had her head on his chest. "I wish it hadn't happened," she said. "I wish she was still here."

She could tell that Theo was crying, a little, and so was she.

After a while he said, "It would be okay if I live with you? If Grandma doesn't come back? I think it would be okay."

"More than okay."

Chapter XVI of *The Mystery of Cabin Island* was called "The Intruders Revenge." Joe, wandering around on the snowy island searching for the persistent, elusive intruders, was bashed on the head by one of them and lost consciousness. His brother Frank and buddies Biff and Chet, also wandering about in the snow, stumbled upon two more intruders, the young hooligans Ike and Tad.

Frank turned to Biff and Chet. "I'm going to find Joe. Something's happened to him. You take those two inside and don't let them go. I want to question them later."

"You think Joe is in danger?" Chet asked fearfully.

Frank looked worried. "I'm afraid so. It's a big island," he added grimly. "I hope we're not too late."

Eighteen

Lydia and France had arranged to meet in the parking lot of Mermaid Springs at five-thirty, after the place had closed for the day. Lydia had a key to the side gate. "If anyone sees us," Lydia said, "I forgot my falsies in the locker room. Kidding!"

In the locker room, they changed into bathing suits—Lydia into her green alien one, France into the turquoise-and-black one she'd probably wear till it was a rag. She couldn't keep her eyes away from the dark hole she had to make herself go down into. She had to do it now or quit trying to be a mermaid. "What do you think about when you're in the chute?" she asked Lydia.

Lydia shook her head. "You're as bad as Elvis, asking questions like that. When I jump in, I'm already there," she said. "I don't think about the here-to-there part." Lydia sashayed over to the chute and slid into the water. "I'll wait for you down at the bend," she said. "We'll go out together." She held up her fist. "Merhags forever!" she said. Then she was gone.

France watched her descend, her white skin glowing in the dark water. At the bottom she took a breath from the bubbling air hose. She beckoned to France.

France lowered herself flippers first into the water, every fiber of her being screaming at her to stop, to get out, to run away. She tried not to think about the chute, but it didn't work. Before she could climb back out she plunged down. The panic that she was expecting washed over her, and she fought herself to keep from propelling back up to the surface. She let out some air, not allowing herself to look at Lydia or back at the lighted opening above her. The chute was squeezing in on her. There wasn't enough room. She heard her mother's voice. "Most mermaids don't make it through training. Most aren't cut out for it."

Then she was squished up beside Lydia, who passed her the air hose and began swimming off into the dark tunnel. France took a quick breath and grabbed Lydia's ankles. Lydia moved in quick bursts toward the opening, pulling France with her. France scissor-kicked, trying to help. Go go go, she kept thinking. Faster. Suddenly they were at the end, emerging into the bright blue spring, and she released Lydia's ankles. The sunlight shone down from above, giving little naked David and the treasure chest a weak glow. She never, ever wanted to get into that chute again. She popped up in the air lock underneath the stage. Lydia, already waiting for her there, flicked an imaginary bug from her shoulder. "Can you do it by yourself at the dress rehearsal?"

France couldn't speak. Her legs were trembling. She had no idea what she could or couldn't do.

When France got home from her practice with Lydia, she noticed that North's rental car was gone. Sisterwoman trotted up to greet her, rubbing against her leg. There was a note on the kitchen table. "Took Theo to the carnival. Back soon." Another good-bye note.

She drove as fast as she could to the Wal-Mart on the edge of town. The carnival spread out in an empty field, its colored lights pulsing. The first ride she came to was the Super Himalaya, which was decorated with painted scenes of the Alps. A train of cars raced around and up and down, and rap music blasted. Theo would never get on such a thing. She strode between other huge rides, seeing them through Theo's eyes. Yo Yo, Thunder Bolt, Hi-Roller, Pharaoh's Fury, Avalanche, Zipper. She couldn't imagine anyone voluntarily boarding one of these monstrosities, although they were packed with shrieking teenagers. Snakes of black cable trailed back and forth over the muddy ground. Sickening smells wafted out from little food stands bedecked with brightly colored flags— fried funnel cakes, onion rings, sausages, chicken on a stick, greasy slices of pizza.

France hurried by the Haunted Railroad and the Creep House. She peeked in the Museum of World Oddities and the tent housing Tiny Jim, the World's Smallest Horse, but decided that even North wouldn't let Theo visit Angel, the Snake Girl. "No bones in her body!" There were booths selling black

T-shirts, clear plastic aliens, and huge, garish stuffed animals—sharks and rottweilers—that nobody was buying. A Drown the Clown booth. North might get into drowning the clown, but they weren't waiting in the line. She found herself wandering between rows of games—Fishing, Pop the Balloon, Shoot-the-Moving-Ducks. Barkers dressed in turquoise polo shirts called out to passersby, "Over here, Mom. Win Junior a prize! Come on, Dad. Let the kids play!" She glanced at everyone she passed, man, woman, child, as if Theo or her father might be disguised, or transformed by some evil spell. There were too many young, very young, couples pushing strollers. She envied them their restrained, portable children.

She stopped at the edge of a large mud puddle, studying the footprints, trying to imagine what Theo's footprints might look like, when the thought struck her. If North really was going to sneak back to Indiana with Theo, wouldn't they be gone already? Why hadn't she checked to see if their clothes were still there? "Theo!" France screamed and a black woman wearing a yellow hat scooted away. "Theo," France yelled again, "Theo! Where are you?"

People were gawking at her now. A few teenage girls started laughing. "Oh, Theo!" one of them yelled. Her T-shirt was emblazoned with rhinestone lips. She began walking in place. "I'm moving my legs," the girl lisped. Her friends collapsed against each other, staggering with hilarity.

France began to jog, scanning the crowd, until finally she was among the kiddie rides, spinning dinosaurs, a little train, the merry-go-round squealing out organ music, airplanes, boats—nothing. Then she saw North, standing in front of a ride called

School Daze—a big box painted like a school bus that went straight up into the air and then around and around, like a hand cleaning a mirror. She didn't bother speaking to her father—she just wanted Theo. She caught a glimpse of him, hunched double, head in his lap.

"Stop the ride!" France yelled. The young ride operator stared at her. He wore wraparound, blue-tinted sunglasses, even though it was nearly dark.

"My nephew," France said. "He's terrified. Let him off."

"Sorry, ma'am," said the kid. He looked like a frat boy gone to seed. "Can't halt the ride till it's officially over. We still have," he checked his watch, "a minute and a half."

The school bus swung by them in a big arc. Other children waved and yelled at their parents, but Theo's head stayed buried in his lap. She eyed the control panel beside the ride operator. There was a big red button labeled Stop. "I'm going to push that," she said, pointing. "Stop this thing now."

Her father suddenly appeared and laid a hand on the young man's shoulder. "This is my daughter. She's very upset. Please do a good deed. You'll be a hero." The young man, evidently liking the word hero, stepped forward and pushed the red button.

Theo's body was tensed into a fetal position, and he wouldn't open his eyes, but France scooped him up and lugged him over underneath a tree, where she cradled him in her arms, kissing him, comforting him. His T-shirt was damp with sweat. A group of people stood around them, watching. The other School Daze riders began yelling in protest until the young man started the ride up again. France ignored everyone except Theo until at last people moved on.

Finally she lifted her head. Her father still stood there in his khakis and pink polo shirt and his polished loafers. Mr. Minister. Mr. Untouchable. "Thanks," she told him grudgingly.

He nodded.

"What the hell was he doing on that ride in the first place?" France asked him.

"I suggested it," said North. "I had no idea it went so far up in the air. I'm sorry."

Theo began to cry now, digging his face into France's shoulder.

"Why didn't you ride it with him?" France said. "Or stop it earlier? Couldn't you see how scared he was?"

"He said he wanted to ride it alone," said North. "I couldn't tell he wanted off. He wasn't screaming or anything."

France could picture her father standing there, watching Theo suffer, a distant little smile on his face. She'd seen that little smile many times before—when she'd fallen off a horse and broken her leg, or when one of Grendy's Great Danes died, or on the day Beauvais showed up on their doorstep, wanting to apologize for her latest misstep, and he had shut the door in her face and watched from the living room window as she walked away. Theo would not be next in line.

"What are you doing here?" North asked her.

"I thought you'd taken him back to Indiana."

"You really do think I'm a villain, don't you?"

"I think you're not taking him back to Indiana."

The little smile again. "And why's that?"

"Because he said he wants to live with me."

"I'm sorry, Grandpa," Theo said. "I love you. I'm sorry." Still sitting in her lap, he began to cry harder.

"You don't have to be sorry," she told Theo. "He's the one who should be sorry." She gave her father a hard look.

He gazed blankly at her, and then said, "See you at home."

France and Theo sat in their spot under the tree and watched till he disappeared into the crowd. "Would you like to see the World's Smallest Horse?" she asked Theo, and he clambered up, ready to go.

North wasn't home when they got there, so France called Bruno. "Everything's haywire," she said. "My father is so weird."

Bruno listened to her story, then said he was glad she'd changed her mind about Theo living with her. "Why don't you and Theo come on home now?" he said. "Since you aren't going to swim in *Mermaids on the Moon*. You can see my doll show."

France told him about sneaking in to practice with Lydia and her plan to appear in the show anyway.

"You're taking some big chances just to be a fake mermaid," he said, but he didn't try to talk her out of it.

"Did you deliver the dolls?" she asked him.

"She went ape shit over the new ones. Kept asking me if you'd made them, 'cause she knew you liked mermaids, and I kept saying no, *I'd* made them. But she wouldn't believe me. Thought I was covering for you."

"Jesus."

"She's way too intense for me. I said I had a doctor's appointment and got the hell out of there."

"She still thinks I made them? Guess that's better than her thinking you made them."

"But you didn't make them. I made them."

She couldn't argue with that. "Are you going to the opening?" she asked him.

"I'd sure like to, since it's my show, but it would be too strange. Like being in disguise at your own funeral."

What kind of position had she put him in? "I'll take care of it," she told him. "I'll call her now and straighten it all out."

France called Naomi, but only got her answering machine. "The dolls really are Bruno's," she said. "He makes them. I didn't want to tell you, for obvious reasons. I hope you won't cancel the show. I hope you won't fire me. I still want to buy into the gallery. Please don't hate me." She'd said enough stupid things, so she hung up.

France took Theo to Mermaid Springs for the dress rehearsal. When they walked into the locker room, Lydia jumped up and applauded. "Here she is," Lydia said, as though she were responsible for France's entrance. "Bigger and better than ever! And fully chute-trained!"

Rose and Coralee, already in their green suits, were leaning into the mirrors, putting on their green makeup. They both turned, startled.

"I can do the chute," France said. "I did it once, with Lydia. I'll do it again. I want to be in the show."

Rose mumbled something about management.

"I took care of Ace," Lydia said.

Coralee said, "What'd you do? Kill him?"

"I wish!" said Lydia. She unbuckled her high-heeled sandal. "I took him out to lunch and promised him the moon if he'd keep his mouth shut. But then he got so drunk I had to take him home."

"Hey," Theo yelled. He stood in the corner of the dressing room, holding a blue-and-green-striped towel. "This is Grandma's. I found it on the floor."

"Lots of people have towels like that," Rose said.

"But lots of people don't come in here," Coralee said. She went over to examine the towel.

Rose snapped a green bathing cap onto her head and began stuffing her hair up underneath it. "It's probably been in here for weeks."

Coralee said, "I would've noticed." She shook out the towel, studied it, then rolled it up, and gave it back to Theo.

"Maybe she's been here," France said. "Maybe recently!"

"You're jumping to all kinds of conclusions," Rose said. "Getting all worked up about nothing." She glowered, her eyes huge and scary in her green face.

Theo hugged the towel. "It smells like her."

"She's been in here swimming," Lydia said, swinging her underpants up with her toes and catching them. "That rat."

"Why would she do that and not tell us?" France said. "Who's she hiding from?" She found herself looking at Rose for the answer.

"Maybe from you," Rose told France. "Who knows?"

The others didn't seem surprised.

"Why? I'm her daughter."

"She must have her reasons," Rose said. "Come on. Let's rehearse."

France could tell by Rose's stiff green face that she'd get nothing more out of her—not now, anyway.

"Who's going to start the tape?" Coralee asked. "With Ace out of commission?" Her green cap had transformed her into Junior Asparagus, a creature from Theo's *VeggieTales* video.

"I can do the music myself," Theo said. "Ace showed me everything."

"Are you sure?" Rose asked him.

"The kid's a little genius, Rose," Lydia said. "Let him go."

Rose glanced at France, who nodded. France had no doubt that Theo could do it.

Theo gave France an awkward hug and raced off for the control booth.

France was so relieved to be back in the show and so worried about the chute that she was able to put aside Rose's remark about her mother avoiding her. Coralee and Rose and Lydia, all three in their green tank suits, their upper bodies and faces caked with green makeup, their green caps in place, carried their green iridescent tails from their lockers to the edge of the chute. One by one they tugged on their flippers and then wriggled into the tight rubbery tails, pulling them up over their flippers and legs and hips like too-tight panty hose. Coralee rolled onto her side so Rose could zip her up, and then Lydia did the same for Rose. France stood watching in her mother's silver astronaut's suit and helmet—a silver football helmet without the face guard—part of her wishing she could wear a tail too, part of her squirming at the thought of having her legs so confined. She zipped up Lydia's tail. Soon she'd be alone with the chute.

Lydia, perched on the edge of the portal, must've noticed her expression. "Pretend there's some real treasure at the bottom," she told France. "Something you really want." She disappeared down the chute.

It'll all go smoothly, France told herself, once I get through the chute. She could already hear "Blue Danube" playing down below.

And, for once, everything did go smoothly.

The next day was Saturday. Showtime.

The theater was already full of people when France and Theo arrived, and more were streaming in. France wanted to flee. She hadn't really thought about the audience before, how many people might be there to watch her screw up. Theo swaggered off to the control booth to join Ace. France stood outside the theater for a moment, gazing at the aqua green water, only half believing that in a few minutes she'd be part of a show performed far underneath that water, a show featuring old women acting like alien mermaids, and she herself an astronaut, riding in a make-believe space capsule. As ridiculous as it all was, she wished that Bruno could be there to see it. Naomi, too. But especially her mother. North had left for Indiana that morning, but she wouldn't have wanted him there anyway.

And she and Theo would be back in Indiana before they knew it. This was her last weekend in Mermaid City, her one and only weekend to be a mermaid. She couldn't stay in Florida any longer. She wasn't any closer to finding her mother than she'd been three weeks ago. She knew more about her mother, but still didn't know where she was. Lynn the medium said that her mother wouldn't be back for a long time. But then there was the towel. Rose probably knew how it got there, and France would see to it that Rose told her.

The underwater theater had a rim of black mold around the roof, just above where it met the water. The white paint on the theater was peeling. If only she could've seen the place in its heyday, everything new, the water even cleaner. The shows back then had big casts and wildly imaginative props and costumes, and Elvis came to watch. She could almost see Elvis's limo pulling up in front of the entrance, the crowd of adoring fans—wholesome, 1950s girls. But at least Mermaid Springs was still open. She was glad she'd gotten to see it. Being part of a show, even a small show, was more fun, and scarier, than she ever could've dreamed. And people were still coming, from somewhere, to see the show. Lots of people.

When France sank down into the chute this time, she was more leery about facing the crowd than going down the chute. How could she have forgotten about stage fright? She dragged herself down into the water, down toward the bend, pretending she was going back in time, to 1961, the last summer her mother was a young mermaid at Mermaid Springs. She was going back, back, back, and she was going to find her mother there.

When she popped up under the stage, nothing happened to disrupt this illusion. We're all young again, France told herself. She was surrounded now by the green faces of the alien mermaids, all breathing loudly, waiting with her in the air lock, listening to Ace begin the show: "Welcome to the City of Live Mermaids. The mermaids can hear your applause, and like any performers, they love it!"

She pictured Theo turning on the music and then it began, the

"Blue Danube," and she ducked into the little space capsule and began worming it up toward the surface. She wondered if Grendy had been this nervous at her first performance. *"Fly me to the moon and let me play among the stars."* She emerged from the capsule into the sunlit water, her air hose clenched between her teeth, carrying her flag and black bag. The theater was all lit up inside and there were rows of people watching and clapping. She twisted her way over to stick the flag into the sand and then jumped—slowly—up and down, fist aloft in triumph. The audience clapped. She took a swig of air and did her slow motion leaps and loops. "Smile!" Ace said over the intercom. The helmet covered her head and the goggles covered her eyes and nose, but her mouth was right out there in the open. France plastered a silly grin on her face, which wasn't hard to do, because this was her mother's favorite song, and her favorite part of the show. She relished the clarity of the water, the dreamy slow motion, feeling alone yet knowing people were watching her. No wonder Coralee wanted to stay down here forever. France began collecting the spray-painted moon rocks, inspecting them with a frown and then smiling as she nestled them into her bag.

Music change. "Blue Moon." The alien mermaids rose up behind her as the audience clapped. France threw up her hands in mock surprise. The audience clapped even more loudly when Rose dumped her rocks out, scolded her, and pushed her down. *"You saw me standing alone."* She sat on the bottom and watched the three mermaids do their stuff. Lydia grinned bigger than France had ever seen her, teeth white in her green face, her moves tight and perfectly timed. Rose had a dreamy expression, and she did her back dolphins in an almost languid manner. Coralee looked a little sad and wistful. Her entire body exuded emotion. "*Without a love of my own.*"

Then it was time for her to join them. This was the scary part, the part where she could mess things up. They beckoned to her with big smiles on their faces. It was impossible to tell what any of them were thinking. Were they worried that she couldn't do it? They probably weren't thinking about anything except how much they were loving their show. Their show. She knew they felt like they were getting away with something. They were still mermaids, after all these years!

"*Moon River.*" In a row they did back dolphins and at times France was a little higher or lower than the rest of them, because she wasn't controlling her breathing correctly. The tower went well. The square went okay. "*Wherever you're going, I'm going your way.*" Just before their cancan move, France sipped from the air hose but didn't get enough. She felt trapped, her arms locked tightly with Lydia's and Rose's, and her chest began to tighten as she kicked along with them. "Smile!" Ace said again, but she couldn't. When they broke she lunged for the air hose. Then it was time for the wheel.

As they began, France saw that her hose had fallen into a dark patch of eelgrass on the stage. If she couldn't find the hose, she'd have to break character and go pawing around for it. Then she heard Theo's voice over the speaker. "The hose will be right underneath you when you come back around." She came out of the wheel, saw the hose, reached down, and tugged on it, and the mouthpiece flew into her hand. She'd done it. Thanks to Theo.

Too soon, the show was over. There were only two more performances after this one! "Blue Danube" again. France swam into place to take her final bow, but the other mermaids stayed back, to the side, their eyes fixed on the surface, and suddenly the audience began clapping, for no reason that France could tell. France turned and looked up too. A big silver star was descending slowly into the water, and sitting on it was someone dressed in a sparkling silver suit and bathing cap.

"It's Grandma!" Theo yelled over the speaker.

Grendy waved at the audience, then waved and blew bubble kisses at France, who started to swim toward her. Suddenly Coralee was there beside her, holding her hand, keeping her back. Lynn was wrong! She was back already! But what else had he said? "Look up and you'll see her." And "She'll be down below."

Grendy dove for an air hose, then came up and did a back dolphin. The alien mermaids and the astronaut and the audience watched her. Grendy was the heaviest, but most graceful, the most natural of all of them. She moved in an effortless manner, at home in the water as if it were her element. And it was her element. She's home, France kept thinking. There was an outpouring of applause. Grendy'd stolen the show once again. She'd always steal the show, if she could. France was so happy to see her, and to see her happy.

Nineteen

In the dressing room France and Theo kissed and hugged Grendy
till they knocked her over, and then demanded an explanation. "I
was staying in a motel up in Chiefland," she told them.

"That close?" France said, her emotions all mixed up. Why had
she stayed away? Especially since she'd only gone to Chiefland.

"Tell you more later," Grendy promised her. "Let's get out of
here before management gets wind of an extra merhag."

Now all the merhags and Theo were sitting in Tiny's Fish
House, a crowded place with a warren of small rooms. Out the
window beside France she could see a canal of dark green water.
Probably full of gators.

Grendy, wearing the yellow shell that showed off her olive skin,
sat directly across from France. She'd cut her white hair short again,
which suited her. She leaned over to whisper to France that she didn't
want to really talk till Theo was out of earshot. Then she added, in

her normal voice, "I'm so tickled you're a mermaid. You, of all people! I'm just tickled pink." She stabbed at an egg in her chef salad.

"I loved it," France said, but the moment felt flat. Was she expecting her mother to make more of a fuss about it? She'd had high expectations of this reunion, she realized, as an opportunity to connect with her mother in a way she never had before. Before, there'd always been North. And Beauvais.

"What are you going to do now?" Coralee asked Grendy. Coralee wore pearl earrings and her sleeveless black linen dress.

"Heading back to Indiana?" Lydia said hopefully. For some reason, Lydia had clipped her hair back in two barrettes. She wore a shirt threaded with strands of gold lurex. Why were they both so dressed up?

"I'm going to stay right where I am," Grendy said. "I'm going to start divorce proceedings." She smiled at France, but France couldn't smile back. She'd been waiting to hear this for years, and yet she still wasn't ready. "Don't worry," Grendy said, as if she could read France's mind. "And Theo will stay right here with me. Right, Winky?"

"Right!" he said, too enthusiastically. He turned sideways in his chair and pulled his knees up under his chin.

"He's not Winky anymore," France said sharply. She can't just snatch him back, France thought. But she said nothing.

After Theo finished eating, dropping half his fried shrimp on the floor as he tipped from one side to the other, Grendy sent him over to play the pinball machine in the corner.

"Now tell me what happened," France said.

"I left because I heard Lydia talking to your dad," she said.

Lydia focused on her salad with new intensity.

Grendy went on. "North was supposed to be out with the

guys, but Theo and I went down to the church to drop something off and heard him and Lydia together, in his office. I came home and packed my bags." She took a big bite of her salad. Please, France thought, nobody interrupt her. She hadn't expected her reunion with Grendy to be so public. "I was really upset," Grendy went on. "I couldn't think. All I could do was act. I hardly remember writing that note or packing or even driving away. Next thing I knew I was sitting at a stop light in Chiefland. I knew I couldn't drive anymore that night. So I checked into a motel, but I didn't sleep. I just sat on the bed, thinking of all the horrible possibilities, things that might happen since North knew the truth."

"But I didn't tell him," Lydia interrupted. "I lost my nerve. I should've told him, but I didn't."

France said, "What should you have told him?"

Grendy held up her finger—one minute. "I started thinking, too," she said, "of all the affairs he's had over the years, and for all I knew he and Lydia were hot and heavy too. Although he usually goes for the young ones."

"Pul-ease," Lydia said. "Give me some credit."

"You knew about Brett?" Coralee said.

Her mother nodded. "Brett was only the latest."

"That's not why you left?" France said.

"That was part of it," Grendy said. "I didn't know where to go, so I just stayed in Chiefland, walking and thinking. People there probably thought I was nuts."

"All this time you were only ten miles away?" France asked. All the scenarios she'd imagined. She'd been worried for weeks, and for nothing. She stared down at the tabletop, where an old map of Florida was preserved under glass.

Grendy said, "I was just a nervous wreck. Wasn't thinking clearly. After about a week I called Rose and told her where I was."

Rose, dressed in diaphanous white, still eating her garlic grouper, wouldn't meet France's eyes. Rose was all dolled up, like the other two.

Grendy looked at France. "Rose told me you had come down, and then I got really nervous. I thought for sure that Lydia, or North, would talk to you. Get France to leave, I told Rose. Try to convince her not to be in the show! I just wanted you to go back home."

"Why did you only call Rose?" Coralee said. "Why Rose? What about the rest of us?"

"Yeah," echoed France stupidly. "Why Rose?"

"Why do you think she called Rose?" Lydia rolled up her napkin, held it in her hair like a bow and said in a girlish falsetto, "My hero!"

Grendy glared at Lydia. "Those barrettes look silly."

Lydia smiled, batting her eyes.

Grendy addressed the table at large. "I know I should've told you all where I was, but I kept on stewing around about what to do. I came over at night a few times to swim in the springs. I hated giving up on the show. It was my baby."

"My baby," said Lydia. "If you want to get technical."

"We don't," said Coralee.

Grendy turned to France again. "Rose got the idea of me reappearing during the show and surprising you. She told the others the day of the show."

Great. They'd all held out on her. France was trying to eat her Italian-style grouper, but it took effort. Everyone had dressed up, she realized, to celebrate Grendy's return, everyone except France, her only daughter, who'd been kept in the dark and was wearing her usual fuddy-duddy overall shorts.

Across the room, Theo hunched over the pinball machine, flipping the flippers. Pinball was the sort of activity he could lock into for hours.

"It *was* a little over the top, your grand entrance," Lydia said. "Overkill."

Grendy hissed. "The whole thing's overkill."

"You couldn't stand not to be center stage," Lydia said. "You had to be the star. You even dropped down on a star." She tossed her head. "Least I have enough hair to wear barrettes."

Grendy rolled her eyes, as if she couldn't be bothered to reply to Lydia's silliness. But Lydia had a point about the star. It was a rather grandiose way to reappear. "I hoped France would think it was neat," Grendy said, sounding like a child.

"You hoped it would soften the blow," Lydia said. "But there ain't no way to soften the blow, Sea Cow."

Grendy didn't react to this slight. She bent over her salad. "I guess I better tell you. Blabbermouth will if I don't."

"Yes, I think you'd better," France said.

So Grendy told her. Back in '61, she said, the summer Elvis came, the summer she was engaged to North, she'd been sleeping around. "I was panicking, I guess. Maybe I knew I shouldn't marry North. I was seeing Wayne Purdy too. And Ace. Can't believe I did that. And a few others who were just passing through."

"No way," France said. Her straitlaced mother? She remembered her father shouting at Beauvais. Whore! Slut! At the time, she'd been sleeping with Mr. Quack. She'd never imagined that her mother had gone through such a period. She gazed out at the palm trees lining the canal. One had a bleached white trunk. Another was covered with poison ivy.

"And there was Elvis," Coralee reminded her. "Don't forget Elvis."

"We won't go into that," her mother said, sweeping her fork across her plate in a show of false modesty.

"So you did go to Elvis's room," France said. "And something happened."

"Something happened, but not what you're thinking. Just some kissing and rolling around. He thought I was too forward. He was probably expecting resistance."

Across the table, Lydia was simmering. "You lied to Coralee. You told her you had sex with Elvis."

"That's the pot calling the kettle," Rose said.

Grendy snapped, "At least we did more than talk."

"Back to the story," France said. "Please."

Grendy continued. "Anyhow, the upshot is, in August, I found myself pregnant. It was right after Linda Huddle died in the air lock. I wasn't sure who the father was. Who your father was. Is."

It took a while for France to understand the meaning of Grendy's words. "So, Dad's not my dad?" She felt as if she were standing at a great height, wavering at the edge.

"He may be your dad," Grendy said. "There's a good possibility he is." She seemed to draw into herself. "I'm so ashamed," she said in a small voice unlike her own. "It's the only time in my life I acted that way. And I'm sorry to tell you like this. But if it weren't for the merhags, I wouldn't have had the courage to tell you at all."

"Think about it this way," Coralee said to France. "Elvis could have been your father."

"If they'd actually done something," Lydia said.

France sighed. "Forget about Elvis," she said.

Lydia went on. "But you wouldn't have been able to *prove* he's your father. You can't get a blood test from Elvis. He's dead."

"Will you shut up?" Rose said. "And take out those stupid barrettes."

Lydia shook her head.

"I thought my secret was safe with Coralee," Grendy said. "But when I moved back down here, we were all having a drink one night and it came out that Rose and Lydia knew all about my sleeping around, and they also knew that I wasn't sure who your father was. Coralee had told them both."

Coralee grimaced. "Don't ever tell me any secrets," she said.

"That's when Lydia pipes up and says I ought to tell North," Grendy said. "That he ought to know the truth. She threatened to tell him if I didn't. I thought she was all bluster."

"I didn't tell him," Lydia protested.

"You are all bluster," Rose said.

"When I heard her in North's office talking, I assumed she was there to tell him."

"I had no intention of telling him," Lydia said. "I went for spiritual guidance."

Rose guffawed.

France studied her mother, who all of a sudden looked like an elfin stranger in her yellow shirt. The other women were concentrating hard on their food. Everyone but Grendy was eating garlic grouper, and the smell of it made France sick. She asked her mother, "Why didn't you let me know you were all right? Theo and I were so worried."

Grendy twisted up her face like she was about to cry.

Oh no you don't, France thought. If anyone gets to cry here, it's me. "We'll talk more later," she told her mother. "When we're alone."

Rose, Coralee, and Lydia gathered up their things, leaving their dinners half eaten. They stopped to tell Theo good-bye, but he didn't break his concentration. Lydia was the last one to get up. Before she left, she dumped the breadbasket in her purse and then hurried away. Grendy looked bereft without her friends.

"Why are you telling me this?" France said. "I had a dad, now I don't."

"I needed to face up to what I'd done. Face up to why I married North in the first place. It will help me make the final break."

"But don't I get a say?" France said, her voice rising. "What if I don't want to know the truth? What am I supposed to do now? Go demand a blood test from Dad?"

"That's up to you," Grendy said.

"Well, thanks," France said. She couldn't think of anything more pointed to say.

"I was a coward," Grendy said. "I admit it. But I finally realized that I should come back and be honest with you." She shimmied in her seat, proud of herself. "I didn't want to be like your father. I didn't want to live a lie anymore."

Why not? France thought. Then she said it aloud. "Why not live a lie?" She realized she wasn't making sense, but she couldn't help it. "At least he has the decency not to tell everybody all the sordid details." Why was she sticking up for her father—or rather her putative father, as they said at Social Services?

Grendy reached over and took France's hand, but she pulled away. She wanted to say more, but right now it seemed like trying to talk would be fruitless, that it would be like trying to talk underwater. She got up and walked out of the restaurant. She stepped out the door into the heat, and it felt good. She veered across the road, away from the canal full of gators, and onto a sandy field that was probably full of fire ants. It was still early evening. On the other side of the field was a baseball diamond. People were watching a game, cheering and calling encouragement. People she didn't know. She walked toward the diamond. There were little kids playing T-ball, kids about Theo's size, in jerseys that said Pablo's Pizza. Theo should be over here playing, France thought, instead of hanging out with a bunch of old kooks.

She walked around to the edge of the aluminum bleachers, climbed up and sat down. The bleachers were in the shade, but they were still warm. There was someone sitting beside her but she didn't acknowledge the person. She fixed her eyes on the game but didn't see it. She wanted to be back in Indiana. Soon it would be fall there, her favorite season.

She remembered a hike she and Beauvais took with their father one afternoon in October, years and years ago. The leaves on the trees were banana yellow and russet red, and the sun dappling through was just warm enough. Her father walked ahead on the trail, swinging his arms, then Beauvais, then her. It was a weekday, and there was nobody else around. They were all playing hooky. Grendy would've been furious if she'd known. Sugar Creek rippled and splashed to their left, to their right were the limestone bluffs, and up ahead she could see their destination, the covered bridge on which she and Beauvais would run back and forth, yelling so their voices would echo. Their father would skip rocks across the water, trying to beat his own score of seven skips. She was happy that day. She liked being last in line. She liked playing with her father and sister. I'll never forget this, she'd told herself.

After a while France walked back across the field to the restaurant. Her mother was waiting in the parking lot, leaning against France's rented Taurus. Theo, sprawled out in the backseat, idly kicking at the ceiling, did not speak. He seemed to have disconnected from her.

"I was keeping an eye on you," her mother said. "I didn't want to bother you. Please don't be so mad, honey."

"I'm not mad anymore," France said, and she wasn't. She didn't know what she was, but it felt more like disappointment and embarrassment. Her mother, by coming back the way she did, dropping down on a star into the middle of their show, into the middle of *my* show, France thought, surrounding herself with friends while she told her story, reclaiming both the show and the friends, and then unloading her big secret on France—all this precluded the intimate, joyful reunion that France, without even being aware of it, had been hoping for. She'd told herself that she'd been searching for her mother for Theo's sake, but that hadn't been the whole truth. Here she was, thirty-eight years old, and still hoping for that elusive closeness with her mother. "I want to go home," she said.

Instead of being in the show the next day, France decided to return to Indiana. Grendy could have her part back.

"Don't do this," Grendy begged her. She still wore her long pink nightgown with the poodle on it. "This time I won't come in at the end. I want to sit in the audience and watch the whole thing. You did such a great job. You're a great mermaid."

France, who was folding shorts and dropping them into her duffel bag, couldn't help but laugh. "Never thought I'd be called a great mermaid," she said.

Grendy came over to hug her, and France allowed herself to be hugged. Grendy smelled of strawberry lotion. She reminded France of a turtle—her back hard and her arms and stomach too soft. She was getting old. "I wish you'd stay longer," Grendy murmured.

"I've been here too long already," France said. She wanted to get home, get back to Bruno, back to her job, if she still had it. And there was Theo. France yanked a dresser drawer open. "I don't know if Theo should stay with you," she said. "I wouldn't mind taking him. In fact, I'd love to." She knew she was talking in a stilted, distant way, but it was the only way she could talk to her mother right now.

"I *do* think he should stay with me," Grendy said. "He's like my own child."

France bent over the drawer, scooping up underwear and white socks. "That's why you went off and left him." She whirled and tossed the pile onto the bed.

Grendy grasped France's arm with a cold hand. "I won't do it again," she said, looking intently at France. "I left because of my bad marriage. That's over now."

"Do you really want to be a single mother?" France asked her.

"Do you?" Grendy said.

France groped around in the drawer, pulled out her turquoise-and-black bathing suit and dropped it into the trash can. "I want to be with Theo," she said.

"We can work something out," Grendy said. "Half and half, if that's what you'd like."

France nodded. "That makes sense."

Grendy sat down on the bed, hiking up her nightgown, crossing her bare tanned legs underneath her. She stroked Sisterwoman, who lay beside her, and whom she professed to already be
crazy about. She seemed relieved to be back in her own room,
with its glittery ceiling, surrounded by all her mermaid items.
North had taken most of his things with him, but the room didn't
seem any emptier without them. Grendy said, "I know your father
doesn't want custody of Theo."

"I wouldn't let him get custody," France said. "But he's right,
Theo does have some problems. We should have him evaluated."

Grendy said, "I just feel so sorry for him."

"That's not going to help him," France said, dumping T-shirts
onto the bed beside her mother. She wadded them up and stuffed
them into the duffel bag. "I feel bad for him too. But he needs
help."

"You're right," Grendy said. She watched France zip up her
bag. "Are you going to tell your father?"

"That he might not be my father? I haven't decided. Do you
want me to?"

"I can't tell you what to do," she said. "Either way, it's fine with
me."

France slung her bag over her shoulder. Her plane didn't leave
until the following morning, but she was spending the night in
Tampa at a hotel near the airport. She stuck her hand into the
pocket of her skirt, the tissue-soft skirt she hadn't worn since her
first day in Florida. She felt a folded piece of paper, and she knew
right away what it was. Grendy's good-bye note. "Why'd you leave
us the first time?" she asked her mother. "The time you went to

Arizona." She heard her voice quaver, but she kept on. "Beauvais and I were really scared."

Grendy clasped her hands together and lifted them up to her mouth. "I made a big mistake," she said. "I should've talked to you girls."

"You shouldn't have left us. Not knowing if you'd come back."

Grendy nodded. "That was the first time I caught him cheating. I should've left him for good that time. And taken you girls with me. I guess I just wasn't ready to make the break. By going alone I set things up so I had to come back. And once I was back, it was too hard to leave again."

In the mermaid lounge, France hugged them all, one by one. She should be mad at them. But how could she? They'd kept things from her, but they'd had their reasons. Sometimes it was better not to tell everything you know. Grendy's revelation was a good example of that. Maybe France would never really understand why Grendy felt the need to dump her secret on her the way she did, at the time she did, but maybe, even if she couldn't understand, she could still forgive her. France herself could use some forgiveness. From Bruno. And Naomi. She'd already forgiven the mermaids. They'd taught her how to be a mermaid. They'd accepted her into the sisterhood of merhags. She didn't know how she could leave, but she was doing it.

"Please come back and swim with us again," said Coralee. "Anytime. We do shows one weekend a month up till Christmas. Maybe you could be in another one. We've got a really cool Halloween show planned. Skeleton suits that glow in the dark!"

"I'll come back," France said. And she knew she would be back—to see her mother and Theo, of course. Where else could she be a mermaid, after all? When Lydia had said that, France had thought Lydia was out of her mind.

"Chin up, girl," Lydia said. "Come stay in my condo anytime. Thanks for being the astronaut, so I didn't have to." Then she whispered in France's ear. "Remember. Elvis is *not* your father."

It was Rose who cried, which caused France to cry too. "I'm sorry I didn't tell you," Rose sobbed. "I wanted to. I really did."

France found herself patting Rose on the back. How would she ever make it out alive? She thanked them all, again and again, feeling like Dorothy saying good-bye to the Lion, the Tin Woodsman, and the Scarecrow, and then ducked out.

Theo was the hardest one. They said good-bye alone, in the living room. He hung his head, eyes averted.

She squatted beside him. "It's best you stay with Grandma for now," she said. "She wants you to. And you want to stay with her."

He nodded. She knew he did want to stay, but he was torn, as she was.

"I'll call you," she said, "and write to you, and I'll see you next month. If you ever need anything, or get scared, call me. Here's my phone number." She handed him a little wooden box. "I wrote it on a piece of paper, inside," she said. "Keep it in the box. So you won't lose it in your room."

He didn't open the box. His face was blank. What was he thinking? Was he just wishing she'd shut up and go away?

But she still hadn't said enough. "You've got Sisterwoman. She'll send you messages from me. Every time you rub her forehead you'll get a message. You can come stay with me for weeks at a time. Months at a time. I'll be a much better aunt. I'll be a super aunt."

He gazed into her eyes in his earnest way. "I really don't want a super aunt," he said. "I just want a regular aunt." He lurched forward, hugged her tightly and then suddenly broke away, grinning impishly. "Did you remember your Kansas plate?"

"Of course."

"Wait here a minute." He ran into his bedroom and came back a few minutes later with another souvenir plate. On it was a map of Florida that had the usual big cities and the Bok Tower and palm trees and flamingos and manatees and gators and water skiers at Cypress Gardens. And a mermaid beside Mermaid City.

"This is mine," he said. "But I want you to have it. Don't break it."

"I wouldn't dream of it," France said.

Naomi, it turned out, took the news about Bruno making the dolls in stride. "I think I'll change our policy a bit," she told France on the phone. "He makes female dolls—I guess they're women—so maybe we could display art that's *about* women, even if it's by men."

"I don't know," France said. "It's a slippery slope. May lead straight to a unisex gallery."

"Ha, ha," Naomi said.

France told her, for the first time, about swimming with the mermaids, and about *Mermaids on the Moon*, and how her mother had reappeared on a star and then announced at dinner that she'd once made out with Elvis.

Naomi didn't speak for a while. Finally she gave a bark of

laughter. "You and your sense of humor," she said. "Just like the humpbacked artist. You're always trying to pull the wool over my eyes."

Before they hung up, Naomi said, "So, still want to buy into WomenSpace?"

"I'll think on it," France said, which wasn't the answer she expected to give at all.

A few days later, Bruno and France sat in Giovanni's Restaurant in downtown Cedar Valley, celebrating France's homecoming and Bruno's successful show—he'd gone to the opening after all. He was dressed up in a bleached-spotted blue oxford cloth shirt and jeans, and looked wonderful, mostly because he kept smiling. Tired of flip-flops and overall shorts and tropical colors, France was wearing all black.

"Who died?" Bruno'd said when he saw her. He thought black was such a pretentious color.

They sat at a window that gave them a view of the monolithic county courthouse across the street. It had finally stopped raining, but the sky was still gray. Bits of paper and dead leaves swirled down the sidewalk. Out of the corner of her eye, France watched for her father—she'd asked him to meet them there. He was thirty minutes late, so they'd already ordered their food. When he came into view it seemed he'd changed into a different man, bent, fragile. His windbreaker whipped around him. Was he trying to look pathetic on purpose? She knew that part of him must dread seeing her.

He gave her a one-armed hug, which she didn't stand up for,

and shook hands with Bruno, trying to act glad to see him, even though he'd always considered Bruno a real flake. North had lost weight, from worry or guilt. Or missing Grendy. Or all three.

He sat down at the table with them. She studied him. Was he her real father? Should she be relieved that he might not be? He was, after all, a lying cheating scumbag. She'd asked him here so she could decide whether or not to tell him the truth.

"I can't stay in Cedar Valley," he blurted out. None of his usual social lubrication.

"I thought you couldn't wait to come back here."

"Too many memories," he said.

"So where are you going?" said Bruno, biting into his chicken tetrazzini.

"Don't know," said North. "Maybe up to the Twin Cities. Or farther up. Away from here. I can't seem to sleep. Or eat." He shrugged, and France could see that he was definitely miserable. "I'll just have a cup of coffee," he told the waitress.

"He'll have the seafood pasta," France told the waitress, and he smiled at her, surprised, thinking that this gesture meant she still loved him, which, on some level, she did. But she was also furious at him and always would be. Maybe in the future she'd have some sympathy for him, but she couldn't summon it up now. If she told him that he might not be her father, what would that do to him? Did she want to see him fall apart even more? Yes, and no.

Bruno was telling North about his show and how well it had gone.

"You're going to keep the doll thing going?"

"Of course," France answered for him.

"I think I'll start carving some male dolls," Bruno said. "Work-ingmen, maybe."

"What?" France said. He hadn't mentioned this before. "Why? Naomi only wants female dolls." Why did Bruno have to be so contrary?

"Don't want to get into a rut," he said, and winked at her.

"You're a pain in the rut," she told him.

"Thank you," he said. "I don't want to be a workingman myself, but I admire them."

"Workingman," North said. "I used to be one of those." He looked totally lost, and that's when France decided not to tell him. Not yet, anyway. For all she knew, he might already have his suspicions but didn't want to bring them up. She wasn't going to try and find out who her real father was. She didn't want to take the time to go back in time, digging up more stuff she didn't want to know, staying overly involved with her parents and the past.

Before France left Florida, her mother had told her more about why she'd stayed hidden away in Chiefland for so long. When she returned to Mermaid Springs as a Mermaid of Yester-year, she'd been so excited, she said, about being a mermaid again, swimming with all her old friends, that she'd forgotten the sad things that had happened there. All the hard parts. You can't go back, she told France, without the hard parts. When she was stay-ing in that dumpy motel in Chiefland she fell into the past and couldn't get out. She started thinking about how she'd fooled North by telling him that he had to be France's father. And she wondered again why she'd put up with his cheating. And she thought about how poorly she'd done with Beauvais, because she knew that her rotten marriage had caused most of Beauvais's problems. So the medium was right about that, France thought. Grendy was communing with Beauvais's spirit. Sort of.

And then Grendy started berating herself again for Linda Huddle's death, because the truth was, she'd hated Linda Huddle, the mermaid-in-training, who was also seeing Wayne Purdy at the time, and she and Linda had gotten into an argument before they realized that the air in the clamshell was bad, and then Grendy swam out and Linda didn't. She kept going over and over her mistakes, sitting on that motel bed, and after a while she felt almost paralyzed. She couldn't do what she needed to do in the here and now, which was to go home, let France and Theo know where she was. "My friends," Grendy said, "my old mermaid friends, helped pull me back into the present again."

France asked her mother what she and her father had ever seen in each other. Grendy explained that North's father was very strict and North had always tried to please him, but never could. "When he was young North acted good," she said, "but he didn't feel good. He always felt bad, so he figured he might as well do some bad things so he'd have a reason to feel bad. That's the way I see it, anyway. I could analyze his behavior till the cows came home but I could never get him to change it. He married me because he thought I was a truly good person, the only one he'd ever met. If he only knew! After a while, my goodness, as he saw it, got suffocating. So, out came the sinner again."

"What did you see in him?"

"He seemed so solid—a minister, for Christ's sake. Sophisticated. And he came from old money. I didn't consider the fact that he was bound to be a bit stuffy. Plus, he had those big blue eyes.

We did have some fun together. All those trips we took. My big mistake wasn't marrying him. My big mistake was staying married to him. I didn't have the sense to leave him the way you did Ray."

Then she went on to talk about Beauvais and all her problems, but France stopped listening. It was the first time her mother had ever mentioned France's divorce in a positive way.

France observed her father now, sipping from his glass of Merlot. His blue eyes were cloudy. Like everyone else, her father was a flawed man, in his case deeply flawed, but he'd never own up to his flaws. She didn't plan to beat her head against the wall anymore trying to get him to admit things. He was guilty—he knew it and she knew it. She remembered what Lydia had told her about saying good-bye to her husband, Del, how she'd given him, and herself, permission to move on. "You can go now," she'd said.

North noticed her staring. "And you?" he asked France. "Will you stay at Women Only?"

"I'm making something myself," France said. "To show at WomenSpace." Which wasn't true, yet, but would be soon, France thought. For some reason, the souvenir plates popped into her head. "Being in the mermaid show got me going," she said. "I may travel. Or go back to school." In truth, she had no idea what she was going to do, but she was enjoying the bracing feeling of uncertainty.

Since she'd returned from Florida she'd begun having her own underwater dream. In it, she was swimming in her astronaut suit in Mermaid Springs. She reached down to pick up a moon rock and it wouldn't budge. She tugged and tugged and tugged, getting more and more anxious, until she suddenly glanced up and saw the merhags standing next to the window in the underwater theater, pointing at her and laughing. At first she was angry, then she realized that all that tugging wasn't necessary—who cared about a silly fake moon rock? But when she looked down again, she held the rock in her hand. And it wasn't fake—it was real. A genuine moon rock.

It was later that week that she got Theo's postcard with a picture of Mermaid Springs on the front. "I got three lovebirds!" he had dictated to Grendy. "Sisterwoman likes to watch them. Grandma and I finished *The Mystery of Cabin Island*. Now we are reading *The Great Airport Mystery*. I like my new school and my teacher Ms. Bev. I miss you. After the Halloween show we are doing *Mermaids of the Old West*. Love, Theo."

She wrote him back: "Dearest Theo, I miss you too. I'll be there for the Halloween show, and I'll come down to watch *Mermaids of the Old West* too. Maybe they'll let me be the sheriff. Bruno says hello. He's carving a farmer doll to dance with a doll called Francie Pants. I've found six more souvenir plates—Ohio, California, Texas, Wyoming, Arkansas, and New York. I love them, but the Florida plate is my favorite. Be good. Kiss Sisterwoman for me and rub her third eye every day. And remember, don't let your birds fly around in the kitchen! Birds are very precious and must be protected by you from dangerous household fumes. Always, always, keep that in mind. Love, Aunt Frances."